PRAISE

'An utterly compelli[ng] ... magic. I simply couldn't put this book down.'

> *– Poorna Bell,*
> *Lifestyle Editor, The Huffington Post, UK*

'A wonderful tale that merges ordinary reality with a magical otherworldliness to create an atmosphere guaranteed to enthrall and delight.'

> *– Shihab Salim,*
> *Editor-in-chief, Asiana*

'By turns poetic, bittersweet, and humorous, *Kabuko the Djinn* takes you into the heart of a culture that is occult and beguiling. A mesmerising debut!'

> *– Ross Heaven,*
> *author of The Way of the Lover*

'Hamraz Ahsan weaves a tale of darkly magical wonderment, a latter-day fairy story for sure; the way Ahsan writes about entities that are other than human, I would suspect him of being part-Djinn himself. *Kabuko the Djinn* is enthralling from start to finish, and destined to be a classic.'

> *– Adele Nozedar,*
> *author of The Secret Language of Birds*

Published by

FiNGERPRINT!

An imprint of Prakash Books India Pvt. Ltd.

113/A, Darya Ganj, New Delhi-110 002,
Tel: (011) 2324 7062 – 65, Fax: (011) 2324 6975
Email: info@prakashbooks.com/sales@prakashbooks.com

facebook www.facebook.com/fingerprintpublishing
twitter www.twitter.com/FingerprintP, www.fingerprintpublishing.com
For manuscript submissions, e-mail: fingerprintsubmissions@gmail.com

Copyright © 2013 Prakash Books India Pvt. Ltd.
Copyright Text © Hamraz Ahsan

ISBN: 978 81 7234 472 6

Processed & printed in India by Nutech Photolithographers

To all the fallen lovers, be they human or djinn.

He created man from potter's clay and the djinn from smokeless fire.
Which of your Lord's blessings would you deny?

The Koran 55:15-16

PROLOGUE

When you were born, wailing and shaking with rage at your rude expulsion from the comfort of the womb, did you know, in your tiny infant brain, the exact trajectory of your life? Had you already decided on which events would shape you and how your personality would be? Had you decided on who would be your first love and who would be your last? On where you would be and on how you would earn your bread? Did you know how you would live? Did you know how you would die? And, after knowing, did you, exhausted at the intelligence of every intimate detail of your life, fall into a deep sleep and then, relieved, jettison all that information to live your short, new life with fresh eyes, acquainted as you are with the notion of surprise? Is that how it happens with humans? Do you just . . . *forget*? I have always been curious to know, you see.

On my part, I have been blessed with an excellent memory. While your memories of infancy blur and fall away, mine remain fresh and precise. Unlike you, I was born without any foreknowledge of the miraculous life that I were to lead, but I can recount every incident of my life to the minutest of details. For instance, I could sing for you the exact sonorous, uplifting song of the bird that sang at my mother's window on the day of my birth. It was a sun-blessed, beautiful morning, and that bird had arrived to bid my mother a good day—a sentiment that she did not fully appreciate while in the midst of her labour. Yes, I understand the speech of birds, insects, and other animals and it is never a cacophony for me since I also know how to focus on one thing to the exclusion of all others—a skill that you humans would do well to cultivate.

Given your narcissism, you probably think that I am miraculous enough anyway, since I am . . . well, who I am. For the modern man, I don't exist, or maybe just exist in the world of make-believe. Don't act affronted, for you must admit that you are obsessed with your own stories and your own existence, and every other creature not approved of by your scientists or your priests is relegated to the realm of fairy tales and dreams. Thankfully, I have spent most of my life in an area of the world where there is a healthy degree of acknowledgement of the existence of my kind—the djinn kind.

I am Kabuko. Kabuko the djinn.

The Indian subcontinent is rife with those who not only believe in djinn but have specialised in capturing or harming them. I used to wonder if it was a human trait to respond with aggression towards anyone not exactly like oneself. I then thought about the division of djinn clans and our own wars and petty conflicts and was humbled into wondering if the gods looked down upon us both with disgust and pity . . . until I read about the jealousies and intrigues of the gods. Perhaps the fault lies with duality, and union is the only peace? But I am getting ahead of myself. I will begin my story at the beginning.

I belong to a clan that speaks like birds. The only concession my mother made to the polite gesture of that small blue bird who sang to ease her birth pangs was to name me after its song: Kabuko. *Ka-boo-ko.* Our clan of djinn are renowned for our fluency in the language of the birds. Kabuko means "mighty hunter" but in bird terms this isn't as impressive as it sounds, given that those winged fellows rarely hunt anything bigger than grubs and worms. Of course, I do not speak of birds of prey, which I feel are another matter entirely. I suspect that the elders who picked my name were mocking me. I was not a particularly robust child and nothing in my demeanour betrayed the unusual course my life would take.

Many of my kind say that it would have been far better for me had I married a nice djinn girl, taken a few human lovers for variety, and lived a quiet, pleasant, ordinary life. The idea of us taking human lovers might surprise you, but we djinn can take on the guise of mortal men to seduce your kind. This is no great difficulty for us as we merely vibrate our energies at a denser level, thereby taking on a human shape. And then there is the small matter of possession.

I may seduce your women—in fact, if I am honest, I have seduced a great many—but I would never possess anyone. A favourite uncle of mine insisted that possession was an immoral act and bid me to never engage in it. He spent forty years as the captive of a Muslim occultist, and some say he even converted to Islam and that this was at the heart of his moral objection, but I wondered if it might not be the tragic tale of his father, my grandfather.

We djinn often fall in love with you humans. However, that love is often unrequited. While you also suffer from unrequited love among your own kind, djinn have made one-way love into an art form. We regularly fall in love with you and then are driven away from you or trapped or even killed. You call our embraces "possession" and our beloveds "victims" and forget that a djinn heart is as capable of love as a human one.

My grandfather was one such ill-fated lover. He fell ardently in love with a young girl from a small village in Ahmedabad, India, and possessed her. Our body energies vibrate at a much faster frequency than yours, so we are able to possess you by just stepping into your denser, slower vibration bodies as easily as one would step into a warm bath. This girl was an obsession with my grandfather and he possessed her in a vain attempt to get closer to her. Aah . . . the naïveté of love.

An *aamal*, a Muslim occultist, was sent for to rid the girl of my grandfather. The occultist was pragmatic in his approach and tried hard to work out some sort of compromise but my grandfather blankly refused his every offer. An old person's love for a young being is a terrible thing. The spirit worker, then, forcefully extracted my grandfather and gave him a chance to run away. But when my grandfather tried to repossess his beloved's body, the occultist performed his ultimate ritual and burnt him alive. He threw his ashes in a nearby river.

This terrible tragedy had a huge impact on me. I became fascinated with the human race. My grandfather was one of the greatest djinn of my clan. Whatever he said, or did, held the credence of being the final word. So, what was it that was so attractive about you that my grandfather would risk everything for the lowliest of your girls? What charm do you possess that one of you could enslave a djinn like my uncle for more than forty years and yet not draw any resentment towards himself? But, more than that, what occult knowledge do you have at your disposal to enslave and kill us? To learn this would be of advantage to all djinn-kind. So I decided to live up to my name and become a mighty hunter of human knowledge.

For years, I stayed in one of you. I have had all the experiences of pain and pleasure, boredom and excitement, tears and laughter, and erections and impotencies that a human body goes through. I have dreamt human dreams and even experienced human nightmares, in which my own kind scared me half to death. In fact, I have become so used to being a human that for some time now I have been unable to dream like a djinn. I have to admit I still need some degree of rehabilitation. But I have no regrets. I am still young and hope to use this wisdom I gathered in my human form to make a mark in my world.

This is the story of those thirty years that I spent with you human beings. In fact it is not my story, it is essentially yours, and my role is more or less that of a narrator. Before entering into the human world, I did not even know that for humans story-telling was an art. If you find any spin to the tale, claim all the credit for yourself, as whatever I know of twists and turns, I've learnt it from you, mankind.

1

Fire in the Belly

From my high perch atop this tree, I can see the woman in the courtyard below making roti, skilfully manipulating the dough and rolling it out into a flat circle. It is a thrice-daily ritual, this making of fresh bread on a griddle. I find my eyes following her practised, unthinking hands. You all look so ordinary, so innocuous, so vulnerable to attack and so utterly self-absorbed. I feel my heart quicken at the thought of my forthcoming dissection of your soul and what treasures I may find there.

My elders told me that the djinn came to this planet long before humans. This does not make us special, as almost all non-human species on the planet are older than man. We all consider man an alien, still a newcomer. The Earth before the human's arrival, though not a paradise as we had our own wars and confrontations with other entities, was still peaceful. But the day humans were struck with the idea that they are the "greatest species" in this universe, everything went horribly wrong.

My mother used to say, 'O, Kabuko, you are unlucky because you were born into bad times.' In my own life, I witnessed many of our clans migrating from one place to another, taking refuge in unfamiliar and inhospitable places, as humans ruined their native habitats. I am not just talking about the djinn who have always lived on mountains or in jungles or other deserted places, but even many of those who lived in the cities and towns and shared their dwellings with humans and their ghosts. They were forced into exile as the modern human lifestyle, full of messy sounds, irritating vibrations, poisonous smells, and dangerously sharp thought forms, became all too intolerable for them. But, thankfully, you humans could not turn us into an endangered species because our natural lifespans are very long.

I, for example, am more than two hundred years old and that is barely middle-aged in djinn terms. I do not have a single grey hair and am still called "young man" by my elders. I don't know my exact age; for neither are we as bureaucratic as you humans nor do we prescribe such inflexible dates to celebrating the miracle of our births. Our perception of time is totally different from yours, too. We can move in the split of one of your seconds to distant places without any vehicle. Many of the things you find miraculous about us have their basis in this fact, but I shall not reveal all, yet.

Being endowed with all these powers, it was surprising to me that humans should still have the upper hand through occult knowledge. It is true that sometimes djinn also kill humans but we always do that through sheer force and not by rituals, by invoking mystical powers that even we cannot see. We can physically possess the weakest among you—mostly females—but we cannot enslave you.

While I have no desire of enslaving anyone, I do have a burning curiosity about that which nobody quite understands.

For many moons now, I have followed my obsession to great lengths. Lengths that have resulted in me sitting here, watching this beautiful, youthful woman with dark, shining hair and smooth skin.

Her figure is curvaceous and her movements, as she goes about her chores, graceful. I do not watch her with lust; I watch her with intense anticipation and the great hope that she will be destined to become my human mother.

I carefully approach the woman as she reaches for a vegetable from a rack behind her. Leaning in close, tensing my body even though I know that she cannot see me, I sniff her breath. I am disappointed. It is not time. I return to the safety of my tree.

Watching her bare forearms as she works, sunlight flashing on her bangles, I remind myself how far I've come and how being impatient now would be foolish in the extreme. Even though I did not have the blessings of my elders in my decision to make the humans my area of study, I had set off in search of my goal exactly one year after the release of my uncle.

I travelled far and wide and met many strange entities in the hope of learning more about humans. While it may have made more sense to learn directly from yo, there are not many of you who can sense us, let alone see us. Those rare few of you who do not react in horror at the sight of us, nevertheless seek to banish us, lest we have some nefarious purpose. One species always regards another with some suspicion. Besides, I am no fool. I know that revealing myself to the wrong human could have me suffer the same fate as my uncle, and that was a risk I wasn't prepared to take, then. So, I contacted wise djinn, djinn with long-term human lovers, and even those tough djinn who lived right in amongst you, in your houses, your buildings, and in your polluted cities where it is impossible to breathe easily for most djinn. But they all were of not much help.

One lucky day, a friend of mine told me of a wise female djinn called Lady Kiya. A recluse who lived in the mountains of Asia, she only rarely broke her solitude by occasionally taking a young djinn as a lover and as a student in occult matters.

I went to her mountainside home immediately. One of our "powers" as djinn is that we can locate anything by desiring it and then naming our desire. I have heard tell that humans can do this too, but they are so ignorant of their true desires that they pine away without ever being able to identify and ask explicitly for what they want. A djinn would never be so stupid. We desire, we ask, and we get. So I asked to meet this old djinn woman and, lo, I found myself immediately at the entrance to her cave dwelling.

It was not an auspicious first meeting. The old lady was impossible; bad-tempered, abusive and foul-mouthed, even in her normal speech. Her appearance was obnoxious too; naked with pendulous breasts and matted hair, she looked scary and feral. But, at the very first sight of her I, somehow, knew in my heart that she was the master who could help me achieve my goal. I put up with her taunts and rejections, prostrating myself in supplication and begging her to accept me as a pupil.

Eventually she grunted, and grabbed and squeezed every part of my body as if I were a mere puppet in her hands. After arousing my genitals, she judged my physical strength and grunted again, this time in satisfaction. The Lady Kiya had certainly earned her reputation for seducing young males and females. She clearly got a kick out of having inexperienced young partners.

For a year and a half I was obliged to lie with my mistress regularly, but only during the night time. During the day, she forced me to take horrible-tasting herbal potions, the ingredients for which she always collected and mixed deftly with her own

16

hands at the campfire outside her dwelling. I knew that without those potions I would have soon lost the sexual strength to satisfy my old mistress. I had many mysteries of life solved for me by her but she never taught me anything about humans. One night, when we were in the midst of coupling, and she was in the throes of ecstasy, might I add, I asked her for a favour. Living with her had made me so crafty that in spite of her insistence, I did not tell her my specific wish at that time. The next day, when the sun had almost set, I told her about my obsession.

'Foolish boy, you'll only be able to obtain such knowledge through a human,' she said, crushing my hopes immediately. 'You like sitting in trees and watching these beings, but only through direct experience can you learn such secrets.'

'I don't want to possess a human,' I replied, my voice taking on the whine of a petulant child as I remembered the harsh words that favourite uncle of mine had used against a djinn who possessed humans.

'Ha! If only it were as easy as possessing one of them,' she retorted. Then, lowering her voice to the husky whisper she used whenever she was about to say something of deep significance, she said, 'The knowledge you seek can only be obtained through direct experience of being a human being. Of actually living within and through a human being, as if you yourself were a human and not merely possessing one of them as a foreign entity.'

I was perplexed. I had no idea what she meant as the only djinn-human contact I was aware of consisted of possessing the human.

'Of course, not just any body will do,' she continued, vigorously poking the fire in front of her and sending up waves of embers. 'You will have to incarnate and be born into the body of a male child of a spiritually high ranking family. Your

17

sojourn in such a body would need to be for the span of a human lifetime. Seventy years or more.'

This had sent me into an even deeper vortex of gloom. To be with a girl might have its pleasures—and I do admit I briefly allowed the thought of being a woman to fill me with an erotic charge—but to be with a man for such a length of time was unthinkable. I was wary of men and attracted to women; it felt like my benefactress had told me to sleep with a man. I could not countenance it and even wondered if she were teasing me.

'Why will a female body not do?' I asked, hoping some caveat might save me.

'Because, you idiot,' she snarled, 'humans hardly ever keep that sort of occult knowledge in female bodies. Women have a natural monthly bleed that means they cannot perform the long and strenuous practices that demand a certain type of purity. It is very dangerous and sometimes even fatal if one is menstruating during some of those rituals. That is the basic reason that very few human females are ever able to have those kinds of powers.' Hesitating and then, staring entranced into the flames, she continued, 'There are, of course, those hardened old birds who only acquire that priceless knowledge after their menopause. Or some gifted neophytes convince their masters to change the whole system of their bodies so they are rid of the monthly cycle for their entire lives.'

Then Lady Kiya looked up at me sharply, and barked, 'O Kabuko, this is not your cup of tea. You do not have the patience for this. Forget it, and one day I will teach you some gimmicks to impress your friends.' Before I could protest, she strode away purposefully to gather night-blooming ingredients for her potions. She did not even lay with me that night. The discussion was evidently over.

I was confused and felt somewhat insulted. That whole

week my performance in bed with my mistress was at its worst. Eventually, with the heaviest of hearts, for it is not my usual practise to give up, I decided to abandon the whole idea altogether and to go back to my clan. When I asked the lady for permission to leave, she started laughing crazily, her eyes becoming wet with tears. Then she said something that I would never forget, 'Kabuko, you dirt on a donkey's hoof, it is too late. You cannot go back now. It is not your destiny. I see you in the human world. It is true that I discouraged you but that was not to stop you from pursuing your obsession. A red hot blade needs to be quenched by cold water if it is to be made into a battle-worthy sword. Of course, your intended adventure is very risky and you could lose your life. But sometimes it is better to lose your life than to lose your heart.'

Her words had instantly made me happy and determined, and I had excitedly asked her, 'My loving mistress, does this mean you will help me in my mission?' She had smiled and said, simply, without adding a customary insult, 'Yes.' Then she gave me another surprise 'Kabuko, the day you showed me your face I knew what brought you here. I am not stupid. And I am not a predator, either. If I was not able to return your gift tenfold I would never have taken you for a lover.'

And that night she slept with me for the last time and after each coupling that night I felt more and more energetic. Early in the morning, she woke me up and took me to a nearby lake where she washed me more thoroughly than my mother had ever done when I was an infant. She washed herself afterwards with the same meticulous perfection. When we came back, without eating or drinking anything, she made a tiny man from clay and then lit a fire and dried the clay man over it. During her ritual, I caught her murmuring some repetitive short sentences in a language alien to me. When the little clay man had become fired in the heat, she took it and forcefully pressed it against my abdomen.

I screamed out loud at the pain but didn't pull away. After that she gave me a potion that I had never tasted before. I immediately fell into a deep, dreamless sleep.

When I awoke, I learnt I had been asleep for seven days and seven nights. I felt like a different being altogether. I could not define this difference but it felt as if a space had been created within me and it was giving me vast reserves of confidence and strength. After that day, my mistress never slept with me again, and she never even cast a lustful look my way. I was impressed at how disciplined and impeccable she was. Even her speech had become cleaner and less abrasive when she spoke to me.

'You have much to learn before you can begin your adventure, child,' she said one night while tending the fire. 'The process by which you'll enter the human body is complicated and dangerous. You must pay attention and not let your impetuous nature get the better of you.' I did not protest at that as I suppose I do have a habit of leaping in without much forethought. She then taught me almost everything that she knew about the human species. She taught me about the anatomy of the human soul and told me that you are not made up solely of a human spirit. There are mineral, vegetable, animal, angelic, and other spirits that live within you and also play an equally vital role in your life.

Before saying goodbye to me, the Lady Kiya gave me a final instruction. 'Do not enter a fully-developed newborn boy, as the settled human spirit in the soul sometimes cannot bear djinn energies. Enter into the human foetus immediately before the human spirit comes to reside there but do it after the arrival of the mineral, vegetable, animal, and other entities. And hide yourself as much as you can in the unborn body until the baby develops recognisable features in the womb.' I again made a mental note of what had already been drummed into me. 'Finally,' my mistress continued in a serious tone of voice, 'some animal and fallen angelic spirits in the human foetus do not like the company of djinn. At first they will be furious and with their body gestures, will give the impression of being stronger than you. Do not lose your temper in that show of muscles and deal with them not by force but only by persuasion.' My mistress emphasised that my basic aim should always be to develop a good relationship with all those entities that have to live together in that human body until the moment of its death.

With this precious knowledge imparted to me by my benefactress, I had carefully chosen a noble female of the highest Muslim ancestry in northern India. She was a good choice, this woman. The wife of an army man and already the mother of healthy children. But it wasn't an easy choice. I selected her after much deliberation. And now I wait.

But this waiting is driving me crazy.

A month of watching and waiting later, at last her breath indicated to me that she was pregnant, and I followed my mistress's detailed instructions on how to enter the human foetus's body.

I was dazzled by the light the second I entered the womb. I could suddenly understand the attraction of possession; this was a firework display like no other. Such vibrant colours, so much happening all at once—light dancing, snaking, leaping, bursts of energy, and rivers of light everywhere. This surely must be heaven, and you, you who are the vessel of all this beauty and drama, can never see it. No wonder so many of you are so very sad.

Once my eyes had adjusted to the dazzle, I saw groups of entities moving about and, remembering my Lady's instructions, I scurried into a relatively dark corner to hide and wait. The entities appeared to be dancing and paid me no mind at all. I watched the dancing for I know not how long and felt very secure and happy. My mission had begun!

After some time, I do not know if it was hours or days, the scene seemed to shift in anticipation of something. I did not think it possible but the colours and lights became brighter and more dazzling and there it was—the human spirit!

How to describe this to you? Oh, words are useless in such a case! The human spirit was a colour that I can never possibly describe. It seemed to be made of just moving light and yet it had discernible features. But more than its appearance was the feeling you got from it, a feeling of great wisdom coupled with child-like innocence. There was also a tremendous benevolence coming from it and I remember thinking 'how could such a spirit ever enter bodies that end up belonging to murderers and villains?' And that if, as I knew, even those evil-doers had such a spirit within them then, at their heart, they must be good.' Such was the intense quality of goodness that emanated from that spirit. I could see that the other entities and spirits in that body felt it too and gathered around the spirit as though greeting a monarch that enjoyed its regal status, not from an unfair accident of birth but as a true divine right.

I must confess I fell in love in a way that I've never fallen in love before or since. This pure, shining being of light made my every sinew sing and before I could control myself, I leapt from my hiding place to get nearer to this being. And that was my first and my biggest mistake.

There was an instant of recognition, a pulse of light, a slight shake of the human spirit's head and it was gone. Immediately it was as if the whole cosmos were being sucked into a black hole, the animal spirits and entities all zipped away, the lights went out cell by cell and there was nothing but darkness and emptiness, where just seconds before it had been light and celebration. 'No! No! Come back!' I beseeched, sobbing at my error. I held my head in my hands and wept for some time before I left the dead body of the foetus.

2

Honouring an Uninvited Guest

Perhaps I should have abandoned my mission
then, but my love for the human spirit did not let
me. My zealous feelings, recurringly, made me want
to encounter such an entity again. To feel that
benevolence again . . .

So, I set about my task with renewed vigour
but events in the wider world of Man were not
conducive to my mission. The Indian subcontinent
was divided into two countries on religious grounds,
and bloody riots had started everywhere. Everyone
was killing everyone else. Thousands of those who
were murdered could not move into the other world
and their ghosts wandered around in rage. The ether
around this part of the world was heavy with despair.

I could not wait much longer and, also, I could
not see myself wasting time looking for another
suitable female in some other part of the world.
I had not chosen my human parents out of a gut
feeling but by the laws of probability. Both of
my would-be parents belonged to the Syed family
and their ancestors were the keepers of the arcane

knowledge that I was seeking. If anyone were likely to have a predisposition towards knowing how to interact with djinn kind, it would be a child of this lineage.

As I said before, my human mother is a beautiful lady. She is, perhaps, in her early thirties. Her beauty has a touch of the sacred about it. She was married at an early age to Subedar Hussain Shah, an army officer, who was already married with four grown-up children.

I waited impatiently for her to fall pregnant again. I was around her all the time, watching with the keen interest and optimism of an explorer in alien territory. Like every other woman of that time and region, she was also a person of fixed routine. In those days I had my routines, too. I used to smell her breath early in the morning to see whether she had conceived again. Sometimes, if I saw her carrying something heavy, I gave her a hand. Though she always noticed the weightlessness, she never suspected anything unusual. When my father made love with my mother, I always left the room because I followed a very strict code of conduct.

During the hot summer, when my would-be mother took her routine mid-day nap, I used to move my body back and forth over her to give her some comfort from the oppressive heat. The different density of my body shifted the air in a way that created a gentle and pleasing breeze. However, not all of my attempts to be of service to my human mother went quite as well.

Once, while cooking the evening meal, she panicked on noticing that there were no onions in the house. The orderly was away and there was nobody else who could go buy the onions. I, Kabuko the djinn, wanting to help her, went to a nearby shop and took two big onions and put them under a bunch of coriander in her vegetable basket. Then, as she brushed past the basket, I made it topple over. She was so relieved to see those two onions, it was as if they were as precious to her as diamonds. That's when I remembered something my benefactress had told me. I realised I had made a great blunder. Those onions were stolen and were prohibited for the Syed family to consume. I felt not so much guilt as fear for my hasty act, performed impetuously in sympathy for my prospective mother. I became very concerned that perhaps my act of stealing had ruined my chances of a second sojourn in her womb. In my desperation, I went to an old friend of mine—okay, truth be told, an old lover, who lived thousands of miles away.

'Do you have any legitimate human money?' I asked, without much preamble.

'Always dashing about,' she replied, as she kissed me on the lips. 'Oh, and always so dashing!' She smiled, pulled back, and sighed when she saw that her kiss had not impacted my desperation at all. 'Kabuko, you have no idea how to make a woman feel loved but I am not so useless. I'd do anything for you, my love.' She pressed two old gold coins into my hand and pecked me on the cheek, still looking at me wistfully. The coins were from the reign of the great king Akbar. She assured me that her father had acquired those coins lawfully. I was in such a hurry that I could not thank her properly but, to show my gratitude, I blew her a flying kiss.

I immediately went to the shop from which I'd stolen the onions and put the two gold coins in the small iron box where the shopkeeper kept his takings. With those coins I could have bought all the stock in the shop many times over but that extraordinary over-payment freed me from any anxiety.

Then, one fortunate day, in the early spring of 1948, the smell of my mother's breath changed. She had become pregnant! Now my only concern was the gender of the child in her womb. I was quite worried by the thought of what I would do if that baby was a girl. Should I wait for another year or two? Or go and look for a new womb? I never thought to abandon my mission but I was a little scared that my impatience would cause problems.

One day, when I was sitting on a branch of the big courtyard tree lost in thought, my old teacher appeared unexpectedly. She was in a good mood and seemed happy with my perseverance, despite my beginner's mistake with the previous pregnancy. She even kissed me on the abdomen and did some massage-like movements with her fingers around the centre of my body. It felt ticklish. Before I could say anything to her, she went inside the house and touched my would-be mother three times gingerly, in the manner of a human touching a naked electricity wire with just the fingernails. Then she declared, 'Kabuko, it is a boy. An extraordinary boy! It is like you and both of you will give each other a very hard time. But that is exactly what you were seeking.' She kissed me on the stomach again and hurried away. With her departure, all my worries were gone and I became much more peaceful and content.

I patiently waited for the multitude of mineral, animal, angelic, and other non-human spirits to settle in the foetus. Then one day, in the middle of the night, I entered into the womb of my adoptive mother very silently and most carefully, like an experienced thief. I found myself a little cave-like space in which to hide and settled down in my new home.

For days I had to fast as seeking my share in the available food would have alarmed the already residing spirits. When I became comfortable and entrenched in the foetus, and was confident that now those spirits could no longer pose any real threat to me, I came out of hiding. All the entities in the unborn baby's body gradually accepted me without any fuss. That was surprising for me as I had expected to face a lot of opposition. At last, just before the birth, the human spirit arrived and entered into the body of the unborn child, as a legitimate owner takes charge of his fresh dwelling. I felt the same pulse of excitement and attraction but this time I steadied myself and kept myself in the background.

The human spirit looked neither young nor old but was exuberantly energetic and, like me, was always looking for new experiences. At first it ignored me altogether and intermingled with the other natural spirits, as if it was instinctively expecting them to be waiting for him. Eventually it turned to me, with a mercurial quality that initially gave me the impression of some hostility. I was anxious at this stage that it not leave in the way the other had. But I need not have worried. The spirit had a lot of volatile energy that could have easily been mistaken for human emotions like rejection or hostility but in actuality it had no emotions; just a benevolent curiosity about everything.

After a while, the human spirit started showing me the colourful patterns of its being. It was breathtaking. I, Kabuko the djinn, could never conjure up in my wildest dreams such a rhythmic dance of colours and geometrical shapes. My love for it deepened and I felt very fortunate to be seeing these miraculous sights.

During one late autumn evening of 1948, my surrogate mother was transferred to a cantonment hospital after having the usual labour pains. A Lieutenant Shamim was on duty in the maternity ward at the time. A very slim lady, her sharp, angular features reminded me of a bird of prey. She was a scarily confident doctor, trained in ignoring the cries of women in labour and capable of holding a fragile newborn baby with the same rough vigour as a fisherman grabbing a big, wriggling fish from the sea.

It was in the early hours of the next morning that Lieutenant Shamim, disguised in her white apron, snatched a human body out of the vagina of my mother. Her firm grasp added to the shock of leaving the comfort and safety of the womb to emerge into this cold, well-lit, agoraphobia-inducing world. My very first human experience was of being manhandled. I felt no love or affection in her otherwise soft, hands.

After the delivery, she washed her hands and elbows in the sink and went to her desk, leaving the dirty work for two female nurses. One of them I quite fancied, the other was too plain for my tastes. But, both were equally appreciative of the healthy body into which I had been born in the human realm.

Then, on the same evening, a man with a black beard came to the hospital accompanied by my human father. The bearded man put a small straw-like tool in the right ear of the baby—I suppose you could say in my right ear as I was now experiencing everything the baby was—and recited something in Arabic, that they called *azaan*. That religious ritual sounded good to me, though I did not understand a word of that recitation.

Ejaz Shah was the boy's proper name and his nickname was Ajee Shah. Ajee Shah was my human body and the being in which I was to reside for a whole human life. His early thoughts were concerned with things I couldn't understand, realms of light, and desires to experience this or that. It seemed as if a very mature person was speaking but in a language I couldn't understand. Certainly it was not the blank slate I thought newborns would be.

We spent three days in the hospital and were looked after very well. On the third day we went home. Everybody in the family was thrilled by the newborn baby. A week later more good news came, creating an atmosphere of celebration in the house. Ajee Shah's father, Subedar Hussain Shah, was promoted to Subedar Major, but despite that he continued to be simply called Subedar Sahib. After that there was no more promotion left for him but only retirement as that was the highest rank in the category of junior commissioned officers.

Ajee Shah's birth was a good omen for his mother too, specially after the previous stillbirth. She was overwhelmed with the thought that God had compensated her for the deceased boy with another boy. Ajee Shah was regularly checked for quite some time for any unusual signs or afflictions. In time his mother and other close female relatives were satisfied that the newborn would not share his dead brother's fate.

To his family, everything appeared to be normal with Ajee Shah, but since I was within him, this was clearly never truly going to be the case. I tried to make my presence as unobtrusive as possible but one thing almost gave me away. While I had free access to all his emotions, sensations, and thoughts, I could not countenance the idea of suckling milk from a human breast. Though naturally I had the previous experience of sucking female bosoms during love-making, those young breasts only released a lovely fragrance and not milk. We djinn do not feed in this way and are born quite capable of taking solid food in the manner of an adult.

Soon I started resisting that activity and Ajee Shah's mother noticed that he did not suckle milk out of her breasts in the same way as her other children had. She was an experienced mother and knew the behaviour of babies very well. She had to push Ajee Shah's head towards her bosom constantly. Unlike her other children, he appeared unaware that this was a feeding source. To her, the way he sucked her milk was also odd. He tried to suck her milk as far away from the nipple as possible, and from the corner of his mouth, without omitting any cries of frustration. It seemed to her that either he didn't like the taste of her milk or he was always more interested in exploring the human body than in filling his little tummy. But she had no idea that the real culprit behind the unusual behaviour of her son was me, Kabuko the djinn. In spite of my distaste, I always made sure that Ajee Shah did not go hungry as the survival of all of us within him depended on that human milk. Ajee Shah's mother considered him a special child and was not much bothered about his eccentric feeding behaviour. In fact, she felt deep down that Ajee was enriching her experience of motherhood. The real challenge for Ajee Shah's mother came on the night my grandmother visited, determined to take me back to the djinn world.

When, in the middle of night, Ajee Shah's mother was again trying to fix his wandering mouth to her left nipple, my grandma took the form of a human female and stood at the foot of the bed. Her demeanour was not friendly but I could see that she was trying hard to appear utterly harmless. She smiled and her facial expression became more amicable. When she opened her mouth, her voice, though distinct and firm, was not at all threatening. She said in a mild manner to Ajee Shah's mother, 'Please, show me your child. I want to see the baby.'

To my surprise, Ajee Shah's mother was not at all scared by the apparition of my grandma. She lifted her half-asleep baby to show his face to the entity while proudly declaring that it was a boy. My grandma looked at the child from every possible angle and made with her index finger some complex patterns in the air that Ajee Shah's mother watched with curiosity. Then she became silent for some time, as if meditating. After a while she abruptly announced, 'He is the same. He is our Kabuko, our missing child. Give us our child back as he belongs only to us!'

The ease with which Ajee Shah's mother had accepted the presence of the stranger evaporated in the time it took my grandmother to finish her declaration. Ignoring the young mother's shrieks of protest, my grandma continued, 'I don't understand Kabuko's problem. This adventure is foolish and ill-advised, I will take him home and I will make sure that he never re-enters the human domain. Give us our child back and we'll leave you in peace.'

Ajee Shah's mother's alarm grew. She held us tight against her chest and her mother's instinct suddenly gave her a burst of energy and strength so strong that she was ready to fight my grandma. She raised her voice and forcefully said to my grandma, 'This is my child and he was in my womb for nine months. I don't know who you are but you have no right whatsoever over my child. I will never allow you to touch him. You have to kill me first to take my son away from me.' When she heard this, my grandma laughed, and this time her face became grotesque. Her reply came like an unearthly hiss, 'This is not a human child. This is not even a child. He is almost a grown-up. If I told you his age you wouldn't believe me for a second. He is a bloody crazy fool to want to explore your human world. I told him many times to stay with us and not enter an alien womb but he never listened to me. I am his grandmother, his real grandmother. Now he must return to where he belongs and you could not keep him anyway.' Her tone softened as she finished with, 'Give me back my Kabuko. It is better for you and for him.'

Ajee Shah's mother was no longer looking at my grandma but praying for help. She recited all the Koranic verses she remembered by heart. She also called on God, the Prophet, the Saints, and all her noble ancestors to help her in the time of this earth-shaking experience. Suddenly a dervish appeared near the headboard of her bed. If Ajee Shah's mother turned her head she could see exactly what he looked like. He was an old man but his voice boomed with authority and resonance, so much so that Ajee Shah's mother took fright and broke out into a sweat. The dervish directly addressed my grandma, ignoring Ajee Shah and his mother. 'I am Hidayat Shah, a descendent of Prophet Mohammad, Peace Be Upon Him, and I am the grandfather of this child. You, the creed of djinn, know me very well. I had many contests with you when I was here on this Earth. I have freed, with the grace of God, many females and males from the possession of you djinn. Now I am on another plane but I was called here to deal with you as I know how to mould you to understand.'

My grandma pulled a frightful face and screeched, 'Do not threaten us, murderer of husbands and destroyer of lives!' To this the dervish calmly responded, 'I have never killed any of your kind in all my life. I know that your grandson has settled in my grandson's body and it would be dangerous to pull him out at this point. It would take the life of my grandson, and I cannot allow this to happen. Not twice. It was he who entered into this child's older brother, making him die as he couldn't bear his strong djinn spirit. Leave this one alone now for he has entered into my family. We hold no grudge against him. He is a part of our child now.'

My grandmother was clearly annoyed but was somewhat pacified with the knowledge that the dervish was not a djinn-killer but a djinn-extractor. I kept quiet, watching this drama unfold. Like a naughty child being discussed by grown-ups, I didn't want to draw attention, or wrath, to myself.

She attempted to reason with the old man, 'You know that this is against the nature of this universe, in which both Man and djinn live. And it is also against the established rules between our two species.' The old man with the white beard snorted at this assertion, and replied, 'Yes, but who has broken the rules in the first place; you or us? I could have allowed you to take him with you but you know that with his departure my grandson will die. So he is no more yours. He is ours. He has been born into us. He is now the grandson of Hidayat Shah, and you know we are strong enough to look after our guests, even the uninvited ones. We do not differentiate between the invited and the uninvited, as all are sent by God.'

My grandmother's face contorted in anger and she mumbled something to her left side, as if consulting an invisible being. Then, my grandmother used her last card and said, 'But, do you realise that we are not Muslims? How can you accept our Kabuko, an infidel, as your grandson?' Hidayat Shah smiled, as if he had expected that argument, and replied mischievously, 'We will circumcise him and make him a Muslim.' The answer was so shocking for my grandmother that she was stunned speechless for a few moments. Then she began keening in mourning, just as humans do at the death of a loved one. It was apparent that she was uncomfortable in her human shape but could not change her appearance. Although she was in no mood for a showdown with the legendary Hidayat Shah, she still reproached him before leaving, 'O Shah, you have not done the right thing. You have not done justice in snatching our child from us.' Hidayat Shah's firm rebuke was heard by Ajee Shah's mother before he too disappeared, 'We did not begin this; he did. We did not do anything wrong but we cannot let him go now. You know, we too have our own laws, our own etiquette.'

After the departure of both terrifying elders, I, Kabuko the djinn, gave a sigh of relief. The defeat of my grandmother gave me no pleasure as I love her very much. But at the same time I was annoyed at the stupid thing she had done. Ajee Shah's mother was also feeling unbearable emptiness over her head and under her feet. She started sobbing in such a loud voice that the whole family woke up. Her garbled explanation through tears only imparted the information that an old woman had tried to snatch her baby. Her husband, who had been sleeping in the same room but on another bed, was listening to his wife while still half-asleep. On hearing that someone had tried to snatch their baby, his knee-jerk reaction was to take the revolver that was always lying under his pillow and begin hunting for the intruder. He searched every corner of his house but found no one. He went outside and called the duty guard and asked him, 'Have you seen anybody around?' The guard saluted him, and said, 'No sir, everything is okay here. Is there any problem?'

Subedar Sahib shook his head in refusal and came back in. When he had heard the full story, he appeared sheepish at his hasty reaction. But, if you ask me, it was not really his fault. He had been in the army for almost all of his adult life. Esoteric and paranormal concerns are far from a life where you only know to take orders from your seniors and, in turn, give them to your juniors.

Though Ajee Shah's father did not take the incident seriously, he did enjoy boasting about his late Sufi father and claiming that having such spiritually powerful ancestors meant that nothing could harm his family. 'Even if they are in another world, you are under their constant protection,' he told anyone who would stop to listen.

After that night, neither my grandmother nor any other member of my family or clan came to try to take me back. I know they all missed me very much but eventually your family just has to let you go, and I suppose they took this as my declaration of independence.

My soul mate, Ajee Shah, grew up to be a healthy, active, and a very good-looking toddler. He even started walking early in comparison to his siblings. His mother faced no further problems either. She didn't see anything else frightening after the apparition of my grandmother and eventually conceded that the event might have been nothing more than a post-natal hallucination, as the army female doctor Lieutenant Shamim had bluntly declared it at the time of the episode.

3

One and A Half
Knot Maketh the Man

Ajee Shah's fourth birthday had passed but he was
still not circumcised. In those days, whenever I
remembered Ajee Shah's late grandfather's remark
that he would make me a Muslim by circumcision,
I always smirked. The idea of conversion into a
religion by cutting off the foreskin of one's penis
was quite amusing to me. I was convinced that Ajee
Shah's grandfather was not serious, that his rebuke
was just meant to shut my grandmother up. Still, I
did sometimes wonder how little Ajee Shah would
take that inevitable experience of circumcision and
how it would affect me.

Although my djinn clan has many elaborate
and well-defined rituals and ceremonies at births,
marriages, deaths, and other important occasions,
we do not follow any specific religion. Our elders
say that religion, no matter how good it is, always
binds your free spirit and thus handicaps you in one
way or the other. However, many other djinn clans
do have their own religions, some of them have
even adopted human religions. There are individuals

among us who practise their religion so strictly that they more or less lose their natural djinn characteristics and become quite odd. But, I have never heard of any djinn, even Muslim or Jew, ever being circumcised. On the top of that, the natural shape of a djinn's phallus does not require it anyway.

Then came autumn and one day Ajee Shah's father announced abruptly that the season was good for circumcision, as wounds would heal quickly. He fixed the coming Sunday for his son's circumcision and invited many guests to the ceremony. Ajee Shah, whose thoughts had changed from the complex, indecipherable ones of just after his birth to more basic ones connected with emotions or his environment, was so embarrassed when the barber did the deed, in the open courtyard in front of all those people, that he screamed and cried inconsolably. Some of the spectators giggled and little Ajee's embarrassment deepened, but that at least distracted him from the pain. At the time of circumcision, I only felt a slight irritation in my genital area and a lot of sympathy for the poor child. But, after a week, when Ajee Shah's penis had completely healed, I felt a big change in myself. The core of my being was transformed in some mysterious way. In the space of just a few days, my whole relationship with Ajee Shah, his parents, his siblings, and his extended family changed tremendously. I felt as though I had a blood relationship with them and had never been an outsider! My djinn identity even became a little blurred in my mind. Then I realised that Ajee Shah's late grandfather had not been joking after all. While I was no convert to Islam, from that moment onwards I was also no longer an infidel . . .

Soon the shock of circumcision became a distant memory in the light of that bane of childhood: education. It had come time for Ajee Shah to be admitted to class one in a primary school where all teachers, except the headteacher, wore army uniform. Subedar Sahib's orderly, Sher Bhadar, fixed a small seat to the main rod of his bicycle and took us to the school. At the last bell of the school, he was always waiting with the other orderlies to take us home. The school had a strict dress code, a uniform with a tie.

Before starting at the school, Ajee Shah's father taught him how to knot a tie. Though he taught him three knots—single, one and a half, and double—he was out-and-out in favour of the one and a half knot. For some reason, that Ajee Shah and I were not able to understand at that stage, his father declared the 'one and a half knot' as an English gentleman's knot. That was the first skill I learnt from humans: to knot a tie. In my whole life I have never seen a djinn wearing a tie. Our sartorial choices are always free-flowing for is it not foolishness in the extreme to allow your clothes to encumber you? We hate knots, particularly around our necks. I pondered it for hours but could not find a single reason for that piece of human attire. Why do you wear ties? Why would you want to squeeze your neck in that way? And why do some of you take a very special kind of pride in wearing a matching tie? I am sure that Ajee Shah himself would have had no problem with the tie but I had serious issues with it. As I had to live in the body of Ajee Shah, for who knew how long, I wanted to live comfortably. So, as soon he wore the tie, I started my protest. Ajee Shah had to face a very confusing situation. No doubt Ajee Shah could knot a tie perfectly and was happy to have this new skill but, as soon as he put his tie on, I would start nagging him from the inside. He experienced this as an inner dialogue so he still had no inkling that I was within him fighting against the tie-wearing.

'Don't wear a tie. It is no good. It stops the flow of your breathing. Doesn't it choke you?' Ajee Shah was fed up with my suggestions but he could not stop them. Even if he loosened his tie, I never let up. I hated the tie so much that I demanded to be rid of it altogether. Now all day at school, Ajee Shah waited impatiently for PE lesson or the last school bell to ring to get rid of the tie. Eventually the battle of the tie went so far that one day Ajee Shah refused to go to school with a tie on. There was a lot of argument in the house but finally Subedar Sahib wrote a letter, in his military-style English, to the headmaster. He asked him to allow Ajee Shah to remain tie-less on health grounds, as he felt suffocated when he wore one. Ajee Shah was given special permission to attend school without a tie and with his collar button untied. I felt, for the very first time, a pride in Ajee Shah at standing out and being distinguished as different from the rest of the school. After that I never needed to bug him on that issue as an aversion to ties became part of his "story", his beliefs about himself, and his likes and dislikes. Such was the blending of our two selves . . .

Subedar Sahib was a fantastic storyteller and I was fascinated by his many anecdotes—some of which were very interesting— but repetition had made all of them equally dull for his principal audience, his immediate family members. Ajee Shah and I were new additions to the audience and, so, were fresh-faced, excited, and unfamiliar with the material. I was perhaps more excited than Ajee as the Lady Kiya had told me that every human story, no matter how tedious, always has something of worth for non-humans.

Ajee Shah's grandfather, Hidayat Shah, was a Sufi master and all his adult life he had never missed any obligatory prayer, five times a day. The first story we heard about him from Ajee Shah's father had me as well as Ajee equally interested. Subedar Sahib started the tale thus: 'My noble father, Hidayat Shah, learnt the holy Koran and got basic religious knowledge in his

childhood from a religious teacher in our native village. When
he was in his teens, my grandfather arranged for his admission
to a reputable religious school for advanced studies that was far
away from his home district . . .'

We listened rapt as our father related how Hidayat Shah
had studied at this school for three years when, one fateful day,
he had an argument with four of his classmates. Our father
continued, 'He lost his temper and made a very big mistake. He
told his friends, "I know who the hell you are and why you are
so nasty to me." They replied, "You have no idea who we are. If
you know anything then tell us who we are?" And he said, "You
are not human beings. You are djinn and have taken on the
appearance of us. You are nothing but disguised clowns." The
faces of his schoolmates turned pale and all four disappeared
right in front of Hidayat Shah's eyes. Within half an hour, the
head of the religious school called him into his office. The
man was in his eighties, but his eyesight, memory, and physique
were astonishingly good. He asked the first question, "Shah
Sahib, how did you know that the four friends with whom you
argued were not human beings? Do not lie as you are Syed, a
direct descendent of the Prophet Mohammad, Peace Be Upon
Him." Hidayat Shah remained silent for a while but couldn't
resist the eyes of his old teacher waiting for an answer. He
said in a low voice, "One day, during the last cold winter, when
we all woke up early in the morning for the first prayer, those
four were sleeping. I went to their beds to wake them up but
when I removed the quilts, there was nothing under them. I
became very suspicious and knew in my heart that this was not
their spiritual advancement but something else. As we went
to perform the first prayer of the day, all four were present
there standing in the first row of the congregation. After that
I watched them and even spied on them. Then eventually I

came to know that they never spend their nights with us but go somewhere else."

"But how did you know that they are djinn?" the old man asked.

"It was very simple. One day I flashed my hand in front of their eyes but they didn't blink and just laughed. I knew from that moment that they are djinn."

The old man's tone immediately changed and became very stern. "Look, Shah Sahib, you are a good student but you are too nosy and, now that you know the truth, we cannot allow you to remain here. Djinn have been studying here for many generations. Until now no pupil recognised them. Nobody outside knows anything about them. Because of you, years of old arrangements could be turned topsy-turvy. And we cannot permit this to happen at any cost. You have to leave this school. I will pray for you that you will get another one suitable for you."

My father, Hidayat Shah, had never thought his innocent curiosity could have led to such a drastic consequence. He started crying while apologising for his behaviour. He promised by God not to tell anyone about those djinn and in future to even keep himself away from them. But, the old teacher replied, "This is out of my power. I cannot do anything besides pray for your future knowledge and spiritual growth, which I will definitely do. Now go and pack your things and leave before the afternoon prayer." Then the old man took a coin out of his right pocket and handed it to him, saying, "You will need this money for your return journey. Keep it safe." My father took the coin, kissed it and put it in his side pocket. He was utterly disoriented but his spiritual manners were automatic by now, and he went to the dormitory to collect his things. He did not say goodbye to anyone and could not stop the tears

42

running down his face. At the main door, when he looked back at his school for the last time, he saw all the four djinn friends standing there. They apologised to him and, while touching his feet, they said that if they had known the consequences, they would never have complained to the headteacher. And all the four of them started crying and shedding even more tears than my father.' Our father's story ended on that sad note.

I was rather affected by this sorry tale but Ajee Shah wasn't particularly saddened by it. But that didn't mean I never experienced sadness within my human compatriot. Occasionally, for no apparent reason, he would become gloomy. In such moments, he was always nostalgic for the things and people with whom he was not familiar with in this life. I had some idea about this phenomenon but I did not want to interfere as I knew that Muslims do not generally believe in reincarnation.

Apart from that occasional gloominess, Ajee Shah was so upbeat and energetic that instead of walking he used to run all the time, and was often told off by his elders for his haste. No one could blame me for that as I played no role in his speediness. He was naturally like that.

Ajee Shah even learnt by himself to climb a small tree that was in the front garden of the house. Whenever he wanted to be alone, you could see him sitting on its branches. Though in reality he was never alone, as I was always with him. Ajee Shah's mother and father often worried that he might fall from the tree and hurt himself. One Sunday when the army maintenance unit were working in the surrounding area, Subedar Sahib asked them to dig the ground at least a foot deep around the tree trunk and soften the clay in that circle. It was an ideal precaution to stop Ajee Shah from hurting himself, should he fall from the tree, but little Ajee had other ideas about that soft pitch. Now he climbed the tree and jumped to the soft ground and made his clothes dirty. Our mother blamed our father for the new trouble of having to change Ajee Shah's clothes three to four times a day. But Subedar Sahib always defended himself by saying that it was better for Ajee to be dirty than to be hurt.

After some days, Ajee Shah became bored with jumping off from the tree and decided to turn the pitch into a mud pool by pouring water on it. For months he played in the mud and put our mother to the greater trouble of washing his muddy clothes. Then one day he climbed the highest tree in the courtyard, the one where I used to sit myself before I entered his body. Ajee Shah's mother immediately saw him from the courtyard, something she had never been able to do with me, despite months of my being there. She took a sharp intake of breath and prayed, 'O God, it is only you who can save this brat from falling to the ground. Please protect him.' Did my own djinn mother ever pray like that for me, perhaps when she had realised that I had left for my human adventure? I doubted it, as I said we're not bound by religion, and so praying is not something we do. I envied you humans this ability to appeal to something greater than yourselves. Did your prayers ever get answered? Perhaps sometimes they did.

Subedar Sahib's orderly, Sher Bhadar, was like a family member. Moreover, he had a special bond with little Ajee Shah. Often Sher Bhadar would take Ajee Shah outside and play with him for hours. They both looked forward to those times. Sher Bhadar was in his mid-thirties but always acted like a child when he played with Ajee Shah. He would cheat, fight, laugh, tease, and pretend like children. Some days they were best friends, sharing their sweets and secrets, and on others they were cross and not on speaking terms with each other.

Sher Bhadar was a nice person but he had a serious

problem. He was a thief, but only of a single item—the bullets of 303 rifles. He was not the only one; there were many such "bullet thieves" in the army. Like Subedar Sahib, he belonged to the traditional soldier-producing region of Punjab where the British recruited their army in the days of the Raj. He lived in a village and his family had generations-old enmity. Many people were killed in those skirmishes between villagers. Those were the days when there were very few firearms around. Only the army or the police used the 303 rifle and no civilian could legally possess it. It was standard army issue. Sher Bhadar's family had a stolen rifle but the bullets were not available from anywhere.

Now, under pressure from his family, Sher Bhadar stole a couple of bullets before going on his annual holidays. But on his third attempt, he was caught red-handed and was sentenced to thirty days' rigorous imprisonment in the army gaol. He was also transferred from the ammunition depot and was made an orderly. But, despite all that, he was still looking for those bullets and used to go to other units in search of someone who could supply him, even if just a bullet or two. Subadar Sahib knew this and sometimes joked with him, 'Sher Bhadar, if you continue with this obsession you will definitely lose your only stripe of Lance Corporal.' He always answered, 'But, Shah Sahib, if I go without bullets to my village, they will break my skull, and my skull is more precious to me than my stripe.' Fortunately, Sher Bhadar was never caught again.

Ajee Shah passed class one successfully, as did all his class fellows. All the children knew about their success before the day of the announcement of the results, and were expected to bring garlands to place around the class teacher's neck. Sher Bhadar had collected many flowers for the occasion from many front gardens, but the garlands were not ready in the morning. Ajee Shah was sent to school with the promise that Sher Bhadar would bring the garlands before the announcement of the result. When he left for school, his mother and older sister were busy in making the garlands. Unfortunately, the results were announced before the orderly's arrival. The teacher didn't even take pains to mention the names of students individually but announced that the whole class one had passed. Every student placed garlands around the neck of the teacher except Ajee Shah. To conceal his embarrassment he kept looking back constantly towards the school gate. The whole show was over in mere minutes and the teacher left the scene.

Ajee Shah came to the school gate and a short while later saw Sher Bhadar coming down the road on his bicycle, with many garlands hanging from its handle. Ajee Shah's little body shook with rage and he shouted at Sher Bhadar, 'Now what is the point of bringing these garlands? It is too late! They are useless now. The teacher has gone.' Sher Bhadar tried to explain but Ajee Shah wrenched all the garlands apart and then, in a frenzy, crushed the flowers under his shoes. He even refused to go home on Sher Bhadar's bicycle and walked all the way back.

On that day he walked so slowly that nobody could believe that he was the same Ajee Shah who ran at breakneck speed at all times. I, Kabuko the djinn, also shared the anger and agony of my soul compatriot but I did not put any oil on the fire. When reporting the whole incident back to the family, Sher Bhadar finished with, 'I have never seen little Shah so wrathful before! As he crushed the beautiful flowers, and all our hard work, it seemed as if a djinn had possessed him.' It was a comment and not a complaint, based on the human belief that djinn possession unleashes rage and uncharacteristic behaviour in those they possess. Of course, you are quick to blame our kind but have you ever thought that perhaps it is your own suppressed human emotions that we permit you to release in a healthy catharsis rather than any strong feeling on our part? Nevertheless, Sher Bhadar's words made me anxious and I started to worry that I was not as well-concealed as I thought I was. I asked myself in awe, 'Am I showing myself to outsiders?'

4
Other Men of Clay

We only spent three months in class two before our father retired from the army after thirty-two years of flawless service. At his recommendation, the orderly Sher Bhadar was not only promoted to corporal but also transferred to a regular unit. But, until the day of Subedar Hussain Shah's departure, he remained with us.

The last few weeks before our father's retirement were a very enjoyable time for me and Ajee Shah. Subedar Sahib sorted out all his stuff, and Ajee got many small metal things to play with, like army badges and other such decorative items. Ajee also collected those long barbs that his father removed from his old papers and replaced with metal pins. I realised that human children are not dissimilar to magpies, when it comes to small, shiny things.

Then the final day came and the family left for the railway station to leave the cantonment for good. They were to return to a town near their ancestral village. On the platform more than one hundred of our father's army colleagues had gathered to bid him goodbye. Though nobody was in uniform, almost all of them were clearly recognisable by their typical army haircuts and the uniformity of their civilian clothes. Before shaking hands, they saluted each other in their habitual manner. Ajee Shah was constantly at his father's side, his neck full of garlands just like Subedar Sahib's. Sher Bhadar had put many garlands around Ajee's neck. There were tears in his eyes and in spite of wiping them away with a handkerchief, he could not hide his emotions. The train came and all our family members took their pre-booked seats in a second class compartment, but Subedar Sahib and little Ajee Shah stood at the door of the carriage. As Subedar Sahib waved to his army colleagues, Ajee Shah saw a hint of tears in his father's eyes.

The train left the small station and both father and son took their seats. Everyone was completely silent for quite a long time. Ajee Shah was thinking about Sher Bhadar. He regretted the day he had shouted at him and that made me feel guilty, too, about my failure to stop him. But then, Ajee Shah took consolation remembering the remark of Sher Bhadar and thought that it must indeed have been the possession of a djinn that made him behave so rudely.

The departure made Subedar Sahib very nostalgic. Also, he was feeling very insecure at having to rejoin civilian life after serving for more than three decades in the army. He knew he had young children and his measly pension would not be enough for their survival, he would have to do a civilian job to run his household. He looked like a worried man.

After a couple of stations, Subedar Sahib returned to his normal self and started talking, first to his wife and then to other family members. What he didn't realise was that the nostalgia for army life was clear in his conversation.

He recalled the time, during the Second World War, when his

name was put forward for a commission. At that time his father, Hidayat Shah, was still alive, so he went to his native village and proudly told him that soon he would be a commissioned officer. On hearing that, Hidayat Shah fell silent and went into a meditative state. He then left for the mosque. Subedar Sahib had not been expecting that sort of reaction from his father. The next day Hidayat Shah called him and asked, "Can you withdraw your name from the commission?" He replied, "Yes, of course, but this is the opportunity of a lifetime. My colleagues would die for this kind of promotion. If I take it, I will definitely retire a Brigadier." Then, after a long silence, Ajee Shah's father gathered the courage to ask Hidayat Shah, "May I ask you why I should withdraw my name?" The elder Shah Sahib said, "You cannot see what I see. Withdraw your name. It is not good for you. And, in any case, this is my order to you." That last sentence shut all doors for further persuasion. It was the norm in those days that if your father ordered you to do something, you had no other choice. At all.

When Subedar Sahib withdrew his name from the commission, his English officer called him and asked, 'Why are you doing this to yourself?' He answered, 'This is the order of my father.' How could he explain to his English officer that, on top of everything else, his father was no ordinary person but a Sufi who had not only studied with djinn but had also cleared many human bodies possessed by male and female djinn?

Even without such cultural eccentricities, the officer did not like that answer but took no further action. Another soldier was included in that batch of seven and sent for training to become a commissioned officer. After a few months all seven were promoted to second lieutenants and were sent to the Burmese front. Minutes after their arrival in Burma, Japanese war planes bombarded the area and all seven officers, along with a few others, were killed on the spot. 'What an unfortunate end,' Subedar Sahib concluded his story, 'But I was saved by the grace of God, which was expressed through the order of my father.'

I had listened rapt to this story, wondering if it was indeed the grace of God or some innate quality in Hidayat Shah that had given him such psychic powers. It was impressive, either way, to be able to know the future in this manner. We djinn often have glimpses of the future but that is only because of our different, more pliable relationship with time. It is not a supernatural power in our eyes, merely the human equivalent of hiccups.

The train reached their town about mid-morning and Subedar Sahib's older brother, Ali Shah, along with many relatives and a band of local musicians, was waiting to welcome the family. We all left the railway station following the band, which was playing in full swing. There were several pre-booked horse carriages waiting to take us into town.

We stayed for a couple of days in Ali Shah's house and had great fun there, what with feasts each night, much laughter, and reminiscences. Then, we moved to another house belonging to Ajee Shah's maternal aunt. Ajee Shah's father, with the help of his brother, started looking for a house to buy. They soon found an old house with spacious land and bought it.

Subedar Sahib borrowed some money from his brother, demolished the dwelling, and built a new house on the land. He returned the money in monthly instalments, though it took years to pay off. On the day the last instalment was to be paid, Ajee Shah's mother performed a special gratitude prayer, which is recited one hundred and one times. She was very happy that their only loan was paid off. She used to say that death could come at any moment and one must not go to the grave with a pending loan. That is misfortune and may God save everybody from that. It made me ponder the debts I had left hanging in both the djinn and human world . . . not all of them financial.

Ajee Shah liked the smell of their newly-built house and loved the homely atmosphere of his new neighbourhood. There were many children around—older, younger, his own age—and most of them became our playmates. Streets and alleyways were the main playgrounds, and the children shared those with donkeys, mules, buffaloes, goats, stray dogs and cats, horse carriages, oxen carts, and male and female passers-by of all temperaments. In this new atmosphere, Ajee Shah never missed the dull and boring life of the army barracks but occasionally remembered Sher Bhader and his playful teasing and departing tears.

Unlike at the cantonment house, here hardly a day passed without some guest turning up at Ajee Shah's new house. Most of them came from their native village. Ajee Shah and I had a favourite among the many visitors and that was his maternal grandmother who lived in another village, just four miles outside the town. I liked his grandmother, who Ajee Shah called Nani, very much because I could see my own grandmother in her. Upright and strong, despite her age, she was a proud and resourceful woman.

Nani loved Ajee Shah, and would not only tell him many interesting stories but would also take him along to spend a day or two at her house in the village. She never came to her only daughter's house empty-handed and would always bring along sweets and other tasty things, made with her own hands, with the know-how of a lifetime. She had a very independent nature and never took instructions from anyone. Her husband had died years ago and since then she had supported herself in every respect and never become a burden on any of her relatives.

During the morning hours, our Nani was a trader and sold sweets and other titbits to the children of a nearby primary school. After that she made coloured straw baskets for shoppers. In the afternoon, she took on the role of a herbalist, preparing many herbal remedies and giving them to anyone who needed it, free of charge. She never even took any favours in return for her medicines, which seemed to be very effective as they were always in demand. She was a hands-on healer as well and used to cure headaches and joint pains. For a healing massage, she prepared her own oils; she would read many verses of the Koran and at the end of each verse would blow into the bottle of oil. Among the mothers of the neighbourhood, Nani's *phhaki* powder was the most popular as it gave instant comfort for an upset stomach. Ajee Shah's mother always kept it in her home for her children.

Like Ajee Shah's father, Nani was also a storyteller but her style was straightforward and her narration simple. Nani never defended any of her stories except one, which she always insisted was one hundred and one percent true. All the other family members had their doubts about Nani's distant memory of the event but Ajee Shah and I, Kabuko the djinn, believed her story and never doubted a word of it.

She told us that in the days of British Raj, when she was a little girl, her family lived in a remote village near the border of Kashmir. The village was very unfortunate in one respect—the water under its soil was salty. Men and animals couldn't drink it and it wasn't even suitable for washing body, hair, or clothes. But sometimes people, in their desperation, did use it for washing up. Whenever they did, it always left salt marks on their hands and caused a lot of itching.

The women had to go a long way, twice a day, to get water from a well that was near another village. They stacked four to five pitchers on their heads and one in each of their arms. It was such hard labour that many parents simply refused to marry their daughters to the men of the village. It had become a joke in the area that whoever wanted to show enmity towards their daughter should marry her into that village. In search of clean drinking water, those people had dug many wells in different places but always found the same salty water. In the end, they accepted their fate and abandoned the search for sweet water.

Years passed like that and then one day a man arrived in the village and stayed in the house of the village head. The man was a *khojee*, a tracker, who offered his services to police and villagers wanting to trace the tracks of thieves. In his early years, he had been a thief and used to steal animals. Then, by chance, he met a wandering yogi who read his forehead and told him the details of his every crime. The yogi advised him to leave off stealing and become *sukhi*, the contended one. He was so impressed by the yogi's mysterious personality that a change occurred in his life then and there. He vowed never to steal even a needle again, and the yogi rewarded him with two gifts. He taught him how to cure milk-giving animals gone dry due to an evil curse and how to find things hidden under the earth. After that he did not come across that yogi again but he also never stole anything again; and went from being a thief to a thief-tracker. He adopted the name Sukhi Khojee.

Sukhi Khojee was a good-natured man and offered his services free of charge to the villagers to help them locate sweet water under the soil. They accepted his offer with a lot of gratitude but with little enthusiasm as they believed the water in the soil was salty all around. Sukhi Khojee asked only for two spades and two strong men to dig the soil. Both were provided by the village chief.

Now Sukhi woke up two hours before sunrise, took his

two helpers along, and went all over the place including the courtyards of houses. His method of exploration was very simple. He washed his hands and forearms thoroughly and then would put his right elbow on the palm of his left hand. Facing North, he closed his eyes and straightened his right arm. Then whichever direction his arm moved towards automatically, he followed with the helpers. Sometimes, he suddenly stopped at a place and asked the helpers to dig the ground a foot or two deep. First, he would smell the soil and, then, taste it. Sukhi's exploration went on for many days and the diggers became bored and thought that the whole activity was just a waste of time. But before they reached the point of not showing up early in the morning, a miracle happened. In a field, just outside the village, under a sheesham tree, Sukhi smelt and tasted sweet soil, an indication of drinkable water beneath. He ordered the men to dig deep and again smelt and tasted fine mud. Then, he climbed the tree and ate many leaves from the branches at the very top. Sukhi came down with a big smile on his face and declared with full confidence that the water under that particular spot was definitely sweet. When he saw doubt in the eyes of the villagers, he announced, "If you don't find sweet water here, on this very spot, you can shave my moustache and paint my face black."

The whole village became excited at that unbelievable prediction and many people joined the two diggers and the spot became crowded. Sakina, a new bride in the village, vowed in her heart that if the prediction came true, she would perform a thousand and one prayers of gratitude. The digging went on at full speed for many days as the water at the spot was located at a great depth. Sukhi was present at the site all the time, smelling and tasting the deeper mud. At last they reached wet mud, and then muddy water. Sukhi took the muddy water and filtered it through a cotton cloth into a clay bowl. He tasted the water first and then many villagers, including the chief, confirmed the sweetness of the water. The joy of the villagers, particularly of the women, was indescribable.

Next day, when the work started, two men were inside the well, digging and filling buckets with muddy water, and three were on the ground, pulling and emptying them, when something strange happened. As they pulled out one bucket, something moved in the muddy water. They noticed but ignored it and poured the bucket out. The thing was still moving in the heap of mud. They thought it was probably a toad or some other reptile. But then they realised that its shape was completely different to anything that they had ever come across before. One of the men tried to catch it but it slipped away from his hands and disappeared into the mud. They stopped the work, and the two men inside the well also came out.

The villagers told Sukhi that there was a strange creature in the mud that had come out of the well in the bucket. Sukhi Khojee smelt the bucket and tasted a little bit of the mud. To utter surprise of the villagers, he became crazy and started jumping up and down, and shouting, "It must be a *bauna*! It must be a *bauna*!" He was so overwhelmed that he could not speak normally. The villagers were confused as to what had happened to an otherwise sane and wise man.

Sukhi told the villagers that the yogi, who imparted this knowledge, had made a prediction that one day Sukhi would meet one of the little men who live deep under the earth, and that this *bauna* must be the one that the yogi had told him about. Even in his frenzy, Sukhi Khojee didn't waste any time. He took off his shirt, rolled up his shalwar, and started searching the watery mud mound with his hands. Minutes later, he found something and brought it out of the mud. He then stepped away from the mud so as not to give the creature any chance to escape again. He shouted, "Bring clean water!" and when somebody poured water from a pitcher onto his hands, the features of the creature became clear.

It was about five inches tall, like a tiny man, but with no hair on his head and also without eyebrows and eyelashes. Sukhi washed the creature carefully, while holding it tightly in his hand. The creature seemed to be very uncomfortable with this and moaned time and again. But its voice was so low that it did not make much impact on human ears. It was trying to break free from Sukhi's grip. Then, Sukhi put a cloth around its body, leaving its face uncovered. In just a short time, all the village had gathered around Sukhi to see the *bauna* with their own eyes. They had only heard tales about the humanoid creatures living deep under the soil and never imagined in their wildest dreams that they would see one with their own eyes.

Sukhi Khojee showed the little man to everyone, including the little ones of the village, but did not allow anyone to touch it. Then, he told the villagers that the *bauna* should be released back into the same well as keeping it overground would bring bad luck to the whole village. A few people initially disagreed with him and suggested keeping it in a small mud container. They argued that it was the common property of the village and that they could sell it to the authorities and get a big reward. But Sukhi refused to do so, and told them, "Look, they are creatures of God just as we are. The only difference is that they live below and we above. But it makes no difference in the eyes of God. God sees all His creations with the same eye." Those few mercenary men had no worth against Sukhi, the discoverer of sweet water in the village.

Then, holding the small creature in his hand, he walked away from the crowd. People saw that he uncovered the creature and kissed it three times on its abdomen and spoke to it, making some strange sounds, and then put the creature to his ear to listen to it. This mysterious activity went on for an hour or so after which Sukhi lowered himself into the well, holding in one hand the creature and in the other, a strong rope. He remained in the well for quite some time and finally shouted for someone to pull him up. Then he closed the mouth of the well with wood, straw, and mud and declared that it should remain closed for another seven days. He and his two original helpers set up their beds near the well to protect it from predators. All seven nights the stray dogs of the village howled continuously, which made the villagers very frightened, but Sukhi remained content.

After seven days, the villagers resumed work and completed the well in a couple of weeks. Before leaving the village, the strange man that Sukhi Khojee was, drew a long line with a wooden stick, starting from the sweet water well. He told the villagers that water under this line was sweet and they could dig as many wells as they liked. But he did not tell anyone of what he had conversed about with the creature from the underworld.

Nani had never claimed to see the *bauna* with her own eyes but she was insistent that her whole family had seen the strange creature. Nani used to say that her father was suspicious of Sukhi Khojee and had accused him of being a black magician. He used to say that Sukhi was a disciple of an infidel yogi and not a proper Muslim. He also doubted his very integrity by saying that trackers and thieves are one and the same thing and only reverse their roles to suit the time.

I, Kabuko the djinn, whenever I heard or remembered Nani's story, felt a strange tickling in my abdomen. My mental image of the *bauna* bore so much resemblance with the tiny clay man my old djinn benefactress had prepared and pushed into my stomach. We djinn, just like humans, have no access to the depths of this Earth. The depths have always been protected from both of us. But, after hearing Nani's tale, I felt pleased that my kind are not alone; there is at least one other species not yet scientifically approved of in the human world.

5

First Impressions Are Not The Last

It was not just formal education that Ajee Shah and I were made to attend. The first thing his family did upon moving to their new neighbourhood was to put him in the early morning class at a local mosque to learn the Koran, the holy book of Muslims. His father took Ajee Shah to the mosque, along with a dish of sweets, a white cloth to make into an outfit, and a rosary of a hundred and one beads. All of those things were presented to the Imam who would be teaching the Koran to Ajee Shah.

Nobody ever asked the Imam what his real name was, and everybody called him Hafiz Sahib, a distinctive title reserved either for one who is blind or for one who has learnt the Koran by heart. Hafiz Sahib was not blind and fell into the latter category. He was in his late fifties and happily received the traditional gifts and a student from a Syed family. He was a good tutor but so lenient that he never punished any of his students. Most of the parents didn't like his mild attitude towards their children but, in spite of their concern, many of his students successfully learnt all thirty parts of the Koran. 'Don't worry, Shah Sahib,' assured Hafiz Sahib, smiling confidently at Subedar Sahib. 'Ajee will, by the grace of God, learn the Koran in Arabic quickly. The words of God are already in his genes through his ancestors.'

Ajee Shah now had to wake up early in the morning to go to the mosque for an hour before having his breakfast. When he missed a couple of lessons due to oversleeping, his mother declared that if in future he missed the mosque without a genuine reason she would not give him breakfast. Ajee Shah did not think this possible and so didn't take his mother's threat seriously. Then, one day, when he again overslept and didn't heed the many calls of his mother to wake up, he was forced to go to school without any breakfast. His mother even refused to give him his pocket money for the day. As that was an added punishment, not included in the original declaration, Ajee Shah protested a lot at that injustice.

He went to school in a very bad mood with both an empty stomach and an empty pocket. Throughout the day at school strange noises came from his stomach. On his way back, he was so hungry that he took a bite of *gachi*, the soft clay that children used in those days on their writing boards. He didn't like the taste and spat it out.

Ajee Shah was confused too as he could not understand why his otherwise loving and caring mother became so strict to teach him the Koran. I, Kabuko the djinn, was equally confused. Not having encountered any religious dogma in my own tribe, I frankly disapproved of this stern insistence on the indoctrination of children. I could not see my little friend in this miserable predicament. I said to Ajee Shah, perhaps out of my djinn ego, 'Name anything you want to eat at this moment.' Ajee Shah started thinking about his favourite things and ended up with *massu*, a sort of sweet. The second he uttered the word *massu*, I zipped over to a sweetshop and, ensuring I legitimately and invisibly paid for the treat, came back and deposited three pieces of the *massu* in Ajee Shah's school bag. Then I proudly said, 'Check your school bag.' Ajee opened the straps of his school bag and found the *massu* in one compartment. He was so astonished that for a while he couldn't think about anything. He tasted the *massu* very carefully as if it were made of very hot chillies. But the sweets were so tasty that he ate all three of them in minutes. Then he thought about their materialisation in his bag and became scared.

'Don't be scared,' I assured him, from within. 'You are a blessed child and nature takes care of you in extraordinary ways.' This idea, so attractive to the solipsist nature of a child, seemed to strike Ajee Shah as perfectly reasonable and he became satisfied. His easy acceptance of this 'miracle' made me realise that children are quite open to magic and that it is only when they reach adulthood that they close themselves off to the idea of the miraculous, preferring to surround themselves with the mundane, and then complaining when life becomes dull and lacklustre.

When he reached home, Ajee's mother was expecting a hungry child looking for food. She had made a special dish for her child but when she offered Ajee Shah the food, he refused to eat and said, 'Mother, I am not hungry at all.' His mother thought that Ajee Shah was saying this in protest but how would she know that he was telling the truth. He had eaten three heavy, greasy *massus*, after all.

Eventually Ajee Shah accepted the new discipline of waking up early and going to the mosque. But then at the mosque, he adopted another strategy. He discovered a "staring game" in which two people stare into each other's eyes and whoever blinks first loses the game. Ajee Shah never lost. Ever. Soon, he began even staring into the eyes of his teacher, making him nervous. Whenever he found any verse of the Koran difficult, he skipped it, and, while staring into the eyes of his tutor, would insist on learning another, more easy, verse. Hafiz Sahib couldn't resist his staring eyes and always surrendered. Ajee Shah went to the mosque for many years but couldn't learn the Koran properly and chronologically, though he knew many short verses well enough to repeat them by heart. In all those years, whenever his mother or father asked Hafiz Sahib about the progress of Ajee Shah, his answer always was, 'To be honest with you, I am scared of younger Shah Sahib. His eyes are strange. Whenever I look into his eyes, his staring looks are like a djinn's. So whichever lesson he tells me to give of the Koran, I give him. But don't worry, one day he will get the hang of it and learn the Koran instantly.' Alas, Hafiz Sahib's prediction never came true.

While Ajee Shah had no qualms in gently intimidating his teacher, he had no taste for cruelty. He never participated in the sadistic games of his peers. His friends would catch hornets, pull out their stings, and then tie a thread around them so that they didn't fly away. They also often hit stray dogs with stones and, sometimes, with their homemade slings, killed birds like crows that were of no use to them as they were *haram*, and therefore prohibited for Muslims to eat. Ajee Shah hated that sort of barbarity, and I, Kabuko the djinn, was proud of his inclination towards creation rather than destruction, believing it to arise from my own benign influence. Shortly afterwards, however, my pride in the influence of djinn on man would be dented by the saddest of tales.

It so happened that most of the houses in that old neighbourhood had three shared walls with neighbours on three sides around a central courtyard. In one part of the neighbourhood, there was a twisted tree that three adjoining houses shared. The roots and about a foot and a half of the lower trunk was in one house, the main trunk was in another, and almost all the shadow of the green branches was in the courtyard of a third house. The fascinating thing about the tree was not its twist and turns but something else entirely. All the three neighbours sharing the tree belonged to different castes, and yet, eventually, became related to each other, a very rare occurrence in those days. The only daughter in the root-holding house was married to one of the boys of the neighbours that enjoyed the shadow of the tree. A couple of years after that, the middle-aged widowed aunt of the boys, who was staying with her brother's family because of the sudden death of her husband who had been struck by lightning, remarried a chronic bachelor living in the house that held the main trunk. Those were the days that in society, in police stations, in court rooms, and almost on every occasion of any consequence you had to reveal your caste in one way or another. Sometimes people would ask your caste first and your name afterwards, without any hesitation or embarrassment. From your caste they determined what type of respect or disrespect you deserved. While we djinn also have classes and castes, we were never as struck with the idea of classifying souls in the way that humans are.

The children of the neighbourhood were fascinated by that old gnarled tree and took every opportunity to show it off to their friends from other localities. Children enjoyed free movement across houses and had access to almost every house in the neighbourhood. Everybody knew everybody else's caste, nickname, financial and marital status, and other more private matters. Though people still tried to hide their secrets, and would say, 'Don't show your naked tummy to the outside world', most of the time they failed miserably.

Ajee Shah was also entranced by that tree, even more so than his friends. If he didn't see that tree at least once a day he became nostalgic for it. Sometimes he used to pat the tree as if it were his pet animal. At times, his special bond with the tree made his little mind very confused. None of his friends shared that sort of eccentricity with him and that made Ajee Shah feel lonely.

Then, one afternoon, when Ajee Shah was in the house that had the shadow of the tree, I saw an old djinn couple, with a young female djinn I presumed was their daughter, hovering over the tree. They looked harmless but I became immediately suspicious and watched them to see exactly what they were doing there. The couple indicated the tree to the girl and explained to her, 'This is the tree where your older sister spent years in mourning. You can look and even touch the tree now but never return to this haunted place again. We have terrible memories of this place.'

The girl started crying and touched the tree's old branches many times as if she were touching the grave of her sister. I, Kabuko the djinn, became very inquisitive and could not control myself. Without a second thought, I projected myself out of the body of Ajee Shah and into my natural shape. All three were stunned to see me, coming out of a small boy's body. They immediately thought that I had possessed the boy. I had noted in passing that the girl was exceptionally beautiful but I ignored her, as etiquette demands, and addressed only the old couple. I introduced myself and asked respectfully what had happened here to the sister of this poor girl. The old man replied, 'I had two daughters. This is the younger one, on whose insistence we came here to show her this place and this tree. About fifty years back this place was not like this. There was a big courtyard of a house, belonging to a Hindu pundit and this tree was young, standing in the middle of that courtyard. The pundit also had two daughters and one very handsome son. When he was eleven years old and was taking a bath in this courtyard, my young daughter, the elder sister of this one here, saw his naked body by chance. God only knows why she was wandering here alone. The boy was beautiful and she instantly fell in love with him. After that she would come to the house and play with the boy in that courtyard and on the rooftop. She always took the shape of a beautiful human girl of the same age as the pundit's child. He also enjoyed her company as she always brought sweets and fruit for him. But she was inexperienced in her passions and pursuits. One noon, when she embraced him, she couldn't resist her sexual passion and she urged the kid to masturbate. And while he was masturbating, she put her vagina on his little erect penis and seduced him. She took the pleasure of his human body but at the end the boy was so young that no semen came out of his penis. That made my fiery djinn daughter so frustrated that in her madness to extract the human semen from his body, she sucked his actual spirit out. The boy became unconscious and went into a coma. He died after three days. In the whole family, only the pundit had some idea about how his lovely son died but he did not know the exact cause of his death. He was so composed a man that he didn't reveal a word, and so compassionate that he didn't take any revenge on my daughter. He was quite proficient enough to have been able to do that, mind you.

The incident made my daughter very sad and guilty; she hadn't meant to kill her handsome, young beloved, after all. In her guilt, she spent many years, crying and keening all the time, on that tree. She lived rough here and turned almost mad with grief. Then with great difficulty, at last, we managed to bring her back home. But she never married and, to punish herself, started living in a well. She died there. The water of the well turned salty and people stopped drinking from the well. They say the ground beneath the well turned salty but the females of our clan believe that the tears of our poor daughter made the whole water salty.' I also wanted to share the poetic belief of the females of that djinn clan but at the same time I knew that our tears cannot turn underground water salty. I was lost in my own thoughts.

The old djinn was silent for a while and then said, 'I appeared before the pundit and offered him many things in return for forgiveness. I even asked him to take my full services for the remainder of his life but he refused. A couple of years after the pundit died, I would come here and check on the family. Then in 1947, when the killings started, I helped the pundit's daughters, their two children and husbands migrate to an Indian village where their relatives lived. I think I did what I could. But I still deeply regret what happened to my daughter and the pundit's boy.'

When the old djinn finished his story, he asked me abruptly, 'But what you are doing here?' I was not prepared for that direct question and remained silent as if I was not yet out of the shock of listening to his story. The old broken-hearted djinn sadly remarked that if I was possessing the boy, I should leave that human soul alone and go home. I assured the old djinn that I was not possessing Ajee Shah but I could see in the eyes of all three that they did not believe me. Then they flew away.

For days I thought about the story and eventually became convinced that some remaining part of that boy, killed accidentally by the old djinn's daughter, now existed in Ajee Shah. His sad attachment to the tree could only be the result of reincarnation of some sort. Of course, there was no opportunity for me to discuss this with him as he was still unaware of my presence and, besides, I did not know if my infidel notions might cause a block in learning the occult methods I was after. I certainly did not wish to influence Ajee Shah in a way that would take him from the knowledge I sought. However, an overheard conversation was soon going to force my hand . . .

One day, Ajee Shah was resting on his bed and in the same room his mother and Nani, who was visiting, sat on another bed, gossiping. His mother thought that Ajee Shah was asleep and repeated the whole mysterious episode of what happened after the birth of Ajee Shah when my djinn grandma had come to snatch me from her. Nani listened to every word of the story very carefully, despite having heard it before, and at the end remarked, 'Be very careful with this child. Those things never go so easily. Put an amulet around his neck so that he will be protected from those airy creatures.' Ajee Shah's mother replied, 'By the grace of God, my son is fully protected. From that day, nothing abnormal has happened to him, though sometimes he gets very angry but that is normal for boys, I think.'

That revelation was exciting for Ajee Shah but scary for me. I did not want that kind of exposure, particularly at this early stage in my mission, and what if such an amulet affected me adversely? But now that I could not do much to hide myself from Ajee Shah, I decided to change my strategy altogether and be open with the boy.

'Yes, Ajee, it is true. I am within you.' I said it in a way that I hoped was dramatic enough to excite him but not too frightening for his young mind to comprehend.

After that discovery, Ajee Shah taxed his wild imagination to the extreme. I did not like the picture of me he created in his head; an ugly djinn with two horns on his head. It looked more like man's imaginary picture of a devil and I resented it very much. Admittedly, I am not as handsome as Ajee Shah but, to be fair to myself, I am quite attractive. We djinn, while not as corporeal as you, are generally taller with narrower faces but we do not have characteristics so dissimilar to your own. And, as we have different races, we differ in looks according to our race. In fact, some say that a djinn in his natural state could pass for an unusually tall human, until you see his eyes and the larger irises give the game away. However, since some of us can change shape or undertake gimmicks that arise from the difference in our body density, you have these wild notions of us being terrifyingly grotesque.

So, to put things right, I entered into the dream world of Ajee Shah. I created a weird dream that felt so close to reality that Ajee Shah took it as real. Ajee Shah saw in his dream that an entity came out of his body from the space between his eyebrows and stood in front of him. After changing my look into many different shapes and forms—some animals he recognised and some creatures he did not—I finally took the shape of a boy of almost his own age, dark-haired with slightly crooked teeth and dimples in his cheeks, just like Ajee's own.

First, I smiled at Ajee Shah and then hugged him excitedly like an old friend meeting him after a long absence. In dream time, we remained in that hug for seven years and three months. Ajee Shah, in the real world, was seven years and one month old. The length of the hug was two months more than his actual age. I did this to impress upon him the idea that I had been with him from before his birth. After that long time in the dream world, I drew apart from him and gave him a very strange look. The power of my look was so majestic that Ajee Shah didn't dare to look up into my eyes again. I stood about three feet away from him and after a while spoke in a voice that did not match my apparent age as a young boy. It was my own voice.

First I asked, 'Do you know who I am?' Ajee Shah shook his

head to indicate that he did not. 'I am not a human being. I was not born out of clay. I am a legitimate son of fire. My lineage is pure. I am a djinn from a very high caste family, just like yours. I am here to have first-hand experience of the journey of a clay being, namely you. I mostly live inside you but sometimes, in extraordinary situations, I have to move outside of your body. You are not possessed by me. I am like your roommate, sharing the same body. I came to have this unique experience off my own back but then your grandfather generously gave me permission to live with you for this lifetime, to watch you, to observe you, and to feel you. You have a beautiful body which I will share with you to your last moment on this plane.' The strangest thing was that Ajee Shah fully understood my every word and nodded his head, as if I were simply confirming what he already knew. Then I said, 'Today, I appeared in front of you, just to introduce myself. And while I am here in front of you I want to tell you that the tree you like very much belongs to your past. When you reach the age of eleven, your attraction will wither away. So do not worry. It is only a matter of four years now.' Immediately after the dream I woke Ajee Shah up so that he would remember the dream consciously. I also wanted to watch his reaction towards that dream.

My strategy was successful. Ajee Shah was happy to have had that dream and felt himself to be very special. I'll admit I did add a little extra zest to my importance, but it was far better that he have an inflated idea of me than that he think me as a devil-horned lout. His acceptance of my dream self was a good sign for my future relationship with him. It seemed that the mention of that tree played an important role in his accepting me. I became convinced that I was right about Ajee Shah having a karmic attachment to that tree.

6

Death Comes Calling

I am not a masochist but my earnest desire was to experience all emotions hidden in human beings. I was particularly interested in the sensation of feeling real grief, and was always waiting for an opportunity to examine that emotion in Ajee Shah. Day by day, my communication with him was becoming more direct and the confidences between us were growing. One morning, I suggested to him that he bunk school. 'Why?' he asked. 'If you go to school today,' I told him, 'you will regret it all your life as you will miss the last sighting of someone close to you.' Ajee Shah became fearful and thought about all his loved ones. Perhaps it was cruel of me to not give him more information but it provided me with the sensation of the anticipation of human loss. The thought of each person he loved made him progressively more scared as he didn't wish to lose any of them. I felt sadness course through my body at the thought that Ajee Shah might never see his siblings again. Then anxiety, that it would be his father who would pass away. Finally, I felt the

71

blind panic and terror of a child scared of what would happen if his mother died. These feelings were sort of distressing yet also strangely piquant, giving me the pleasant sensation you get when you worry a loose tooth with your tongue. In all his fears, the one person, or entity I should say, Ajee Shah didn't think of was the old stray bitch of his neighbourhood. The bitch whose death would give him such a wound that he would carry a deep scar inside him all his life.

There were many stray dogs in the neighbourhood and nobody ever took any real notice of them. They were an integral yet unspoken part of this rustic and slow-moving world that was filled with the jaded voices of street vendors. The infant mortality rate in the stray dogs was far lower than that in the local human population. They were everywhere. The reason for their mushrooming growth may have been free sex, for they were exempt from the newly-introduced family planning campaigns for humans. Or perhaps, the most vital factor was their strong survival instinct that included knowledge of the local environment and its inhabitants. Each year, without fail, the old bitch would give birth to many puppies, male and female. Nobody ever adopted her offspring. They were born strays and died strays. The old bitch had no pedigree and no one knew her breed. There was not a single derelict, secluded, or shadowy place left in the neighbourhood that she had not had a delivery in at one time or another. Her sex partners always looked much younger and stronger than she. She was obviously blessed in many ways; many young partners and many children.

Ajee Shah had noticed that no dog of the neighbourhood ever fought with the bitch. It seemed as if she was the mother of them all. Either out of her natural instinct or due to her long experience of the local human psyche or for some other reason known only to stray animals, she had adopted a few houses of the neighbourhood. In her days of pregnancy, when she could not grab her food in open competition, she would knock on those chosen doors with her paw and get her food. Ajee Shah's house was one of them.

She often lay in an open drain by the mosque. The water in that drain was comparatively clear and cold to the other drains in the vicinity as it came from the mosque well that was the deepest in the whole neighbourhood. During winter season, it was enjoyably lukewarm and during the heat of the summer, it was pleasantly cold.

The bitch's retreat to the open drain would sometimes cause an annoyance for people coming for prayers. Her body blocked the drain and the water ran out into the street. Sometimes, in a joyous mood, she soaked herself in the open drain and sprayed water all over the place as she shook herself dry. It was quite difficult to save one's clean dress from that exuberant spray of drain water.

She had become a nuisance for passers-by and, especially, for the people coming to the mosque five times a day for their obligatory prayers. Some of those people got very angry when children or animals ruined their clean outfits. They had a genuine reason for their anger as they had to change their clothes before prayer if even a single unclean sprinkle landed on their dress. Often an angry man coming for prayer threw a stone at the bitch, making her leave the place crying. Despite that, she never left off her habit of sitting in the open drain. She would always be back the very next day, occupying her favourite spot, as if nothing had happened.

Then I came to know through the conversation of people in the neighbourhood that a new deputy commissioner of the city had been appointed who was quite different from his predecessors, being extraordinarily efficient. He not only ordered streets to be built with proper bricks but he also ensured the speedy progress of everything within his jurisdiction. Each year the municipal committee workers used to run a short campaign to kill stray dogs in the city by giving them *datura*, a locally-made poison. But that year, there was a real kill under the new deputy commissioner.

As soon as the executioners, the municipal committee workers, entered the neighbourhood, the stray dogs felt the presence of danger and began to flee. Many of them took refuge in the adjoining old cemetery with lot of bushes and pits, places from where it was almost impossible to catch a stray dog. As such, all the refugees in the cemetery were saved from death. The old bitch was captured from *daara*, a small open place adjoining the mosque. She did not try to escape and surrendered herself in a dignified way. Ajee Shah was sure that she knew her fate and had accepted it gracefully. Perhaps she had already lived too long and there was no charm left in eating, mating, and giving birth to more stray dogs. The municipal workers put a string around her neck and took her to an open place where many stray dogs lay, already dying in agony. The old bitch was tied to a small pole and had a pot of poison put in front of her. Ajee Shah witnessed that though she was calm, she resisted her hunger and only touched the poison after more than three hours. As he watched her, great sadness apparent in his heart, she gave him many strange looks. He thought she knew a friend was at her side and perhaps also knew that her friend was helpless and too young to rescue her. When at last she took the poison, she did not cry like the other dying dogs but her eyes started gradually closing. When they came to a point of complete closure, a strange meek sound escaped her mouth and she threw her neck away from where Ajee Shah stood. She died.

Ajee walked around to see her "death face". Her lifeless eyes were wide open. They were saying something, not to him or to her executioners and not even to death. But to the great beyond, far beyond this melodrama of life and death. Ajee Shah couldn't forget that look and each time he remembered it, he felt a pain in his heart.

On his way back home, Ajee Shah sat on the steps of the door of a closed shop in front of the mosque. His elbows were on his knees and he was holding his head in his hands. He sat there in that position for a long time. During that time a question came to his mind, 'How did the djinn inside me know that today the old bitch would be killed?' I could have easily convinced Ajee Shah that I have natural psychic powers but I did not want to lie to him in his emotional state. Besides, I was also feeling the pain of loss through Ajee Shah and it affected my reason quite a bit, making it hard for me to sustain any artifice at all. So I told him the truth.

'That old bitch was not an ordinary dog. She was half djinn and half animal. Her mother was a pure bitch but her father was a djinn. In the djinn realm, there are many who are like your animals but we do not call them animals. They are djinn but of a different, more animal-like type. That old bitch had half the powers of a djinn. Then in her life, through seducing hundreds of dogs in the vicinity, she accumulated so much personal power that she became more than a djinn. Sex gives power if it is done in the proper way, and the bitch somehow knew that genetically. She knew that the moment of her death had come, that is why she did not try to escape. We djinn sense the imminent demise of our nearby fellow djinn, perhaps this is why we deal with death with more equanimity than you humans. But don't be sad any longer. I am sure that she will definitely grow in the other world into someone very special.' Ajee Shah didn't believe me and thought that I was trying to console him through false and baseless notions.

Apart from this great emotional hurt, Ajee Shah also endured many cuts, scrapes, and injuries in the manner of all young humans. Perhaps he had more than the usual, as he would climb any tree available in a heartbeat. I, in spite of giving it my full concentration, could not figure out his craze for climbing trees. However, despite his enduring love for the activity, my prediction came true and at the age of eleven, Ajee Shah began losing interest in that twisted tree. The tree itself was losing its life force and looked very old and tired of being alive. But now Ajee Shah developed many other interests. He would now go much more often to his native village.

The village itself was named after one of Ajee Shah's ancestors—Pir Shah. Pir Shah lived in the time before even Ajee Shah's father was born. He was a strong young man but had not married. He had a spacious house in the village, in which he lived with his old mother who was looking for a bride for her son. Pir Shah's ancestors had left agricultural lands for him, more than enough for his needs. He cultivated his lands and was a hardworking farmer. Though he belonged to a spiritual family, he personally had no interest in prayers or other spiritual practises. By nature he had no interest in women either. He did not hate women or tobacco, but he touched neither, even though in his village almost all the adult males used to smoke waterpipes called *huka*. On the other hand he ate like a djinn and worked like a djinn. No one in the village could compete with him in eating or in hard work.

One day when Pir Shah was tilling his lands and intoning the monotonous sounds that would guide the ploughing oxen, something very strange happened to him. A white bird akin to a falcon flew over to where he was in the field and started circling over his head, making very unusual noises. Pir Shah watched the bird with interest and stopped ploughing. But the bird did not stop and eventually Pir Shah's eyes got fixed on the bird, and after a while he started moving in circles along with the bird in the same rhythm. Then he sat on the ground and looked at the sky. The sky was clear, only the "falcon" was in between him and infinity. Then Pir Shah saw something in that infinity and started shouting. Other villagers working in nearby fields took their staffs and other weapons to hand and ran towards his land, thinking there might be some snake or other dangerous reptile there. But there was nothing to fight with. Their immediate reaction was that something "outer" had attacked Pir Shah as his hands and feet were twisted. A few of them ran towards the village to get some proper help while others started massaging his hands and feet. The bird was still flying over their heads but nobody noticed the sky. Pir Shah lost his consciousness and his pulse became so weak that everyone got very concerned. Then suddenly he stood up with full force and frenetically started moving in circles again. As the bird started expanding its circular flight with every circle, so did Pir Shah. It seemed as if he was a puppet whose string the bird was holding in its claws. After some time the bird flew towards *maira*, the swampy area outside the village, and Pir Shah followed it, running with speed. The villagers tried following him for a couple of miles but then he turned towards the wilderness and they had to stop, though they watched him until he disappeared from their sight. The villagers returned to the village, taking his oxen and plough with them, and informed his mother and other elders what had happened.

For days, weeks, and months, his relatives searched everywhere for him. They gathered the shepherds of many villages who knew every corner of that wilderness and sought their help. But all their efforts proved futile as nobody returned with even the slightest clue about his whereabouts. Over time, Pir Shah became history. He was only remembered at marriage and death ceremonies, and only by the nobles and elders of the village.

Forty years passed and then one day an old dervish came and sat down on the sandy banks of a seasonal river about a mile away from the village. People used to be proud and take it as a blessing if a dervish, or fakir, came to their vicinity. They would do whatever they could to please him. For many weeks, people of the village, especially the women, provided him with food and water, and asked him to pray for their family and their animals' well-being and prosperity. Then one day, an old woman from the village came to ask for the dervish's blessings and recognised him as none other than Pir Shah. All the elders of the village, most of them in one way or the other related to him, went to the banks of the seasonal river and brought him back to his own dwelling. His big house was now derelict but the walls were still standing. Though in the years people had stolen all the wood and other usable stuff from the house, they still put Pir Shah within the four walls of his own house, which was now under a withered tree in the courtyard.

Pir Shah was silent all this time and remained so until his death, but, sometimes, a spiritual euphoria would overtake him and he would rotate his hands clockwise and anti-clockwise. The speed of the movement was so fast that it surpassed all normal human movement. A woman of the village, with a big mouth, one day commented that if Pir Shah was a dervish then why did he always sit under the scorching sun? Why did he not make the withered tree green over his head for shade? A few days later the same woman passed by the dwelling of Pir Shah and was amazed by what she saw. The withered tree not only had become verdant but was providing so much shade that, along with Pir Shah, at least two dozen people could sit within its shadow. The news of Pir Shah's *karamat,* or miracle, spread fast and people from the whole area came to see the green tree with their own eyes. Eventually they named the village "the village of Pir Shah" after this revered ancestor of Ajee Shah.

7

A Duty-bound Djinn

Ajee Shah's father, Subedar Sahib, had two wives.
When he married Ajee Shah's mother, his first wife
veiled herself from him. Many a devout women
would practise this sort of celibacy and never again
have any physical contact with her husband after he
had married another woman. It was a sort of passive
protest as divorce was not the norm in those days.
But Ajee Shah's Badi Ma, elder mother, had always
loved the younger wife and her children as if they
all were her own flesh and blood. The word "step"
was never mentioned in the family and the protocol
of the family hierarchy was always observed without
any protest from anyone. Badi Ma used to visit Ajee
Shah's house and all the youngsters would spend
some of their holidays at her house.

She lived in their native village; her house had
three rooms, one leading to another. In the third
back room, there was a built-in storage space for
wheat and other grains, a hand mill made of two
round stones on a clay base, and a few other things,
mostly broken or rusted, that were once useful but

were now lying there as if the room was their graveyard. In that room there also lived a python called "Babaji" by the women of the village. "Babaji" being a term of respect for an elder and generally used for all pythons. Badi Ma always gave Ajee Shah, and other children visiting from the city, instructions about the python dwelling within. 'Never go in the back room and if, for any odd reason, you have to go to the room, always take off your shoes, do not stay there any longer than needed. If you see Babaji, do not be scared, just greet him and immediately leave. But walk out of the room backwards so that you do not show your back to him. It would be disrespectful to do so.' Badi Ma believed that the python was a saint in the disguise of a snake. The python was not always visible and she herself had only seen it four times in many years. But its appearance always preceded some big news, good or bad. Whenever she saw the python, she would tell everyone in the village that something was going to happen. And somehow or the other, something tangible did follow all the sightings.

Ajee Shah was so curious that he never missed any opportunity to go into that forbidden room. Whenever Badi Ma was absent, he opened the door and looked for the python. But the python never appeared before him. Then eventually he lost interest and stopped entering into that dark room. On one visit, he did not even bother going into it. The night before his return to the city, a python appeared in his dream and asked him, 'Why are you no longer visiting me?' Ajee Shah knew that it was the same python that lived in the back room. He answered, 'You have never shown yourself to me, even once. That is why I no longer go into that room.' The python raised its head as if it were a hooded cobra, and circled it many times. Then he changed his shape and became a middle-aged man with a small beard and no moustache. He pressed Ajee Shah's right hand in his hands for few seconds, and said, 'We will meet again.' Ajee Shah did not relate the dream to Badi Ma as it would have exposed his prohibited visits to the room. But the dream remained with him and he used to often remember what the touch of the python's hands had felt like in his dream.

I, Kabuko the djinn, knew much more than Ajee Shah about that python. He was no saint but a duty-bound djinn from the race of mountain-dwellers. Every time Ajee Shah entered that room, he made himself invisible to him but I could see him. He was a famous and illustrious djinn so I knew his tale and also how he was linked to Ajee Shah's ancestor. It was not for nothing that I chose to be born into Ajee Shah's family, after all.

This djinn had not always taken the shape of a snake but had settled upon it through some inner inclination at a very early age. In his youth, this royal djinn—for he was a prince among his people—agreed to protect two big copper cauldrons buried deep in the ground. Those cauldrons were full of many precious items like gold and silver jewellery and coins, pearls, diamonds, and other precious stones. But these items are not worth protecting for a djinn, much less a royal djinn, as they are worthless to us. Whenever we want such things, we can get them with ease.

What was interesting about these cauldrons was what was hidden in among the treasure. Both the cauldrons had some small plates of copper, gold, and silver, carved with mystical symbols and writings. Many hundreds of years ago, an Indian prince, who was equipped with arcane secret knowledge, buried them when he was seriously injured in a fight with the army of his rival brother. To bury his secret assets in a copper cauldron instead of clay pots showed how knowledgeable the prince was. He definitely knew that clay pots, buried deep in the ground, stay for centuries in the same position but metal pots change their position after some time. The royal djinn knew the prince very well and promised him that he will look after his secret plates after his death. When Pir Shah came back after forty years, the cauldrons had moved directly under the exact place where above ground he was sitting silently under that tree. The snake djinn paid his respects to the saint and sat there for a long time in the state of meditation. When he returned back to his cauldrons, both were not there. The djinn searched for them all around the place but could not find any clue. He returned to Pir Shah and asked for help. Pir Shah, without uttering a word, told him, 'Your duty is now over. I have sent the cauldrons where they had to go eventually. You are free now and can go wherever you like. Nobody will ask you any question.' But the python djinn never went back and remained in the village. Eventually he settled in the back room of Badi Ma's home.

A couple of years after his retirement from the army, Ajee Shah's father had been allotted some land across the River Sutlej near the India-Pakistan border. Once Ajee Shah and his friend Anwar went to visit that place. To reach there they had to travel by bus to a town called Khudian and then had to walk for about seven or eight miles to the banks of Sutlej. There was no bridge and people used to cross the river by boat. After that they had to again walk for about four miles through the wilderness to reach the land. When Ajee Shah and Anwar stepped off the boat, a soldier from the rangers' post happened to be coming back from his holidays. He offered to go along with them because they did not know their way in the wilderness and he feared that if they were to get lost, they might accidentally cross the border. There were no clear demarcations on the border and only on every fourth mile one would find small posts indicating the actual border.

When they had walked about a mile, the soldier suddenly

stopped and took a few steps back. He said to them, 'Do not go any further, Babaji is sitting in our way.' They saw a python sitting in the middle of the path. Its body was so huge that it covered almost the entire way. The soldier was not panicked, but he was also not sure about what to do next. They waited there for a few minutes in the hope that the python would move away but it did not. Then the soldier approached the python and in loud voice addressed it: 'O Babaji, please move, we have to pass through.' He repeated his request many times as if he was chanting a prayer. But the python didn't move an inch. The solider then suggested that they go with him to the border post and spend the night there. 'Tomorrow someone will take you to your land,' he assured them. Anwar thought it was good idea but Ajee Shah insisted that they go to the lands today. Then Ajee Shah did something so shocking that both the soldier and his friend became horrified. Both were so stunned that they did not even try to stop him. Ajee Shah moved straight up to the python and touched him with his right hand and started stroking his body without any fear. Then he asked in a loud voice, 'Oh, Babaji, is this the second meeting you promised me in the dream?' Then, surprisingly, the python started moving. It took quite some time to move his huge, long body. When the python finally disappeared into the woods, Ajee Shah came back to both and said it was okay to pass now. But the soldier was very angry and thought that Ajee Shah had done a most dangerous thing. It was, in his opinion, even more dangerous than crossing the border into India.

Babaji, this particular python, was a well-known entity in that area. Most of the people had seen him at one time or the other but nobody had ever dared to touch him. Hence, many people came to the land to meet Ajee Shah, the young son of a Syed who had touched and stroked Babaji. They told Ajee

Shah that the respected python was very fond of fresh milk. There were a lot of cattle grazing in that wilderness and when someone could not find any milk in the udders of his buffalo in the evening, it was believed that in the day the python had drank all the milk. This was considered a lucky omen for the buffalo and for the owner of that animal. But Babaji, apart from drinking milk, never harmed any animal, not even the wild pigs, which were in abundance in that wilderness.

On their return from the lands, Anwar told everyone about the great act of bravery performed by Ajee Shah. My young compatriot took pride in that. He believed in his heart that it was only with the blessing of the Babaji living in his native village home that he was able to touch that other python. The confidence with which Ajee Shah held such beliefs led me to hope that he would become very adept at the occult knowledge that was at the heart of my quest.

8

Never Walk Straight

When Ajee Shah went from primary school to the high school, beatings at home and at school increased, but then again so did his misbehaviour. Those were the times when parents and teachers used to think that teenage children were most vulnerable to being spoiled. If they were not put on a correct path at that stage, they would go astray and ruin their lives. So they tried very hard to make them, and in many cases, their strictness broke the younger ones. But in spite of the best possible efforts of Ajee Shah's parents, teachers, and the local Imam, they could neither make nor break him. He was made of a different material. As his mother used to say, 'Ajee is like the twisted tail of a dog. You put it for a hundred years in a straight iron pipe and when you pull it out, it will be the same old twisted tail.' Ajee never took that for a contemptuous remark and was never offended by it. In fact, he took it as a compliment and seemed proud of it.

Around this time, Ajee Shah developed a sort of fascination with snakes and in particular with big snakes. This new interest did not just stem from his experience with Babaji the python, since I recall a spark of interest in Ajee Shah when I had shown him the many different shapes I could take in my introductory dream and had briefly changed into a snake.

Ajee Shah could not understand the contradiction in man's relationship with snakes and pythons. Most people respected pythons in one way or the other, but the little version of them, the small snakes, were not tolerated at any cost. Leaving the *jogis* and other snake wranglers aside, everyone feared snakes; some people would even feel a cold wave of revulsion running through the spinal cord on seeing those creatures. Ajee Shah used to think in his childish confusion that all small snakes eventually became pythons if they lived to a hundred years of age. He thought that perhaps the bigger you grow, the more respected you become.

As a result of his fascination, Ajee Shah developed a friendship with "the king of snakes"—known to him only as Raja or King. He was a middle-aged man who had hundreds of snakes and a python. He used to sell "snake oils" and other remedies made of snakes in street gatherings, not only in his own town but in the whole province. He would hold a python in his hands and put many poisonous snakes around his neck to attract the public around him. In his youth, he had run away from his home to escape the beatings of his father. Eventually, he was adopted by a group of wandering *jogis*, the traditional snake charmers. He spent years with them wandering all around India, and had seen so much in his life that he became somewhat contented. Nothing could shock or disturb him. He learned the art of keeping an even keel in all circumstances. The only time he behaved differently was when he was playing *talang* raga on his old *been*, the jogi's flute.

Raja had a vast knowledge of snakes as he had caught thousands of them in his life. Ajee Shah was very disappointed when Raja told him that a snake always remains the breed of snake that it is and would never become a python. He also revealed that hardly any snake lives for a hundred years, and even after a hundred years, it is not able to change its shape—as was the universal folklore belief at the time. These were only superstitions, declared Raja, knowledgeably. Ajee Shah was convinced that the King knew almost every other thing about snakes but had somehow missed that mysterious aspect of their lives. If Ajee had to accept that snakes and pythons do not have that mysterious power of shape-shifting, then there could be no charm left in them for him. I began to understand why Ajee had been so quick to accept me with my shape-shifting skills.

Leaving that small difference of opinion aside, Ajee Shah found the conversation and the first-hand knowledge of the King very interesting. He was astonished to learn that snakes have no ears and they only feel the vibrations of sound on their body. So many poisonous snakes had bitten the King and many a times he was so close to death that he no longer feared it. He often said, 'Now the snakes are afraid of me. As I have so much poison in my body that if some less poisonous snake bites me, it will die on the spot.'

With time, Ajee Shah's friendship with the king of snakes grew stronger and Ajee Shah learnt many other aspects of a snake's nature. Once, Raja told Ajee Shah that he had saved an illegitimate new born baby that had been thrown on top of a trash heap by her mother. When Raja picked up the baby she was in such bad shape that it was almost impossible for her to survive. He took her to the nearest hospital and the lady doctor washed her with some lotions and treated her. She did not even inform the police to save the King from trouble. That baby not only survived but also became healthy very soon. Then she was adopted by someone in the same hospital. After telling the story, the King said, 'Snakes are like illegitimate babies. The mother is their first and foremost enemy as she would eat her own eggs and babies. All snakes that live in the world have escaped from their mother's mouth. Just like when an illegitimate human baby is born, the mother tries to get rid of it and throws it away in some derelict place or on the trash heap. These babies naturally have greater survival strength than normal babies. And they sometimes survive in such circumstances that it could only be interpreted as a miracle. So the survival of snakes is also a miracle of nature.'

Then, another day Raja told Ajee Shah, 'You can learn much from the way of snakes. They evolved the best survival strategy at a time when even man had not yet been thrown to this Earth.' This put Ajee Shah in mind of a poem his teacher had once read out in class, which seemed to summarise the entire survival instinct story that Raja attributed to snakes.

Live like a snake
Never walk straight
Leave the main path aside
On your left or right
Sit with the full spread of your hood
Be aware all the time
Fickle chance brought you here

I, Kabuko the djinn, was sure that the snake's strategy of survival while living among their worst enemy, Man, was very useful for other species like the djinn. We could learn much from snakes.

9

The Curse of Being Loved

Time, or perhaps the python's touch, had made Ajee Shah so over-confident that one day he got himself involved in a ferocious argument with a djinn: a djinn who had fallen in love with a beautiful teenage girl of Ajee's neighbourhood. Her name was Nasreen and she lived with her large family in a big house three streets away. The courtyard of their house was huge and there were two trees, the big one was a jujuba and the smaller one was a fig tree. Those trees were a great attraction for the neighbourhood children. Nasreen's mother was a fat and fair woman in her early fifties. She was not only bad-tempered but also very abusive. She swore a lot. But the fruit called *sew bair* of the jujuba tree was worth taking a risk for. The best time to steal the fruit was at noon, during the height of summer when all the family members were inside the house. Ajee Shah was once caught red-handed stealing *sew bair*. He was quite high up on the tree when Nasreen's mother came out of the room, making it impossible for him to escape. If he jumped from the tree he would definitely break his limbs, so Ajee Shah decided to face her, confident in the certain knowledge that she would not physically touch him. When she saw that somebody was on the tree, she started swearing and cursing. But as soon as she realised that it was Ajee Shah, she instantly stopped and clamped her hand across her mouth. Ajee had come down from the tree and did not try to run away. When he faced her, she said in a humble tone, 'O, younger Shah, why do you make me a sinner? I did not know that that was you on the tree and I swore at you. Look at yourself and look at your background.' Ajee knew that by "background" she meant his ancestors.

'Next time you want *bair*,' she continued, 'you just ask me and pluck as many as you like. But do not bring along your worthless friends. I am fed up with them all.' Ajee knew that most people always avoided swearing at a person belonging to the Syed caste, the direct descendants of the Holy Prophet. Many times he had promised himself he would not do anything that would reflect badly on his ancestral status but he could not keep his vow. But then again, he was just a child. After that conditional permission from the lady of the house, he fully enjoyed his special status of being a Syed and filled all of his pockets with the sweetest berries. Ajee had no need to bring along his "worthless" friends as they were always waiting around the corner to take their share of the fruit. After a time Ajee became so used to it that he didn't even bother to take permission to climb the tree, and behaved as though that was the courtyard of his own house.

Nasreen was unlike her mother. She was thin, fragile, and had a loving face. She never swore and was so mild that when her mother was not around she always allowed the children to climb the trees. She went to a girls' school wearing a white and blue uniform, and was either in eighth or ninth form. Then a horrible thing happened and her whole life turned topsy-turvy.

The story of Nasreen cemented my belief that my uncle had been right about the evils of possession. It also helped me understand why you fear us djinn so much.

It was late afternoon on a hot summer day. That hour of the day, called *zawal*, is considered to be "declining" time. Old folk would advise youngsters and vulnerable adults not to take a nap or, in a girl's case, not to go to derelict or lonely places during those ambivalent hours. They believed that we djinn have an advantage over weaker human beings during the time of ascending darkness—as far as I know, this isn't true but I began to realise that humans restrict a lot of their behaviour with ideas that become true because they believe in them so fervently.

Coming back to Nasreen, neither was she taking a nap nor was she roaming outside. She was very much in her own home and was washing dishes in the corner of the courtyard where there was a hand pump and a small concrete platform called *khurra*. It was here that a passing djinn saw her and immediately took possession of her. Instantly, she fainted and fell to the ground. All the family members in the house ran towards her and put her on the bed, massaging her hands and feet and sprinkling water on her face. Her mother was very disturbed and it seemed as if she knew in her mother's heart that something was drastically wrong with her daughter. In haste, she burnt seven cloves in a small clay tray and moved it clockwise over her daughter's body.

This "first aid" worked and Nasreen opened her eyes. Her eyelids were so heavy that she blinked her eyes many times before finally opening them. But then the real problems started. When she spoke and mumbled a few words, her voice had changed completely and she was talking in a young male's voice. Her whole family was stunned. After some time her speech became clearer. Her mother spoke to Nasreen but in reality she was addressing the spirit possessing her daughter, 'Who are you? Introduce yourself to me.' The male voice replied, 'I belong to *Qoum-e-Jinnat.*' *Qoum-e-Jinnat* meant "the nation of djinn". The djinn in the body of Nasreen did not utter a word of his own accord. He only answered the questions put to her, very briefly. It seemed as though the djinn was being very cautious as if he were a person giving an interview at a police station, where every word counts. After a few minutes, Nasreen suddenly became normal, though she looked exhausted. Her normal soft female voice also returned.

Nasreen's family at first tried to conceal her condition but soon everybody in the neighbourhood knew about it. A few even suggested remedies and the others speculated about the caste, tribe, and religion of Nasreen's possessor. There was no agreement on the caste and tribe but there was unanimity on the religion of the djinn. Nasreen's djinn was definitely not a Muslim, though he himself had never revealed to which religion he belonged. On that question he usually remained silent or reacted in a manner that was most uncomfortable for Nasreen's possessed body. He was a clever guy.

Now once or twice a week Nasreen had to bear the agony of possession. At other times the djinn would not possess her but only play with her. She could see her uninvited lover but nobody else ever glimpsed that spirit. Many *aamal* came and tried their best to exorcise Nasreen but the djinn was not ready to leave her at any cost. They informed the distressed family that the djinn was young, very energetic, and stubborn. He was the son of a chieftain of a clan of djinn. As this was his first encounter with a human spirit and body, he had no idea of the risks involved in this game. He went for the beautiful appearance of the girl but did not consider that he could lose his life in this sort of mingling. The real problem was that the djinn was so young and inexperienced that he did not know any of that. At one point, while answering Nasreen's mother queries, the djinn naively offered to take Nasreen along and marry her according to their customs. But Nasreen's mother said in clear terms to him that they would prefer their daughter dead than to be married to a non-Muslim.

The djinn was not ready to convert to Islam. He always avoided discussing these matters. On the other hand, he tried many times to bribe Nasreen's family with offers to provide them with gold, silver, and other precious metals. As a proof of his access to these things, the djinn many times produced out-of-season fruits and other small things like gold rings and bangles. Nobody ever dared to touch those things and afterwards Nasreen always buried the gifts under the jujuba tree. Nasreen's mother used to say that the djinn had ruined the whole reputation of her family and if he had been a human being she would have killed him with her own hands. But this traumatic experience also changed her tremendously and she not only cried a lot but also stopped swearing at people. But now the children of the locality were too scared to climb the trees of Nasreen's house. Ajee Shah was the only exception.

One day when Ajee entered the house to climb the tree, Nasreen's mother saw him and said, 'O, little Shah, please pray for my daughter. God listens to you Syeds more than us. If my daughter is cured from this curse, I will fill your mouth with sweets.' Ajee Shah felt a strange feeling in his heart. He realised that free access to the berries also demanded from him a responsibility that he be trustworthy, someone whose prayers are answered. He knew that though he was Syed and his family kept a lineage chart, he was not the sort to fulfil all those hopes that Nasreen's mother had of him. He promised himself that from now on he would not pluck berries for free from any tree belonging to someone else.

Ajee Shah often saw that poor girl in the possession of her spirit-abuser. One day, when he was visiting, he saw Nasreen standing under the jujuba tree. He noticed that she was waiting for something to happen or for somebody to arrive. And soon it happened. She became possessed. When Ajee saw her struggling and in a bad way, he got very angry at the djinn and yelled, 'Why don't you leave this poor girl alone? Why don't you go away?' To his utter astonishment, Nasreen answered in a male voice, 'Who the bloody hell are you to ask me to leave her alone? She is my beloved. I will never leave her. You are not her family member. You have no right to say anything. Now get lost.' Ajee Shah was annoyed, very annoyed. He said, 'I am a Syed. I have a birth right to ask you to leave.' 'Syed? So what? I am not a Muslim. Your rules and your precious "ancestorship" do not apply to me. Now get lost, otherwise you will regret it all your life.' But Ajee Shah was in no mood to leave the argument. He threatened the djinn as if he were arguing with a peer, 'You don't know me. My grandfather had the power to send your kind packing! I will ask my ancestors to kill you and you *will* be killed.' Nasreen laughed and the djinn, in his contemptuous anger, snarled at Ajee Shah, 'Look, I know who you are. I have seen you around here many times. You are not a human being. You are one of us but you are old and your clan has much lesser status than mine.' Ajee Shah was confused by this, in his youthful exuberance forgetting that I lived within him, and that the djinn was addressing me. My initial assessment about the possessing djinn was correct. He was a smart guy and had seen through me even though whenever he was around I always hid myself behind the animal spirits in Ajee Shah. I remembered the instruction of my benefactress and, at any cost, did not want to involve myself in this pointless brawl. This was not on my agenda. I kept myself in hiding and did not utter a word either to Ajee Shah or to the djinn.

Suddenly, Ajee Shah became frightened and thought he should leave the place as he knew nothing about djinn and their powers. At this I felt a surge of compassion for my young friend and from a protective impulse said, 'Do not run, stay where you are; stay, stay, you are under my protection. If you run away, the entity will take you away and will consume you alive. Be calm. Don't open your mouth but stay exactly where you are. Do not move your feet at all. Be like a statue. Don't move but stay. And look directly into the eyes of Nasreen.' Ajee Shah could not become like a statue but he stayed where he was and started staring into Nasreen's eyes. Through playing staring games in the mosque, Ajee Shah had become perfect in his fixed gaze. This was the very first lesson of human powers against the djinn that my benefactress had given me, and here I saw it in action for the first time. The djinn becomes helpless to take any powerful action under the strong stare of a human being. We cannot even change our shape. The competition did not go on too long and the djinn retreated and disappeared. Nasreen became silent but foam started coming out of her mouth. After some time Nasreen's brother came and picked her up and went inside the house. He told Ajee, 'O, Syed, go home.' Ajee went to his home and for three days burned with a temperature. He did not tell anybody what had happened but his mother knew that he had caught the temperature in Nasreen's house. She told him strictly not to ever go into that house again. But he didn't listen to her.

Then one day an exorcist came from Sialkot, a town about forty miles away. He was a *dendar*, which is the term used for someone newly converted to Islam. He had all the paraphernalia with him including a rattle, a small staff, many clay pots, and pieces of black cloth, a special knife, cloves, and many other things. Ajee Shah was called to help him. The exorcist needed leaves from the top branches of the jujuba tree. No one in the vicinity could climb to that point except Ajee Shah. His pride touched the sky that day. He would do anything to beat that djinn. It had become his personal fight. The exorcist asked only for a few leaves but Ajee Shah, in his excitement, stripped the top of the tree bald. The man, then, boiled the leaves and started his long exorcism. He was alone, without any disciple or pupil but was very confident. He carved a circle in the courtyard with a special knife and then called Nasreen to sit in the middle of it on the ground. After doing many rituals he called the djinn and then opened a dialogue with him. At first his tone was very mild and he made many passionate requests. But the djinn not only refused to leave Nasreen but also threatened the exorcist with dire consequences. Every time the djinn threatened him, he simply smiled and said, 'Let's see what happens.' At the end he became angry and took his staff and started beating Nasreen.

The scene was unbearable for Ajee Shah and Nasreen's whole family. Nasreen was sobbing and screaming. There were tears in Ajee's eyes and he turned his face away. When he turned his eyes back towards the man, he saw him hit Nasreen's left leg forcefully with his staff. A cry came out of her mouth. Now the djinn was asking for forgiveness. Even at that point, he tried in vain to negotiate with the exorcist. But now the exorcist did not want to hear anything other than him saying goodbye to Nasreen. He also demanded he take a vow to not come near her again, and asked for some sort of sign from the djinn to seal his vow. At that point the exorcist threatened the djinn and declared that if he wasted any more time, he would burn him. The djinn's voice came out of Nasreen for the last time, 'You have not done a good thing to me. You have broken my leg. Now I cannot appear before my beloved. I am leaving her and giving you a sign for that. But I will sit on the jujuba tree and watch her. You cannot stop me from doing that. You have no power to stop me from watching her. She cannot see me any longer but at least I can see her. That is the deal. Do you accept it or not?' The exorcist bowed his head in agreement. Suddenly a big branch of the jujuba tree fell down to the ground as if some force had pulled and separated it from the main trunk.

For many days after the final departure of the djinn, Nasreen remained silent and very sad. She used to rub her hands all the time as if she had lost something very precious. Now she could not see the djinn and was not even allowed to go near the jujuba tree. That tree also became sad. No child, including Ajee Shah, would dare climb it. One morning, Nasreen's older brother brought four burly men to uproot the tree. The men cut it to many pieces and took all the branches and leaves away with them on a cart.

Nasreen became normal. She did not finish her schooling but was married to her cousin who lived in Sialkot, from where the *dendar* exorcist came. What a coincidence. The courtyard of Nasreen's house was left with one tree. The figs would rot on the tree and fall. Nobody plucked them. Nobody picked them up. Even the children never climbed it again. Children of the neighbourhood did not like figs anyway. They preferred *sew bair* of the jujuba tree. But there was no longer a jujuba tree there. In its place was another concrete platform.

10

A Deadly Betrayal

Achhu was one of Ajee Shah's closest friends. They were class fellows and sat next to each at school. They walked to school together each morning and would spend most of their free time together, loitering or playing as the mood took them. Achhu was the son of a priest, and one of his hobbies was going for Friday prayers to a different mosque each week to listen to the sermons of the Imam and other speakers. The noontime prayer was the same everywhere but the style and delivery of the accompanying sermons was different mosque to mosque. Some of the speakers had mastered the art of oratory and their Friday sermons were very impressive. People would travel miles to listen to them. Ajee joined Achhu on his weekly visits to a different mosque and that activity gave Ajee Shah the chance to develop his own natural oratorical abilities.

In a year's time, after listening to so many sermons, Ajee Shah was able to himself speak on religious subjects before an adult audience. Achhu

99

had no talent or aptitude for public speaking, and he eventually took the role of a promoter for Ajee Shah. In some mosques they'd arrive a bit too early but Achhu somehow always managed to drum up a crowd for Ajee Shah's small speech before the arrival of the main speaker. He had discovered a couple of small suburban mosques without anyone to give a sermon to for the Friday congregations. Thus Ajee Shah became the main speaker in those mosques they would visit on alternate Fridays. The caretaker of one of the mosques started giving Ajee Shah a rupee for the horse carriage fare as that mosque was far away from their neighbourhood. But Ajee and Achhu always walked back, and spent the money on sweets, picture cards, and other play things. Achhu was more than satisfied with his self-acquired role as Ajee Shah always gave him his share in the perks. He even helped Ajee organise children's gatherings in their own neighbourhood where the only speaker was Ajee Shah.

Ajee Shah was speaking to one such gathering of about a dozen children in an open space adjoining the tomb of Fakir Sian, when a white-bearded dervish appeared and stood nearby. He listened to Ajee Shah's whole speech attentively and excitedly shouted the slogan of 'Haq Hoo!', meaning 'O, Truth!', many times. That slogan inspired Ajee Shah so much that he spoke about almost all that he could remember on any religious subject. When Ajee Shah finished his long speech, the old dervish came to him and kissed him on his forehead. Then he tried to search for the side pocket of his green maxi-like dress but he found no pocket there. He tried again and again and soon became irritated. Then he said, 'Oh, I have forgotten that we fakirs don't have pockets. He always keeps our belongings. Sometimes He loses them and sometimes He doubles them. It is entirely up to Him.' The dervish anxiously raised another slogan of 'Haq Hoo!' and looked towards the sky. He said in a loud voice, 'I have nothing to offer him. Give me something to give him.' He gestured skyward as though he were demanding the return of his own assets from someone. Then he grasped something from thin air in his right hand, and when he opened it, saw there were two one-rupee coins. He gave both the coins to Ajee Shah and blessed him. But, before leaving, he again looked at the sky and said something that was beyond the perception of Ajee, Achhu, or anybody in that young crowd. 'Oh, you have again put me to water duty. I am looking for fire. Your fire, to burn in, to become ashes. But you never promote me. What can I do? What can I do?' And with that, still muttering to himself, the dervish went away. Ajee Shah held his reward in his hand and was so happy that for a while he forgot about everything and everyone, including Achhu. Two rupees was big money for a child in those days. Now all the children around him wanted to have their share in the reward but Achhu had something else in mind.

He whispered in Ajee Shah's ear, suggesting that he run away from the scene with the money, and that he would deal with the children. Afterwards, they would divide the money equally. But Ajee Shah felt so light with the two coins in his hands as if his feet were not on the ground and he was levitating. Ajee Shah realised that his promoter-cum-friend had no idea of the root of his present weightlessness, the significance of the gift. He was too dense, too mundane to cope with it. Ajee Shah shunned the suggestion with a gesture of his shoulders and started walking towards his home. Achhu was very angry but followed Ajee Shah as did all the other children who had been his audience.

When they all were inside the house, Ajee Shah opened his fist and handed over the two rupees to his mother. He told her the whole story but in an abridged version. His mother was very happy with him and straight away gave one rupee to Ajee and with the other rupee she sent someone to bring locally made biscuits that she distributed equally among all the children, including Ajee and Achhu. The next day Achhu demanded his half share of the rupee but it was too late: Ajee had already bought two fairy-tale books. At that time, he was enthralled by tales of djinn, demons, and fairies, and could often be found with his head in a book of this sort. He offered Achhu one of the story books, titled "The Djinn of Kohqaf", as he had read it but Achhu was interested in money, not in stories.

From that day, Ajee Shah's friendship with Achhu started going downhill. From then on, most of the time they were cross with each other and not on speaking terms. They even had fisticuffs a couple of times over some trivial issues, and Ajee, being the stronger lad, beat him up a bit. Achhu was physically no match for Ajee Shah but he was one of those who believed that everything was justified in love and war.

One day they had a verbal argument and the next day, when Ajee was in his local mosque, Achhu came from behind and gave Ajee a strong blow on his left eye and quickly ran away. Ajee could not chase him as he was in pain and, more than that, shocked by the sudden, unprovoked attack. The Imam of the mosque had seen it all and complained to Achhu's father. When Achhu got home his father gave him a good beating. Achhu thought that Ajee had complained to his father even though he knew tattling was against Ajee Shah's principles. In response, Achhu decided to do something that was completely unthinkable. He decided to try to kill Ajee Shah. While I might have been able to predict a cunning plan in a djinn's mind, the devious nature of human children was still beyond my powers at this time.

Achhu made up with Ajee and, after a few days, suggested

that they go visit Achhu's uncle who worked as a water gauge man on the River Chenab dam. It was a popular picnic spot as there was also a cable car over the water reservoir. Ajee Shah accepted the offer excitedly as he had never been in a cable car before. Ajee took his parents' permission and they both went to the dam by train. They spent the day joyfully and rode the cable car. Next morning, after breakfast, they went for a walk along a long pier that had been constructed along the middle of the water reservoir. The scene was beautiful and lively with many birds fishing in the water and making pleasurable noises. Achhu looked around carefully and after making sure that nobody was watching them, he suddenly pushed Ajee Shah into the water. The water was very deep and fast, and Ajee Shah didn't know how to swim at that time. I was as shocked and alarmed as Ajee at what had just happened and so was not of much help.

First we plummeted a few feet down into the water, but, with desperate thrashing of Ajee's arms and legs, soon surfaced for a few seconds. But, despite his best efforts, he couldn't keep his head above water and went down under the surface again. At that moment, Ajee Shah became convinced that he would drown and that there was no chance of escape. He became terrified, not by death itself but by the manner in which he was dying. A thought zipped into his mind that his body would never be found and would be eaten by fish. I, Kabuko the djinn, was also in a state of terror and was wracking my brains to think of a way to save Ajee.

Suddenly, under the water, the dervish, who had given him the two rupees, appeared. Ajee Shah assumed it was the hallucination of a dying boy. But when the dervish's hands grabbed his arms and felt solid to the touch, he was sure that divine help had come to his rescue. He instantly became confident that he was not going to die in that water. The dervish pushed him towards the edge of the reservoir and struck something with his feet. Ajee Shah touched that thing and found that it was a fishing net. He clutched it as tight as he could, the dervish helping him by pushing him upwards. When his head emerged from the water, he saw that the rope of the net was tied to an iron hook, fixed to the edge of the pier wall. The dervish did not come out of water and when Ajee looked back he was nowhere to be seen. Ajee Shah waited there holding the rope tightly in both his hands, coughing and spluttering to clear his mouth and nose of water. Both of us felt palpable relief.

In a few minutes, Ajee's usual strength came back and he pulled himself out of water. Then he walked to the station and sat on a homebound train without a ticket. He reached home safely but didn't tell anybody what had happened to him. Achhu had seen Ajee Shah coming out of water as he was hiding behind the bushes. He was so fearful of Ajee Shah that he stayed at the dam with his uncle for more than a week. Even after returning home, he didn't show his face for many days.

Ajee Shah was flummoxed by how to take his revenge on Achhu. He didn't want to kill him but he certainly wanted to teach him the lesson of a lifetime. He was constantly thinking about revenge and became very irritated at the whole situation that he had been thrown into unwillingly. Then Friday came, and Ajee Shah went alone to the biggest mosque of the city, where the best sermons were given. When the Imam started his sermon, he read the verse of the Koran that says that all life came out of water. It was a strange coincidence that created a great fascination for water in Ajee Shah's heart. Then and there he vowed that he would learn to swim and explore the water. He also decided not to take revenge on Achhu and leave the whole matter in the hands of God.

Achhu changed his seat in school and went from the front

to the last but one desk in the classroom. Another boy came in to share the two-seat bench with Ajee Shah. His name was Afzal and he lived in a village about five miles away from the school. He had a bicycle but often its tyres were either punctured, or it was being borrowed, and he had to walk all the way to school. His village had a dreadful reputation in the whole province. The villagers fiercely fought each other as they had old enmities between themselves. They always took revenge for their murdered folk and never left these matters to God or for that matter to anybody else. Sometimes twelve to fourteen people were killed from both sides in a major fight and dozens of villagers arrested. Such fights were usually followed by a period of peace, but soon enough the revenge killings would begin again. Many of Afzal's relatives had been murdered or were in jail, but for him this was a routine matter. When Afzal missed school, the class teacher asked students, 'Do you know how many people were killed in Afzal's village?' The figure was always more than one.

Afzal was a very good swimmer, and Ajee Shah soon replaced Achhu with him, and they became fast friends. There was no swimming pool in the city but on the outskirts of Ajee's neighbourhood there were many rain water ponds in the low fields. Ajee Shah started going there with Afzal. Afzal was a good swimmer but a bad trainer, and Ajee Shah had many painful dunkings while following his instructions. Afzal believed that without dunking nobody could ever learn to swim. After a lot of practise, one day Afzal declared that Ajee Shah could now swim in deep waters. They both went to the River Chenab on his bicycle and, under the watchful eye of Afzal, Ajee Shah swam not in the main river but in a side stream that was nevertheless deep enough to drown him. When after a long swim Ajee came out of the water, he had become a swimmer.

After that Ajee Shah used to go at least once a week to the river and swim the deepest and fastest waters. The first time he swam across the river, he thought about the famous love story, *Sohni Mahiwal*, in which the potter girl Sohni had drowned. Sohni did not know how to swim and always used a pitcher as a float to help her across the river to see her lover Mahiwal. One day, her rival changed the pitcher and replaced it with an unfired clay pitcher that dissolved in the water, drowning Sohni. Suddenly a question came to Ajee Shah's mind, 'How could a potter girl not differentiate between a fired and an unfired pitcher?' 'Maybe it was the dark of the night or maybe love rendered even her hands blind,' I, Kabuko the djinn, suggested to him from within.

11

Shamim's Seduction

At the start of one summer, a young couple and an old man moved into the ground portion of a small house in Ajee Shah's neighbourhood. The place they rented consisted of two small rooms, a toilet, and a bathroom but no separate kitchen. The husband was a junior clerk in a government department and had recently been transferred from another city. His wife loved him very much but, with similar intensity, hated her father-in-law, the old man living with them. The old man had chronic asthma and was always coughing. At night-times she would put his bed outside in the street. Perhaps it was not so much because of cruelty as for not wanting any disturbance during her intimate moments at night.

By now, Ajee Shah had turned into a handsome teenager. He was old enough to know that like other wives, young or old, she had to do nothing during the night, except take off her shalwar and sometimes, perhaps, her kurta, too, and then lie down on her back. Most husbands liked their wives to be completely passive in bed, like a dead body. If a young wife reciprocated in any way and actively participated in the love-making, she was often suspiciously looked upon as being of loose character. During love-making, husbands always loved to hear "be slow" requests from their wives, particularly the young ones. Some young females somehow knew the art of exploiting this weakness and so, with fake "be slow" refrains, made their husbands boastfully happy, sometimes over the moon. The morning after always brought some sort of material reward, no matter how small it was, from the fulfilled husbands to the faking wives. They received the gifts with pride as if they had played a major part in winning their husbands a game of solitaire.

Ajee Shah soon became acquainted with the old man lying on a bed in the street. For him, that ailing man was somehow important because of a strange notion in the back of his mind. He believed that old people knew the secrets of life and that when they were on their last legs they always transferred those secrets to someone younger like him. Oddly enough, this was a notion that emerged from Ajee rather than myself and I was keen to know if his suspicion was right. But the old man had no secret to keep or to give away. He only had inflammation and anger against his daughter-in-law. Whenever Ajee Shah talked to him, the old man cursed his daughter-in-law but never said a word against his own son, who was equally responsible for the mistreatment of his father, if not more. The old man coughed repeatedly all night and with renewed intensity in the early morning. Often he produced from his mouth and nose different kinds of sounds, which were like a mixture of a snore and a fatigued breath coming out of his inflamed windpipe.

Ajee Shah wondered what would happen to the old man in winter. Would he be allowed inside the house to spend the cold nights there or would he remain in the street? But before the season could even change, the old man disappeared into the darkness of the night. At first, Ajee Shah thought that the fear of God had somehow entered into the heart of the daughter-in-law and she had allowed the old man to sleep under the roof. But that was not the case. The old man was admitted to a free government hospital where he died a few days later. His body never returned to the rented portion of the house and was taken directly from the hospital to his native village, where he must have had his own dwelling of mud bricks. After burial, the couple returned and the people of the street went to their house for condolences as is the custom. Ajee Shah was surprised to learn that the cruel daughter-in-law was not an outsider but the niece of the dead man. He had yet to learn from life that warmth or cold-bloodedness have very little to do with blood ties.

About a couple of months after the death of her father-in-law, Ajee Shah saw the woman standing on the doorstep of her house. She did not know Ajee's name so called him with a gesture of her beautiful hand and asked him to buy four oven chapattis for her. In spite of his dislike of the cruel woman, Ajee Shah could not refuse because in those days you were not supposed to deny those sorts of requests from a housebound woman of the neighbourhood. He extended his hand to take the exact money from her and as he did, her right hand slightly touched his left palm. Perhaps she intentionally did so, to introduce her sensual touch, but Ajee Shah didn't mind it one bit, in fact he received it with gratitude. It took him hardly five minutes to get chapattis from the oven that was run by an old woman in her dwelling. As he returned, he expected her to be waiting at her doorstep but she was not there. He knocked on the door that was left slightly ajar and heard her say from inside, 'Come in.' Ajee went in and asked where he should put the chapattis.

'In the kitchen,' she replied, while sitting indolently on her bed. There was no kitchen but Ajee knew what she meant. In the corner of her veranda, a hearth made of mud was placed for cooking, alongside which two tiny seats, bottles of spices, and other kitchen stuff were neatly placed. Ajee placed the chapattis in the *chabi*, a round straw basket with a lid similar to those used by snake charmers. As he was leaving, she called him into the room and asked his name. She was smiling for no apparent reason and was constantly looking at him with "sweetness in her eyes". 'Sit down,' she said, politely. Ajee looked around the room and found no other place to sit, except the same bed upon which she was sitting. He hesitated for a moment but her smiling insistence encouraged him to take a seat. He sat down on the edge of the bed and took a lengthy look around the room to avoid looking at her. There were hooks on the adjacent wall, on which male and female clothes hung. Sheets of newspapers were stuck to the wall to shield the hanging clothes from dust. Below the hanging clothes were two boxes, a small box on top of a bigger box. There was a table at the side of the bed on which an alarm clock, a medium-sized mirror, a bottle of mustard oil, some cheap make-up stuff, and many other everyday useable things were placed. Ajee sat as far away from her as he could but she engaged him in chatting by asking many innocent questions, and gradually moved towards him. She was now so close to him that he could feel her breath on him, breath that was gradually becoming heavy. She didn't try to conceal her emotional state, and that made Ajee Shah very nervous. Glancing at the man's clothes hanging on the wall, he feared what would happen if her husband should come home unexpectedly. Ajee stood up to leave, and she, without wasting a moment, gently pinched Ajee's cheek and rushed to her makeshift kitchen as if she were a criminal escaping the crime scene. Ajee did not feel any particular sensation because of his fear, but Shamim, for that was her name, made him internally very cheerful.

Ajee's first illicit relationship with a woman was brought about by the four oven chapattis and was fostered by almost all basic grocery items, reaching its culmination point when Shamim asked him to bring her a yard of elastic band. She told him cheekily that all her bras were loose and she wanted to fix them. Ajee Shah had nothing to do with the loosening of her bras. The real culprit must be her husband who in his excitement could not wait for her to take off the bra and pushed it downwards. The bra was the only garment that took some time to remove, but then the cheap material hooks would sometimes also play their own delaying tactics.

Shamim was kind to Ajee Shah—she kissed him on his cheeks, embraced him many times, allowed him to massage her breasts over the bra, and once had even let him put his hand under her shirt. But that was all. Beyond that the territory belonged to a single man, her husband. Ajee Shah knew that Shamim was not of loose character but either she couldn't resist Ajee's handsomeness or her husband was not sexually powerful enough to fulfil her appetite. Ajee's relationship with Shamim had a peculiar effect on him. Every time he embraced Shamim, he had to go to the toilet to get some release. Sometimes, after masturbation, Ajee felt a burning sensation in his penis. Before Ajee could ponder this mystery too deeply, his relationship with Shamim ended abruptly. Her husband had given some sort of exam and been promoted to an assistant senior clerk in his department. Shamim distributed sweets to celebrate his promotion. After a couple of weeks her husband was transferred back to the same city from which he came. The couple left the neighbourhood with their belongings on a horse and carriage to the railway station. Shamim left Ajee's neighbourhood without even giving him a departing hug. But Ajee Shah had no remorse. On the other hand, whenever he passed by the shop where he had bought a yard of elastic band for Shamim, he always smiled. He thought of the bra, which was tightly holding her ample bosom in check. Sometimes he tried to visualise those unexplored peaks but found it difficult because, until that time, he had not touched a single breast, except as a babe at his mother's teat.

Shamim had gone for good and along with her so had Ajee Shah's convulsions. He became normal. He no longer had to make an urgent dash for a toilet to soothe the physical urges awakened by her now. After a while, his body also became less and less demanding and the usual early morning erections reduced. Ajee was shy and never spoke about sexual matters openly, but he wanted to confide in somebody. And a boy, two or three years older than him and known as the "One-Handed Clapper", was a safe bet. The boy had practically refuted the age-old saying "it takes two hands to clap". He had mastered the art of a single-hand clapping and produced a sound that was a little louder than that produced by traditional two-handed clappers. He unashamedly claimed that he had acquired the art only through the extensive practise of masturbation. Some believed him and some not, but nobody could deny the acrobatic ability of his hands.

One day Ajee Shah took him to one side and explained his problem of reduced erection. He did not mention the cold-blooded Shamim, who used to heat him up and then leave him alone to deal with his fire. The One-Handed Clapper laughed at first and, thus, trivialised Ajee's problem, but after a while, became serious and nodded many times like the local herbalists. Then in a serious tone he advised Ajee to eat a knob of butter first thing in the morning and to always use oil when dealing with himself. 'One should not only butter up others but should also deal with oneself in a moisturised way,' he said. The crux of his advice was followed by a half-hour lecture on the intricacies of mind, body, and spirit.

One-Handed Clapper's advice was not easy for Ajee Shah. How could he tell him that mind and body were very much there but the evoking spirit, Shamim, was missing? And that he did not like butter on its own? He could look at taking it as a medicine but moisturising that wildly spontaneous part of the body was a risky business! There were no washing machines in those days and, like all mothers, Ajee's mother washed all the clothes by hand. What would happen if she noticed something? On the spot Ajee Shah decided not to heed the advice of the One-Handed Clapper and to leave the things as they were and to simply "be brave".

The One-Handed Clapper was not so wrong about moisturising the body inside and out. There is an ancient tradition around these parts that pertains to getting health and healing through moisturising, and it has become an integral part of the collective psyche. For headache, migraine, heaviness, falling hair, tired eyes, blurred vision, nightmares, even depression, the immediate remedy is *champi*, a head massage with oil. Lukewarm oil is also put in ears to clear the eardrums. And then the whole body massage is so popular that every day you see men lying in parks, grounds, and on shop platforms with the local masseurs massaging them with all four limbs. Though Ajee Shah was too inhibited to use those public place remedies, he had become terrified at the thought of becoming impotent. Shamim, his first lover, had put him in a real bind. I must confess that I did nothing to alleviate his predicament as this was surely a primal human male fear, and I was sure that it would teach me much.

12

The King of Snakes

Ajee Shah's fear of having become permanently impotent became so potently disturbing that it broke through the shell of his reserve and came out in the open. One day he went to his old friend, the king of snakes, and revealed his problem quite openly. Ajee Shah felt such an unburdening at telling his whole story to Raja that he naïvely thought that no secret in the world should be so clandestine that it be kept in one's heart for a lifetime. Ajee Shah's tale of his encounters with Shamim was so detailed and repetitive that the King, on a couple of occasions, mildly suggested he cut the long story short. But Ajee Shah ignored his suggestion, intent as he was in reliving the whole experience lest he miss out on sharing any crucial detail. He even tried to explain the texture of Shamim's silky skin and said, 'If you put a drop of water on her forehead, it would slowly travel downwards to her feet and then will go into the ground.' Raja said, jokingly, 'It means that her skin is like a snake's.' Ajee Shah did not appreciate that repulsive joke and protested, 'If you're going to be like that, I will not tell you the rest of my story.' Raja laughed and said, 'Okay, I am sorry. Don't be so touchy.' Then Ajee excitedly made a gesture with both hands to indicate the size of Shamim's generous bosom, though he had never been blessed with seeing the full generosity of her breasts, as they had never been revealed to him naked. Even at that moment, Ajee Shah cursed the person who invented that lousy looking thing to hide the most beautiful part of a female body. When Ajee Shah reached the tangible and (anti-) climatic consequence of his platonic affair with Shamim, he was very precise and with grief in his voice, said, 'Raja, she has made me impotent. She took all my early morning erections with her. I am utterly ruined. Please help me, and do something.' When Raja, usually a serious person, also laughed like the One-Handed Clapper, a terrible thought came to Ajee Shah's mind, 'The world around me is so different and alienated from me that it will never appreciate any of my problems, any of my concerns'.

Ajee Shah became sad and regretful of the fact that although he had shared his only secret this confidently and elaborately with him, the end result was only laughter. What Ajee Shah didn't know was that the King was very clever; he had, after all, lived his whole life with snakes, which are, perhaps, the oldest species on earth. The King had immediately noticed the discomfort Ajee Shah was feeling, possibly provoked by his laugh. He, then, became so serious that Ajee Shah thought his problem was so grave that even Raja had no solution for it! But then he said, 'I laughed because you are worried for such a trivial matter. It is nothing. She made you impotent and I will make you the most potent boy in the whole town. That is my promise, and this poisonous man with hundreds of snake bites on his body, and even on his soul, always keeps his promises.'

Ajee Shah was instantly relieved. He was so overwhelmed

with the words of the King, who he thought meant to give him some snake oil remedy to instantly turn him into the most potent boy in the whole town. Ajee Shah imagined Shamim in front of him, naked and inviting, and him making love to her. Many scenes came to his mind and some of them were sexually so violent that he couldn't dare to imagine them in a normal state. Raja asked for some time to think about all aspects of Ajee Shah's problem and told him to come back the day after tomorrow. Before leaving, he asked Ajee Shah to have *doodpati, or* milky tea. The King joked, 'In *doodpati,* there is no water to pour either on the forehead or on the feet, but only milk, pure milk. And you don't disrespect pure milk . . . to be wasted like that, just for an experiment.' His joke was delivered so seriously that Ajee didn't enjoy it but passionately consumed the *doodpati* as he thought it might be an allusive remedy for the impotency.

At their next meeting Raja told Ajee Shah, 'There is a simple solution to your problem. You must have sex with a girl who knows how to make you hot, a girl without any inhibitions.' Ajee Shah blushed and said, 'That is impossible. How can I find that sort of girl and a place to have that sort of sex?' Raja answered, 'Don't worry, I have already arranged a girl and a place. I will take you to my own favourite girl and she will make you a man again. A strong man. That is not a problem at all.' Ajee Shah wondered and asked in excitement, 'But who is that girl? Where she does she live? And why would she do me this big favour?' The King explained that the girl was young, beautiful, and above all very experienced in raising the spirit of men. She came about three months ago to *chakla,* the local brothel house, and he had visited her many times. Ajee Shah was shocked to hear the word *chakla,* and a wave of fear went through his body. That was the most prohibited place for youngsters of his age. If someone saw him there, the result would be a hundred times more disastrous than staying impotent. But Ajee Shah had no choice, so, he agreed.

Ajee Shah and many of his classmates used to go to the class teacher's house in the evening for tuition. He bunked and the King took him to the *chakla*. All the way to the *chakla*, Ajee Shah was thinking about the menacing proximity of the brothel to his town, a town where most people knew each other. He remembered the day when he had bunked from school and watched the matinee show of a film in the cinema, a person had informed his family. And he was severely beaten by his father. There were many self-appointed informers in the city who thought it was their duty as an adult to report all acts of delinquency to the relevant parents. Sometimes they took so much trouble to locate the address of a juvenile delinquent that Ajee Shah wondered if they might be taking some sort of sadistic gratification in changing the kids' pleasure into pain. But then, the kids were not the only victims of that tightly-knit society, adults had their share too. They had to be very cautious to save their reputations. If an adult drank alcohol, even once in a lifetime, and came out of his hideout without having a fragrant *pan* or a guava, and somebody smelt his spirituous breath, then soon he was categorised as a drunkard. One had no choice other than to live with the perceived notion of one's character because it was humanly impossible to otherwise convince half the city that believed the hearsay.

The *chakla* was situated at one edge of the town but one or two new localities were further away from it as the town was spreading outwards on all sides. It was not a well-lit place at all, but rather dim and shadowy. There were no more than twenty brothel rooms and as the King and Ajee Shah entered one of the rooms, the first thing they saw was a dog and a middle-aged pimp. The dog looked at them once and then ignored their

presence by moving its face to the other side. The pimp nodded
to the King, bidding him and Ajee Shah to sit on the bed, and
called out to the girl who was doing something behind a curtain
that divided the room equally. The girl came out in full make-
up. She so warmly welcomed the King that it was as if she had
met an old lover after a long time. She embraced him and sat on
the bed between Ajee and Raja, and put one arm around Ajee's
shoulder and the other around King's. Meanwhile the pimp left
the room with the dog without saying a word. The girl looked
Ajee up and down and examined with her penetrating eyes his
whole body. Then she joked with the King, 'O, Raja, I didn't
know that your friend is so young. Since when are you making
such young and handsome friends?' Ajee Shah took offence at
her joke and shrugged her hand from his shoulder. She laughed
and kissed Ajee's cheek and said, 'Don't mind my stupid remarks.
I was just joking. I am free with your friend. I know he is not gay
and that neither are you. Raja has told me everything. But you
are too handsome. I fear I will fall in love, close up my shop,
and run away with you. The end.' And she recited the first line
of the national anthem that was always played at the end of film
shows in the cinemas.

Her uninhibited way of chatting had a very pleasant effect
on Ajee Shah. His whole mood changed, making him so relaxed
that he wanted to lie down on her bed. Then the King took her
behind the curtain and kissed her. He also gave some money
to her, and said, 'I don't want to have any complaints. Make
my young friend happy and you will not regret it.' She just said,
'Okay, Okay.'

The King came out from behind the curtain and whispered
to Ajee Shah, 'Don't worry about anything. I have opened an
account for you with her. She will not demand anything from
you. Enjoy yourself and I will be back within an hour. Today,

I will check out someone else, the only woman I have never visited before in this *chakla*.' Raja left with many promises and Ajee Shah believed every word he said. She closed the door behind him.

Ajee Shah's first sexual intercourse started with the question, 'What is your name?' Instead of answering his simple question, she said something strange, something entirely unexpected. 'Our names don't matter at all. We prostitutes change our names all the time. We enter each new *chakla* with a different name. But I will tell you my real name that my parents gave me and which now nobody knows. Sometimes that name sounds unfamiliar even to me. My name is Janti. You know the meaning of my name? It means that I will reside in paradise after my death. You are the first person in this town to whom I have revealed my original name. Even Raja doesn't know it. He thinks I am Jamila. He is a very good customer of mine but you are my beloved.'

She took off all her clothes and then started undressing Ajee Shah. First she took off his shoes, kissed his feet, and put her forehead on his feet. Then, she massaged the top of his feet with her forehead. After that, the trousers were off and, lastly, his shirt. She then put her right breast in Ajee Shah's mouth and he began sucking it. She put her hands behind his head, leading him to suck deeply. She kissed almost every part of his body except his penis, but she did massage that area which did the trick. Ajee Shah became so erect that he found it difficult to control himself. Finally, he entered her and climaxed three times in a row. He was ready for his fourth one but a knock on the door spoiled the continuity. The King had returned but the pimp and the dog were still away.

Raja asked his first question in such a way that it was not addressed to anyone particular, 'Did everything go all right?' Ajee Shah simply nodded but Janti/Jamila was in a jolly mood.

119

She again joked with the King, 'You cheated me. You said that your young friend was impotent but he has shaken my whole body. You must be giving him some of your nasty remedies.' Ajee Shah was pleased to hear her joke but Raja rebutted, 'Jamila, you have not yet seen the performance of my remedies. Once my remedy works, afterwards you will not be able to work for at least a week.' Before leaving the room, the King said to Ajee Shah, 'Now I have opened the door for you. Whenever you want, come here without any hesitation.' Then he addressed Jamila and instructed her in a serious way, 'Don't you ever dare to deal with my friend in a prostitute's way. Write everything in my account and I will pay you on my visits. But I want to have no complaint.' She ignored his warnings and asked, 'How was your new girl?' 'Not like you. Not a pinch of you,' the King answered before grabbing Ajee Shah by the arm and leaving hurriedly.

13
Prayer for a Prostitute

You may be wondering about my role in this most
important first experience of Ajee Shah's, but you
see I had been forced to be nothing but an observer
through a very unexpected request, or perhaps it was
a command, but I had no inclination towards denying
it so have no idea what would have happened had
I refused. The human spirit, that beloved of mine,
never addressed any entity within Ajee Shah directly
but I felt a very strong sensation that seemed to say
that this was the time that I should step back from
interfering in Ajee's life. In any case, a prolonged
silence from me at the time of his puberty meant that
Ajee had convinced himself that his conversations
with me when he was a child had been a figment of
his over-heated imagination. I missed our little chats
but I was by no means bored at experiencing the
sexual adventures of my human host, even if they
weren't a patch on my own experience. I assumed that
the reason the human spirit asked me to keep a low
profile was to enable Ajee Shah to develop normally
at this crucial and sensitive time in his life.

Ajee Shah now bunked at least once a week from the tuition class to visit Janti. His sexual urges had increased so much that he had almost forgotten the purpose of his initial visit to that prohibited place. The only time Ajee Shah felt any discomfort was when Janti behaved just like Shamim, refusing access to a particular part of her body for no obvious reason. Perhaps that was the only mystery that she, in her nakedness, could still evoke. Ajee Shah was very cautious not to ever be caught in the *chakla* but, with his keen sense of observation, he learnt many things about the peripheral and prohibited world of *chakla*.

The first thing Ajee Shah noticed was that nobody ever alighted from their horse carriage in front of the main entrance to the *chakla*. They always went a little further and pretended to be visiting new localities there, then came back by foot and entered the *chakla* from a side street. Some of the visitors covered their faces with a scarf or a small cloth. They were not necessarily religious people but they had a beard, and going to the *chakla* with a beard was considered very shameful. Ajee Shah did not even have a moustache at the time but he also used the technique and found it very protective. The system of the brothel house, which was devised during the British Raj, fulfilled men's natural need for change. One girl vanished after every few months and another would take her place. Most of the girls lived in one room, either alone or with a pimp or a pet, and their sleeping bed was also used for their business. Four or five women permanently resided in the *chakla*. They had passed the stage of menopause and were exempt from closing their business for almost a week each month unlike their younger colleagues. But, on the other hand, they were left with few clients because of their age and the body's natural decay. As their breasts dropped, so did their rates. Most of their clients were older and they also had to spend a fair amount of money on *kushtas* to keep their sexual performance, which the herbalist prepared especially for them. *Kushtas* were made of calcified metal and, while these might have been effective, they were very dangerous as well. If a metal was not properly processed then it worked worse than poison in the body and the consequences were obvious. But people still often took the risk, perhaps it was worth it. Any *chakla* girl, with a little bit of experience, immediately knew if her client was using *kushtas* and doubled her rate in the middle of the sexual act. The equation of time being money was a norm there. Another rule of the place, unthinkable to be waived, was that a client, new or familiar, had to pay first and then do whatever he could, either on his own physical strength or with the help of his wild imagination or some local remedy. Although this rule didn't apply to Ajee Shah as he was probably the only client on permanent account.

Ajee Shah always went alone to the *chakla* except for his very first visit when the King had introduced him to Janti. But some men would come to the *chakla* in small groups of three or four friends and, after selecting one girl, they negotiated a package deal with her. That way they saved twenty to thirty percent of the price. When one of them came out of the girl's room, all the others would ask him to tell them everything. Their appetite for all the details persisted despite the fact that everyone knew these stories were always concocted and exaggerated when it came to the sexual performance of the storyteller. Ajee Shah, through overhearing those boastful tales, also learned that kissing on the mouth was not always allowed in the *chakla*. He speculated that perhaps this was the reason that Janti sometimes avoided kissing him on the mouth by saying there was something wrong with her lips or teeth.

Ajee Shah found nothing grotesque about the brothel. The girls who stood at their doors were friendly to every passer-by. They would invite everybody in and, at a refusal, would sometimes taunt the man accusing him of impotency, but then that was just to provoke his pride; a selling trick. They knew that impotent men would never come to the *chakla* and were much more likely to be found in a crowd around the street vendor selling sanda oil. Sanda is a type of lizard, the oil of which is supposed to have restorative powers for gout and impotence. The *chakla* girls had no visible professional rivalry or jealousy between them and along with the rest of that society they also repeatedly declared that 'whatever is written in one's fate will come to be anyway, so why worry?'

For a few weeks everything went fine for Ajee Shah and he started to become blasé about his visits to the *chakla*. On a very unlucky day, fate took Ajee Shah to the *chakla* after school. It was the first time he was visiting that place in the daylight. As soon as he entered Janti's room, he was shocked to see an electrician from his own neighbourhood, fixing some wires in her room. Ajee Shah's face turned ashen and he could clearly hear his own heartbeat. He tried to turn around but his feet, in his terror, had become like lead and before he could move anywhere, the electrician had spotted and recognised him. Janti instantly realised what was happening and tried to behave as if Ajee was a stranger to her. She asked, in a harsh voice, 'O boy, what are doing in my room?' Ajee answered, hesitantly, 'I am looking for a classmate who lives somewhere here.' 'Get lost, nobody lives here. You don't know what this place is.'

As Ajee Shah made to leave, the electrician jumped down from his ladder and grabbed Ajee's left arm tightly so that he couldn't escape. Then he slapped his face three or four times and said, 'You should die with the shame. You are a Syed and you are in such a place. What will happen to your noble parents when they find out about your evil act?' Ajee Shah replied, 'But I have done nothing. I was just looking for the house of my friend to borrow a book from him.' The electrician was in no humour to listen to excuses or pleas. Ajee Shah remembered afterwards that when the electrician had mentioned his high spiritual caste, Janti had become very uncomfortable as she hadn't known that about him. Ajee Shah, at the instruction of the King, had given her a fake name.

After his citizen's arrest, the electrician brought Ajee Shah on his bicycle to his home. That was the most terrible journey of his life. He handed over Ajee Shah to his mother and told her the whole story as if he had done something of national pride. After the electrician left, Ajee's mother beat him. She cursed Ajee Shah, herself, and the fate that had ensured she had to see this day. Then in the evening Ajee's father came and, before even changing his clothes, beat Ajee Shah very severely. Ajee was not given any food that evening either but he never changed his initial story. He claimed constantly that he was innocent. He was insistent that his only crime was that he had strayed into the wrong place at the wrong time. Nobody believed him but still Ajee Shah was happy. He knew that none had any clue of his sexual adventures in the *chakla* and that the only thing they had caught him doing was wandering in that sinful place.

Ajee Shah stopped going to the *chakla* and told Raja the whole story about his capture. The King was not alarmed at all and said, 'You had already got what you wanted. Now you don't need to go to that place. I don't want you to become addicted at this young age and ruin your life. Your capture was a blessing in disguise for you.'

Then came *Muharam*, the Muslim month of mourning. One evening, when Ajee Shah was going to his tuition class, a woman in a black veil stopped him. As she removed the thin layers of her veil, Ajee Shah became nervous. It was Janti in the black mourning dress. She was going to the *majlis*, a religious gathering. She was very upset and told Ajee Shah that her pimp and dog had both died one after the other, and that she was left alone in this whole world. She was confused about what to do. She could either stay here or go to Lahore's Heera Mandi, the "diamond market" of dancing girls and prostitutes. She asked Ajee Shah to pray for her. Now that she knew Ajee was a Syed, she—like many others—asked him to pray for her, believing that the prayers of a Syed were more readily answered than those of normal folk. Then she left with tears in her eyes and Ajee Shah was relieved of her presence.

A few days after that roadside meeting, Ajee Shah went to visit the King and, to his utter astonishment, Raja asked, 'Did you pray for that poor girl?' Ajee Shah couldn't recall Janti's request immediately and asked, 'W h poor girl?' The King cheekily answered, 'The same one who restored your potency.' Ajee Shah hadn't prayed for her but he lied, 'Oh, yes, of course.' Raja didn't believe him but he laughed it away. Then the King said something that was so unbelievable that you couldn't even laugh at it. But Ajee Shah knew from his experience that he was totally serious. He told Ajee Shah that he was going to marry Janti and would take her away from that cursed world. 'She will become the mother of my boys.'

Ajee Shah was perplexed as to what to say but he also couldn't afford to remain silent, so he said, 'But how will it be possible?' Raja gave him a strange logic that Ajee Shah was not expecting, 'Look, I was a *haram khor*, a person who eats prohibited food, and she was a *haram kar*, a fornicator, and we both decided to amend our ways.' Ajee Shah replied, 'But you are not *haram khor* as you earn your living by hard work.' Raja again laughed and said, 'You know that eating snake meat is forbidden in our religion. For many years I used to eat snake's meat twice a month. It is just like fish but I never offered it to anyone else. I cooked it by myself and ate it all.' Ajee Shah was not at all shocked by this revelation but was very embarrassed to hear about the King's decision. He knew in his heart that Raja was capable of doing anything as he had gone through life experiences that normal people couldn't afford to have. 'As you wish,' Ajee Shah closed the conversation. But the King was perhaps enjoying his embarrassment, and asked, 'Will you not be my best man?' Ajee Shah was very much obliged to Raja for his kind act of taking him to Janti and spending a lot of money on him but he refused plainly to be his best man. Then the King explained that he was just joking and explained that there would be no marriage procession, no band, no best man, no garlands, nothing. 'I have only arranged for the four witnesses and the Imam to perform the marriage ceremony,' said Raja, 'I would have definitely included you but you are not yet of the age to become a witness and sign my marriage contract.' Then he again joked, 'But don't worry, our religion has given us permission to have four marriages and on my next marriage, you will be a witness from my side.' Ajee Shah left the King with a heavy heart and heavier feet.

Ajee Shah didn't sleep well that night and had many weird dreams while drifting in and out of a troubled sleep. He saw Raja and Janti as two snakes making love like humans and saw himself as a big cobra, whose hood overlooked them both. But strangely all his wild dreams didn't create any guilt in him and he was perfectly normal in the morning, albeit a little bit tired.

The King left their town with his wife and shifted to a city about thirty miles away, but he never changed his profession. A couple of years later, when Ajee Shah visited that city to see the editor of a weekly newspaper that published his fictional stories in the children's section, he met Raja again. He was selling his remedies on a roadside to the crowd gathered around him. As soon as he saw Ajee Shah, he came to him, embraced him, and left the rest of the selling to his assistant. He took him to the tea shop and ordered two cups of milky tea. Raja was very happy and contented. He told Ajee Shah that they had a son now and Janti had become a real Janti, "one who belongs to paradise". She prayed five times a day and taught the Koran to the little children of the neighbourhood. 'I knew that she was a good girl. She was only plunged into those unfortunate circumstances. Her heart had always remained like that of an angel.' And while saying that the King's eyes became wet, and I, Kabuko the djinn, thought, in wonder, that human beings are a strange species for, in both pain and pleasure, they cry. They can't bear any emotions. They are too vulnerable.

Raja insisted that Ajee Shah should go with him and have dinner at his home but Ajee Shah refused. He couldn't face Janti, the restorer of his potency.

14

The Teacher-less Apprentice

Karam Shah was one of Ajee Shah's older half-brothers from his Badi Ma. After leaving his job as a police head constable, he returned to live in their native village and never held a permanent job after that. However, he did occasionally do piecemeal work in various factories on the Grand Track Road that was on the outskirts of the village. His lean body structure and sunken eyes made him look like a worn-out person tired of life, but this was quite misleading. He was strong and energetic on the inside. Considering his middle-age and the tough struggle he had endured for years to survive, his physical powers were amazing. Sometimes, he effortlessly carried so much weight that Ajee Shah, who was blooming with youthful energy, couldn't compete without losing his breath.

After Ajee Shah's family moved back to the neighbourhood, Karam Shah became a frequent visitor to their place, sometimes even staying a few days with them. Because of those visits, Karam Shah managed to develop a strong bond of friendship with a local blacksmith named Bao Lohar. He would often spend more time with Bao Lohar than with his own family. Apart from chain smoking, Karam Shah didn't have any bad habits, and in those days smoking was not considered such a bad habit either. In fact non-smoking men were sometimes taunted by brassy women for being akin to eunuchs. Smoking was a manly trait but many old women also smoked the *hukka*. Karam Shah always smoked the cheapest and strongest brand of cigarettes, and his index and the middle finger had become permanently stained. But the problem was not his chain smoking but the smoke of his makeshift kilns, which burnt up all his casual earnings.

From his police days, he was obsessed with the desire to make gold from other much cheaper metals. Karam Shah was always short of money and was perpetually looking for sponsors for his gold-making venture. In the early years, Karam Shah had no problem getting sponsorship and even Ajee Shah's mother had twice lent him fifty rupees from her savings. Many people, in and out of the family, had invested quite a large sum of money in Karam Shah's project. But, unfortunately, he couldn't deliver the goods by tripling the borrowed money and eventually lost all his supporters, whose greed couldn't go any further as they were not millionaires. Karam Shah was so used to scarcity that a simple lack of resources could never kill his inner fire. He adamantly pursued his obsession and, somehow or the other, always found someone to back him. And he was so honest that he wouldn't spend a penny on himself out of the money he borrowed for his pet venture.

Karam Shah had a habit of always scanning the ground while walking. Whenever he found any metal, rubber, nut, or any other small thing, he stopped to pick it up. He, then, examined it carefully and would either throw it away or put it in his pocket. He never threw away any piece of metal, though, and would always spit on it and then rub it with his fingers before putting it in his pocket. Ajee Shah found the spitting so disgusting that he always turned his face away, but Karam Shah was not ready to change his habit. He saw nothing wrong or repulsive about it. When Karam Shah's spirits were low, he often admitted with regret that he was "without a teacher". This showed immense courage and honesty because in those days and in that society "being without a teacher" or *bai ustada* was a cursed predicament. Karam Shah had tried very hard and gone to many places in search of an alchemy teacher but to no avail. He had to pursue the elusive study of alchemy by himself through trial and error, which was very difficult and costly. Karam Shah was regretful of the fact that none of the elders of his own knowledgeable spiritual family had practised the art of alchemy. His regret was understandable as alchemists rarely imparted that sort of secret knowledge to anyone outside their own families.

Karam Shah was unable to make pure gold but one day, accidentally, he had achieved a magical thing that other alchemists in the area could hardly even dream of: he had solidified mercury and made two small balls out of the resulting substance. When Karam Shah had showed those balls to "the alchemist mafia" they had been stunned and had offered to impart to him all the knowledge of making gold in exchange for his method of making mercury solid. But Karam Shah never remembered or wrote down his experimental ingredients or the method. He told them that the discovery was an accident and he didn't really know the formula to reproduce it. They hadn't believed him as it was a lifetime discovery for an alchemist. Thereafter, Karam Shah always kept the two balls of solidified mercury with him as a good omen and a reward for his lifetime obsession.

Karam Shah liked his younger brother Ajee Shah and they had a strange affinity between them but Ajee Shah was no real help to his brother as, like him, he was also always short of money. Ajee Shah was the only one in the whole family who never reproached his brother for anything and, apart from his distaste at the spitting on pieces of metal, always supported him and boasted to others of his achievements.

One time Karam Shah came to Ajee Shah's house with enough money to throw about. He told the family that he had achieved making ordinary metal into seventy percent gold and that 24 carat gold was just round the corner. The family forgot their annoyance with him and even praised the spirit of his persistence. Only Ajee Shah knew that his obsessed brother was so mad that even if he were successful in making gold he couldn't repeat the process and that it would be only a one-off thing. Ajee Shah was convinced that Karam Shah was not really interested in his final achievement but was immersed in the process of alchemy itself, which gave him a greater intoxication than that from a snake bite.

Ajee Shah started going with Karam Shah to his blacksmith friend Bao Lohar, who had a shop in the main street of neighbourhood. It was not a big shop but somehow it comfortably accommodated his old furnace, his battered tools, his few finished and many unfinished products, his sleeping mat on the floor, a few small tin boxes of his personal belongings, and a straw mat for visitors. One could always find a couple of visitors in his shop. Bao Lohar was in his late fifties and at times some very strange looking characters visited him. They seldom talked to anyone except him and their conversation was too peculiar for ordinary folk to understand. They talked about strange things and unbelievable experiences of magical worlds that were beyond Ajee Shah's grasp.

A tea kettle was always lying on the side of the furnace and Bao would drink dozens of cups every day. Most of his visitors were also very fond of tea. The tea was always strong and made with a lot of tea leaves, generous portions of sugar, and with little milk. Nobody knew how the poor Bao Lohar could afford all that. Bao Lohar often talked to himself but that was not a strange characteristic in that society; many people used to do that. For bathing and washing, Bao Lohar always used the public facilities of the local mosque. He also regularly visited the street barber for a shave once a week. After every fresh shave his face looked as pale as a ghost's as the barber would put a liberal dusting of cheap powder on him to stop the bleeding from the inevitable blade cuts.

Some locals, including a few young men, were regular visitors at Bao Lohar's place. They would sit there on the mat for hours and drink many rounds of tea. In the evening a small group listened to folk stories and often a young man called Khadim sang the couplets of Heer, a popular love story of Punjab. Sometimes Bao Lohar made a special herbal tonic for himself in the same tea kettle and never offered it to anyone else.

It was an open secret that Bao Lohar had been in search of a unique magical flower for many years without any luck. No one had seen that nameless flower but Bao insisted that if one were to put that flower in flowing water, it would move against the flow. And that was the only way to identify this flower. After every couple of months he closed his shop, put a big padlock on the door, and disappeared for weeks, sometimes even for months. Everybody knew that Bao Lohar had gone into the wilderness in the search of that unique flower. His sudden disappearance always saddened the permanent visitors of his shop. However, for their comfort, they had the sure knowledge that upon his return Bao would have even more unbelievable stories though, regrettably, not the flower. No one had ever seen Bao depressed or disappointed upon returning from his unsuccessful missions. On his return he was always more determined. Whenever Bao Lohar mentioned that particular flower, his eyes lit up even more. He claimed that the magical flower had many more powers than the alchemist's philosopher's stone, and having said that, he would recount about a dozen attributes of that magical flower. Out of which Ajee Shah and most others could only remember that the holder of the flower could become rich instantly and that the smell of the flower could make any girl on the Earth fall in love with him. It never occurred to any of them that it could happen vice versa. A girl could also find the flower and make a man her slave instantly. Humans . . .

Ajee Shah soon realised that his brother Karam Shah was looking for "his would-be mentor" in Bao Lohar, and was convinced that Bao Lohar knew all the secrets of alchemy. Karam Shah argued that if that was not the case how on Earth was it that Bao Lohar was never short of money? But Ajee Shah didn't agree with his brother's assessment. He insisted that Bao was a lone person in the world, and since he didn't have many expenses and his only intoxication was the tea, he could afford that in his meagre resources. Ajee believed, for his part, that Bao's modest income was not gained through making gold. But Karam Shah never agreed with his younger brother and always shunned him for being still a child. Karam Shah proudly claimed that his judgement about Bao Lohar was one hundred and one percent correct and that one day he would prove the validity of his point beyond any doubt.

That day never came in Karam Shah's lifetime but what did come was one of the worst floods in the country's history. Karam Shah, along with a friend from the village, was returning from factory work one day, and they had to cross the Bhimbar, a seasonal river, to reach their village. The river was so flooded that they couldn't see the other bank. In fact, the river's water overflowed and reached almost up to the village, which by virtue of being on high ground, was never directly hit by the floods. Both judged the situation and decided to go further up about a mile and then swim with the flow of water to reach the village. When they went into the water, the current was so strong that Karam Shah's friend turned back after few yards and pleaded with Karam Shah to do the same. He shouted to Karam Shah the oft-quoted advice of elders, 'Always refrain when the Divine is wrathful'. But Karam Shah wanted to check the temperature and the fire of his furnace at home and didn't heed his friend's or the elders' advice.

After swimming a few hundred yards, Karam Shah reached a sandy high ground in the water. There he sat and smoked a cigarette, his last cigarette, and waved to his friend, who was still hoping for his return. Then Karam Shah started his last journey with two legs and one arm as he was holding his clothes in the other hand, which he kept out of water for miles. When he was mid-river, he realised that he couldn't make it and tried to turn back but the strong current didn't allow him to change his course. Thus he swam for almost three miles, with occasional shouting for help. Many people saw him but it was impossible to help him in any way. After that a juncture came, where another branch of the same river joined the main stream. To survive that juncture in such a flood would be a miracle, but Karam Shah not only survived that but also didn't let go of his clothes.

About four miles away there was a bridge over the river on the Grand Trunk Road. Karam Shah must have thought that he would make it there by catching the bridge's edge, for as he neared the bridge, he finally let go of his clothes and starting using both arms. There were many people on the bridge and they saw a man in the water, swimming and shouting.

Afterwards, the witness account was that he jumped a couple of feet out of the water to try to catch the edge of the bridge but didn't make it, even though the water was almost touching the bridge's edge. When he fell back in the water, the pressure of water caused his head to strike the concrete edge of the bridge and he sunk down into the water. The people on the other side of the bridge saw the red trails of Karam Shah's blood but his body never emerged.

The next day, the flood waters receded and many search parties from the village went looking for his body. Almost all of Ajee Shah's family in the city reached the village the next day, although it took two to three days for other relatives from further afield places to come. Ajee Shah joined the search party in spite of objections from the villagers that he was a city boy and couldn't bear the hardships of that undertaking. They walked many miles on wet, swampy ground. Almost every other tree had a snake in it, brought there with the flood waters, having escaped the wrath of the Divine. When Ajee Shah's search party reached a village about twelve miles further up the bridge, a man told them that he had seen a body near the bank of the river on the same day and ran for help to recover it. But when he came back with the other villagers they found nothing there. The search went on for many days but the body of Karam Shah was never found.

Karam Shah became a legend. No one could fight with such speedy and wrathful water and survive for seven miles. People would remember Karam Shah's courage and strength for many generations in that area as the adults were in the habit of telling those sorts of true stories to youngsters.

The "fireplace" or "the furnace", or whatever one would like to call that smoky corner of the courtyard in the village house where Karam Shah used to burn fire to make gold, mysteriously smoked for seven days after his death; no matter how wispy it became, it did not go out. Nobody went near that place for months. His mother did not allow anyone near it. One night, Badi Ma saw somebody enter the house and she was sure that he was not a thief. The apparition came in and sat on the ground and checked the fire with the stroking of his hand. There was no fire but, the next morning, she saw fresh signs of the ash having been stoked. She told everyone in the village, 'My son came last night and checked his gold.'

15

Tea and Magic

After Karam Shah's death, Ajee Shah took the place of his brother and became a regular visitor to Bao Lohar's Shop. Bao often remembered Karam Shah with sadness and used to say that if he had not been seduced by alchemy, he would have achieved 'something' much more substantial. He had potential, wit and, an ancestral background for such a 'something' but a lesser something had entangled him. Bao always concluded his remorseful remembrance of Karam Shah by saying, 'But that is life. Whatever is written up there in the skies, will happen. Whether you go straight or through twist and turns, you can't change your fate.' Ajee Shah didn't like Bao Lohar's fatalistic view of life, so predetermined that there was no room for free will. In time, however, Ajee Shah came to realise that Bao Lohar's expressed that popular view about life just to comfort himself and others, and that it really meant nothing at all. Just as Bao Lohar used to repeat another popular phrase, 'God only helps men of courage and initiative.'

Only after a few visits did Ajee Shah sense that Bao Lohar wanted to convey something important to him through his remarks about Karam Shah. Perhaps Bao was assessing him as a promising apprentice. At Bao Lohar's age, unusual characters such as he, often looked for someone younger to whom they could impart their knowledge. Ajee Shah was also encouraged to think expectantly by the changed behaviour of Bao Lohar. Before, in the presence of Karam Shah, he didn't talk directly to Ajee Shah and ignored him and his questions. But now he took him more seriously and talked to Ajee as if he were an adult. His more approachable attitude created a space for Ajee Shah to push himself nearer to Bao Lohar. But Ajee Shah was not sure whether Bao was truly a knowledgeable person or just impersonating being wise and mysterious. And if he really knew something, then what was it?

One day, Ajee Shah went to Bao's shop when there was no one else around. He sat on the mat, and without wasting any time abruptly asked Bao Lohar, 'People say that you know how to make gold but you hide your abilities. Is it true that you can make gold?' Bao Lohar laughed weakly with his sad eyes and answered, 'No, I am not an alchemist but my grandfather was a great one. In my younger days, he tried many times to teach me his art. He even attempted to bribe me, punish me, encourage me through various incentives but he couldn't get anything out of this son of blacksmith. I had no aptitude or patience for those sort of endeavours. At last my grandfather got fed up with me and left me alone. That was my first win and his last defeat. He died soon after that and couldn't transfer his valuable knowledge to anyone in the family. After his death my father taught me our family profession of moulding metal. And I am still moulding it, although I cannot transform it.'

Ajee Shah asked, 'Bao ji, have you ever regretted later on in your life that you missed such a marvellous opportunity?' Bao answered, without emotion, 'No, not even once.' Ajee Shah was surprised to hear that; he thought only a mad person would not regret that sort of missed opportunity. Was Bao Lohar such a mad person or was he still hiding the truth? In his confused state, Ajee Shah became silent. Bao Lohar asked him if he wanted tea and he nodded his head in an affirmative gesture. Bao Lohar put the water in his kettle and stood up to get the milk from the shop that was just round the corner. Ajee Shah instantly took the glass from his hand and went to get the milk. Bao asked him to take the money but Ajee replied that he had enough money for the milk. Before that Bao had never allowed Ajee Shah, the son of a Syed, to bring him anything from the shop. This was another sign of Bao Lohar's possible intention to make Ajee Shah his pupil.

After taking a few sips of the tea, Bao Lohar himself started the conversation and said that alchemy was a great knowledge but people had forgotten its true meaning. Now even the few people who knew it well, used it only to transform base metal, not the essence of life. A long time ago wise men used alchemy mainly for its original purpose of overall transformation. Bao paused for a few seconds and said confidently, 'But there are many other things, more desirable and more powerful than alchemy. God's world is full of knowledge. In fact it is nothing but knowledge. That is why our prophet, peace be upon him, said, "It is a duty of every faithful male and female to seek knowledge". But nowadays we have forgotten everything.' Ajee Shah didn't understand fully what exactly Bao was trying to convey but he kept silent and pretended as if he understood every word. Bao asked Ajee Shah to come tomorrow, saying he would show him something from another type of knowledge. Then he smiled and said, 'Not the real knowledge but just a gimmick.' He also advised Ajee Shah to come at a time when there was no one else in the shop.

The next day Ajee Shah went to the shop many times and turned back to see one or two people sitting there. At last he became so irritated that he decided not to waste any more time and went to see a friend who had promised to lend him a book. But it was not Ajee Shah's day, his friend was not at home and he had to return in disappointment. During the next two days, Ajee Shah tried to find Bao Lohar alone in the shop but had no success.

On the third day, Ajee Shah went in the morning and was fortunate to find Bao alone. He went into the shop, greeted Bao, and sat on the mat. Bao Lohar didn't offer him tea but gave him a half rupee coin and asked him to bring a packet of cigarettes wrapped in cellophane. In those days, only packets of ten cigarettes were available, and Capstan was the only brand with that sort of wrapper. The two small shops in the neighbourhood sold the cheap brands of cigarettes but Capstan was expensive and there were no customers of that brand around. To get that brand Ajee Shah would have to walk more than half a mile to the main square of the town where there was a shop that sold almost every brand of cigarettes.

Ajee Shah asked Bao Lohar, 'But why do you need that brand of cigarette, anyway? I have never seen you smoke a cigarette. You only occasionally take a puff or two of *hukka*.' Bao Lohar became serious and said in a severe tone, 'Don't ask questions. Do what you are asked to do.' Ajee Shah was not used to that sort of tone but he didn't take offence and went to get a packet of Capstan. Those were the days when Ajee Shah could not endure normal walking. He had so much energy to burn that he would run, whether in a hurry or not. He came back within twenty minutes, holding a packet of Capstan in his hand and hardly out of breath at all. Bao Lohar noticed his speed and energy, and his smile, at seeing Ajee Shah back so soon, was more than expressive.

Ajee Shah presented the packet to Bao Lohar but he refused to touch it and asked him to hold the packet in both his hands. 'Okay, tell me anything in the world, whatever you can think of, and that will be inside the wrapped packet. The only condition is that it should not be bigger than this packet of cigarettes you are holding in your hands.' Bao Lohar said this to Ajee Shah in the manner of a performer challenging a suspicious audience. Ajee Shah thought for a while and the most unlikely thing that came to his mind was a hundred rupee note. He said out loud, 'A hundred rupee note.' The last sound of the word "note" was still on his tongue, yet to be delivered, yet to be materialised, when a strange movement happened within the packet, which Ajee Shah was still tightly holding in both hands.

Bao Lohar then asked Ajee Shah, with complete confidence, to open the cellophane of the packet. He opened it. Then Bao ordered him to open the packet itself. Ajee Shah did it robotically. 'Now look for yourself in the back sleeve of the packet. Is there something there?' asked Bao. Ajee Shah took out a new hundred rupee note, folded in four layers and stuck behind the silvery leaf of the packet. He opened it and examined it for a long time. The note seemed to be real. Then Bao Lohar asked Ajee Shah to hand over the note to him and said, 'This is yours but the time has not yet come for you to spend it. When you will be capable of spending it, I will give it you. Meanwhile I will keep it in your trust.' Ajee Shah was not interested in the money at all but was entranced by the magic Bao Lohar had performed in front of his very own eyes.

This episode made me, Kabuko the djinn, very confused. Up until that time I believed that only djinn could perform that kind of swift materialisation. But the entity that performed this "miracle", invisible to Ajee Shah but very visible to me, I was sure was not a djinn. The entity resembled Bao Lohar but looked much more translucent and brighter than him. So it was not only the djinn that human beings could enslave, other non-human invisible species were also under their control. My work seemed to be expanding with this discovery. But, at the same time as being pleased with my progress, I could clearly see that Ajee Shah was heading towards the same area of knowledge and the same people who held those hidden secrets of which my kind are so envious.

Ajee Shah was now convinced that even if, as he claimed, Bao Lohar did not know alchemy, he knew something at least as extraordinary. For days he pondered very hard as to how Bao Lohar did that without even touching the packet. He told, in confidence, one of his friends the whole story. To the sheer astonishment of Ajee Shah, his friend was not impressed at all by that incredible incident and said, 'It's not a big deal, only a gimmick of *nazar bindi*.' His friend explained that *nazar bindi*, or "seized vision", is a conjured state in which sight is controlled temporarily to induce imaginary or false vision. Ajee Shah didn't understand this or perhaps he was not ready to listen to anything that would cast doubt on the wonderful knowledge of Bao Lohar. However, Ajee Shah's friend wanted to prove his point and said, 'There was an old beggar woman who used to come, once or twice a year, to our locality. If you have not seen her, ask your mother, she would definitely have come across her one time or another. The old woman never took any grain or food but always asked for money. And women were compelled to give her money, more than any beggar could expect. You know why? Because she was a conjurer. Her technique was simple. She used to ask the woman of the house to bring a few grains of rice, wheat or lentil and then she rubbed those grains in her hands and increased their quantity. She would give back that handful of grain to the woman and instructed her to put it in the pot and the fortune of the house would be multiplied as were the grains. Obviously after that she would ask for money and always got the best deal because the women were easily impressed by this sort of conjuration.'

Ajee Shah asked his sceptical friend, 'But how could the beggar woman multiply the grains? Obviously she knew something.' The friend told Ajee Shah that the grains were never increased in quantity at any time but it looked like that to the housewives. Ajee Shah was not ready to accept his friend's explanation and said, 'It proved the old woman had some power to change the observer's vision and make her see something that was not actually there. That itself is a magical thing.' His friend had no convincing answer to that as he had no idea how the old woman used to do this. In the end he said, 'I don't want to waste my time discussing that trickery. Let us talk about something more interesting.'

When Ajee Shah came home, he went straight to the kitchen and asked his mother about the old woman. She remembered her and said, 'But she has not returned for a long time. She was very old and I imagine has probably passed away.' Ajee Shah was not interested in the woman but in her craft. 'Was she a trickster or a genuine person?' Ajee Shah asked. His mother said in a humble tone, 'Only God knows what is in a person's heart but once she blessed our house with multiplied grains and soon after many good things happened. Your father got a very good job in a foreign construction company that was building the cantonment area. Your elder sister passed her graduation exams with high marks and your younger brother's chronic cough was cured with the same medicine that he was using for a long time but which was not effective before. So I don't know, only God knows better.' Ajee Shah was much more comforted by his mother's words. Mothers always soothe their children.

16

A Fairy At The Well

After witnessing a hundred rupee note being materialised in a packet of cigarettes, Ajee Shah noticed another strange coincidence that happened time and again. Before it was difficult, and at times impossible, to find Bao Lohar alone in his shop but now it became easy for Ajee Shah to spend as much time alone with Bao as he would like. Strangely the regular visitors started avoiding coming into the shop when Ajee Shah was there. They walked down the street but, upon seeing them together, would pretend that they were going somewhere else. Ajee Shah became convinced that Bao Lohar must have the power to control other people's minds. Ajee now spent more and more time in the shop as he found the company of Bao Lohar much more alluring than that of his own age group. He was definitely growing up. But he had no idea he would grow so rapidly that after some time he couldn't recognise himself as the same Ajee Shah.

Ajee didn't wish to annoy Bao Lohar but one day he couldn't resist asking him, 'Did you induce

146

a false vision in me that day when you put a hundred rupee note in that sealed packet of cigarettes?' Bao Lohar didn't mind his question, but asked curiously, 'From where did you get this stupid idea? Who told you that?' Ajee Shah was not ready for this question and, so, lied, 'Nobody. I guessed it myself.' Bao Lohar stood up and opened one of the tin boxes behind him. He searched for a while with his left hand and then took out the hundred rupee note. He handed over the note to Ajee Shah and asked him, 'Here is the note. Check it carefully and tell me what is false in it.' Ajee took the note and rubbed it in his hand and said, 'Yes, it is a real note.' Bao Lohar smiled and said, 'Now take this note and spend it. Perhaps then you will really believe that it was not an induced vision but a real thing that you observed.'

Ajee Shah hesitantly took the note and put it in the front pocket of his shirt. Then Bao Lohar said, 'You should change the note. If you are seen with such a big bill, your family or other people might get suspicious. Go to Munir's shop and tell him that Bao Lohar asked for change and he will readily give it you.' Munir's shop was the biggest in the main street of the neighbourhood and he sold all sorts of things, from green groceries to tin pots. Even Bao Lohar sometimes supplied him with tin mugs and other metal pots to sell. Ajee Shah got the change and went on a shopping spree straight away. However, a hundred rupees was such a large amount in those days that it took Ajee almost a month to spend that money. In that month, Ajee Shah hardly ever went to Bao Lohar's shop as he was so busy enjoying his fortune and showing it off to his friends.

After spending the last penny of the hundred rupees, Ajee Shah went to Bao Lohar's shop, fully convinced of Bao's mysterious powers. But now Ajee felt so inhibited that he couldn't ask Bao any bold questions. Whenever a question came to his mind something stopped him asking it. Ajee Shah thought he had sold his freedom to question very cheaply. He regretted accepting that hundred rupee note but now it was too late. Bao Lohar was not the person he appeared to be. He caught Ajee Shah red-handed thinking that and responded, 'That hundred rupees was just an advance, the real thing will follow. I never cheated anyone and you are a Syed. How on earth can I cheat you?'

Ajee Shah had no idea what Bao Lohar was saying to him. Ajee Shah said, 'Bao ji, I don't know what you are talking about? Please tell me in simple words so that I can understand.' Bao smiled and assured Ajee Shah that he was not playing any games with him but that he needed something from him and was trying to strike a deal. The first thing that came to Ajee Shah's mind on hearing this was something so shocking that he instantly lost all his belief and trust in Bao. Despite trying to strike out that thought from his mind, he was unable to do so, and was scared that Bao would read his mind. Just the thought of this embarrassed Ajee Shah to no end. However, Bao Lohar was much too clever, he plainly said to Ajee Shah while directly looking into his eyes, 'I am not after what you are thinking about. I can sleep with the most beautiful girl and the most handsome boy on this earth any time I want, but I have left sex far behind. And to tell you honestly I haven't had sex with anybody, male or female, or even masturbated for at least ten years. That is not my concern. Can't you see that I am in a much bigger game?'

Then Bao uttered some words and phrases as if he was talking to himself or to some invisible being. Ajee Shah felt guilty at messing up the whole thing. He tried to alter his thought but was unable to do so in his presence. So, he left the shop in utter confusion, even without saying goodbye to Bao Lohar. That night was too heavy and disturbing for him to bear and he carried over the residues of the dreams of that night for many days.

Ajee Shah was not only embarrassed but he had also become fearful of Bao Lohar. He was unsure where the association with him would take him. Eventually, Ajee Shah gathered his strength and decided that he was not meant for those sorts of things. He stopped going to Bao Lohar's shop and also vowed to himself that he would not read any more books of mysterious stories. He even gifted all his books of djinn, fairy, and demon stories to his friends. Ajee Shah had adopted a new lifestyle and started concentrating on his studies. He was in the final year of high school and had set his eyes on getting the first position in the whole district for the matriculation examination. Now, after school, he spent most of his time doing homework and studying general knowledge books at home. He no more wandered aimlessly in the city and even got rid of many of his wastrel friends. Before Ajee Shah could not wake up early in the morning, but now he started going for an early morning walk in the nearby fields to be active and effective all day long. His family was surprised and quite happy to see these positive changes in his attitude. In the evening, before going to bed, Ajee Shah's mother started giving him a glass of hot milk with Ovaltine. No other person in the house got this favoured treatment. That was either a reward for his good behaviour or to encourage him to keep on going in that fashion.

For a couple of months, all the changes went so smoothly that it astonished even Ajee Shah. As he became sure that his new impeccable way of living would stay permanently with him, something out of the blue happened that turned all his plans topsy-turvy, and also put me, Kabuko the djinn, in great trouble.

Ajee Shah usually woke up for his early morning walk with the call to morning prayers on the loudspeaker of the local mosque. On that fateful morning he heard the call and woke up. Afterwards Ajee Shah would concede that he didn't actually hear the call but dreamt that he had. When he came out of his house, it was still dark outside but it never occurred to him that it was not morning twilight he was seeing but at least a couple of hours before the usual time of calling. Oblivious to this, he started walking on the path leading to the fields.

Where the actual fields started and the dust disappeared, there was an old well wheel to water the surrounding fields. Ajee Shah had taken a shower under the water of that wheel many times before. Normally, an ox or two would work the wheel, moving around in a small circle. But, sometimes just to take a shower under the falling water, a person could run the well physically. Ajee Shah was surprised to hear the sound of falling water and wondered why the well was running that early in the morning, but then thought that perhaps it was necessary to water the fields at that time of the year. When Ajee Shah actually passed by the well, he saw the well was running without any oxen or man pulling it. He became frightened but then calmed himself down with the thought that this must be an illusion of the dark and that the oxen were cloaked in the inky black before dawn.

He went closer to the well and what he saw there was so bewildering that all his faculties of thought and action became suspended. He tried to move but was so rigidly frozen that he was unable to go back even a step. In panic, he started reciting the usual simple prayers that Muslims chant when faced with that sort of situation. Ajee Shah saw a young girl taking a shower under the water of the well. Her naked body was so illuminated that Ajee could see her nakedness clearly, even though he was yards away from her. She had very long hair falling down to her ankles. Her gestures of taking a shower were also abnormal. It seemed as if she was not taking a shower but was dancing to the music of falling water. She was so beautiful and fair that she looked like a creature from the world of the fairies. Ajee Shah was convinced that she was supernatural as no human girl ever took a shower at the well, even in clothes.

He was so enchanted by the scene that he would have wished, if his mind allowed him to do so, to spend the rest of his life just observing her. Ajee Shah couldn't tell how long he stood watching that naked girl but when he heard the call for morning prayer from another mosque's loudspeaker, he immediately realised that he had woken up by mistake much earlier than his usual time. During the call, the sound of the falling water stopped and the girl disappeared. Everything suddenly became normal and Ajee Shah felt as if he had returned from somewhere beyond reality to his own world. He went to the well and was stunned to see no sign of any water in the small pool of the well, where a little while ago the girl had been taking a shower. The caretaker of the well was still sleeping nearby and the animals were also not disturbed. The only tangible residue of the incident was Ajee Shah's clothes which were soaked through with the sweat of his fear.

Ajee Shah returned home, but how he came back he couldn't say. When he entered the house, all the family were still asleep except his mother. She was working in the kitchen, and when she saw Ajee sweating and bewildered, she became panicked. She asked Ajee what had happened to him and why he was sweating so profusely. Before Ajee could say a word, a female voice sounded in his ears, 'Don't tell your mother anything, otherwise I will not appear before you again.' Without thinking, Ajee Shah told a lie and said to his mother, 'Today I ran fast for three miles just to check my stamina and that is why I am sweating.' His mother advised him, 'Don't do such a thing in future and go and take a bath with cold water.'

Ajee Shah went to the bathroom and thought about the

voice. Somehow he was convinced that the voice he had heard belonged to the girl he had seen at the well. The voice was as beautiful as the naked body of the girl. Ajee Shah thought that she must be a *pari,* a female djinn or fairy, and assumed that the whole mysterious drama was created just for him. That thought gave him such joy that suddenly all the residues of the horrifying experience were relinquished and only the beautiful fairy remained in his mind. Ajee Shah came out of the bathroom a happy and contended person.

That day he had a heavy breakfast, and he ate so slowly that he enjoyed every bit of his food, perhaps for the first time in his life. His mother noticed the change and thought that her son was acquiring more and more good habits each day. She thanked God for making Ajee Shah so virtuous and discerning.

All the way to school Ajee Shah thought of nothing else but the *pari.* He was so lost in his thoughts that he passed by the left side of the electric pole, which stood in the middle of the street. There was a superstition among the students that if you passed by that pole from the right, you would have a trouble free day at school. But if you went by the left side, all the trouble and brutal teachers were waiting for you. But Ajee Shah not only had a fantastic day at school but also got an extra holiday for the next day as the school's volleyball team had won the district competition.

I, Kabuko the djinn, was not at all happy with this unexpected development. I could see trouble ahead for me. Ajee Shah was right that this was a female djinn in the shape of a beautiful girl, but he did not have any idea who she was. She was the same girl that I had met, in the company of her parents, hovering over that twisted tree. At the time I had thought she was an innocent young girl but she had created that elaborate enchantment at the well so successfully that now I was afraid of her intentions.

Questions came to my mind. Did she know that Ajee Shah was the same boy of the pundit who had been killed by her older sister? Had she fallen in love with Ajee Shah or did she want to do something for his reincarnated soul to pay off the crime her sister committed so many years ago? The most disturbing factor for me was her craftiness in creating such a real glamour. I wondered from where she had learned that art. But my real fear was that if she started messing around with Ajee Shah, what would be my position? How would I deal with her? She had already shown her superiority.

Questions upon questions! I was losing my mind.

17

The Double's Miracle

At the age of sixteen, humans appear to have the greatest vulnerability towards falling in love at first sight. As such Ajee Shah hadn't stood a chance when his teenage eyes first encountered the beautiful *pari*. He barely gave a thought to the fact that his dream girl was not human but djinn. The spell that radiant white being had cast was so overwhelming that her other-worldliness seemed no great obstacle to Ajee Shah. In just one appearance, the "well *pari*" had snatched away all chance of Ajee Shah having a normal love affair with an ordinary girl. This vexed me greatly as human romantic love was one of the areas of study that I was most interested in. In that blooming youth, had the encounter not taken place, Ajee Shah would have fallen in love with any of his good looking cousins or one of the lovely girls from his neighbourhood, who often smiled invitingly at seeing him. There were reasons other than beauty and charm that would have attracted Ajee Shah to start a romance with one of the younger sisters of his friends. The opportunity to touch, and perhaps kiss, a young girl in the dark stairwell of a courtyard was itself enough to start a romance.

The cosy world of romance with a span of at least a couple of years passed him by and Ajee Shah didn't even feel a pang of loss. His desires and thoughts, which together had the ability to weave dreams of unimaginable scenarios, were all in the service of a girl who had no fixed abode. He was deprived of all that a romance entailed in those days. He would not be the recipient of scented letters with poor grammar, sent from a young girl. Some such letters were signed in blood, usually extracted from an index finger and not even from the more apt little finger, the "pinkie" which is ruled by planet of communication, Mercury. Venus rules not one of the fingers of the hand but the fleshy mound under the thumb, in the palm of the hand. No girl ever drew blood from that place; perhaps the pain of pricking such a soft spot was too much, even for those ardent romantics. Ajee Shah would never receive a rose, dried in the pages of a romantic Urdu novel, or a handkerchief with a heart embroidered on the left hand corner, or any other love token. Ajee Shah was stripped of all his possible and probable innocent liaisons but with no regret. To fall in love with a being from another world had its own advantages. Compatibility was guaranteed from the very beginning as Ajee Shah had a strong feeling of déjà vu. He spent hours every day trying to decipher why the *pari* had this sense of familiarity but he couldn't figure it out. Unfortunately, innocent Ajee Shah didn't know at the time that djinn are even more deceiving than human beings. We are much cleverer at cheating, shifting places, shapes, and moods, to play games with other species, and can hide our real identities and, of course, our real motives. Humans need masks to conceal themselves but our whole being is capable of becoming a mask.

Ajee Shah was neither aware of these pitfalls nor was he

concerned about his beloved's alien origins. He was in love with the *pari* and, like a fallen angel, he slipped from his familiar and comfortable position. There is a tradition that you should name your beloved, and so Ajee Shah called her "*khoh wali pari*", well *pari*, for a while but it didn't sound right in the Punjabi language to his aesthetic ears. He changed it to *jal pari*, mermaid. *Jal* means water and *pari* means fairy. Pari also means the most beautiful girl. The name sounded so musical to him and articulated in a sense that he had his first vision of that beauty soaked in water. The only difference was that there was no tail but two beautiful legs. However, Ajee Shah was well aware of the difference between a *pari* and a *jal pari*, as he had read many stories of both and, now, had even seen one.

The *jal pari* knew the art of lying low, but Ajee Shah didn't. He thought about her all the time but she never appeared in his dreams or in a vision. The dreams he dreamt were not what he wanted them to be. At night he saw nothing but a cluttered mish-mash of the days prior to his first sighting of her. The symptoms of those odd dream-packed nights started to appear in the daytime. He had swollen eyes, little appetite, pale-coloured urine, and constipation. Not to mention a lack of motivation and sheer annoyance. Ajee Shah had no one with whom to share his night realities or day dreams. The only person was Bao Lohar but he was too complex and too complicated to deal with. Ajee Shah was sure that Bao would create more problems than solve his present ones. Also, he was still scared of him.

Ajee Shah resisted going to Bao for many weeks and suffered in his loneliness but that could have happened in a normal love affair, too. Before the sighting he had been determined to come first in the whole district but now he knew that he would be lucky to even pass the matriculation examination. All his will and vows had become widowed. In a normal love affair he could have played at the ritual of a romance, which could have had a soothing effect on his health and well-being. But, in this case, he couldn't pretend to write a love letter that he consciously knew would never reach its intended destination.

In a few days, the agony reached a point where Ajee Shah had to surrender. He went to Bao Lohar's shop in a miserable shape and, without saying a word, sat on the dirty mat. Bao didn't say anything but his pleasant silence was as welcoming as before. Ajee Shah sat there for an hour but Bao didn't ask him if he wanted tea, instead he looked at him from time to time with curious eyes. At last, Bao asked him, 'Do you want to say something to me?' Ajee Shah remained silent but his eyes became wet. Bao said in a level tone, 'I know that something extraordinary has happened to you but you do not have the courage to tell me that straightaway. That is not very unusual. Take it easy and go home. Write it in a few sentences in simple Urdu on a piece of paper and burn it there and then. And then come back to me.' Ajee Shah stood up immediately and as he was about to leave the shop, Bao said, 'Write it in plain Urdu. You know that I am not well educated. I ran away from the school in seventh class. And be careful that nobody should see what you write on that paper.' Ajee Shah had almost left the shop when he heard the last instruction of Bao Lohar, 'Don't use lined paper. Use plain paper.'

Ajee Shah came home in a state that was more empty than confused. He searched for a plain piece of paper and noticed for the first time that all the papers available to him were lined. The only plain paper to be found was in his drawing book which was so rough and absorbent that it was difficult to write on it with a normal ink pen. But Ajee Shah, with a lot of effort, managed to write a full sentence, 'I am madly in love with a *pari* who I saw at the well a few days ago, very early in the morning.' He folded the paper many times and then went into the kitchen and burnt it all up. Then he washed the ashes away under a running tap.

When Ajee Shah returned to the shop, Bao Lohar was smiling. There was a dark-complexioned man in the shop whom Ajee had never seen before. His appearance resembled Bao Lohar somewhat, but his complexion was completely different. The presence of the stranger was quite disturbing for Ajee Shah. Bao Lohar noticed his discomfort immediately and said to him, 'Do not mind him, he is an old friend and has nothing to do with any of your business.' Ajee Shah became relaxed at that. Then Bao asked, 'Which well was it where you met that *pari* with whom you have fallen madly in love?' Ajee Shah was open-mouthed with amazement and became speechless. 'How on earth did Bao know that I am in love with a *pari*?' thought Ajee Shah. 'How could he have read that sentence on a rough drawing paper written in complete secrecy? Does he read minds? And who is he really? A man or a djinn?' Many questions came to Ajee Shah's mind but he was even more concerned with his love affair and anything that could help him reach his destiny. Ajee answered after a while, 'I saw the pari at the well where the fields start.'

Bao asked him to relate every detail of the encounter with the *pari* and instructed him to not hesitate in the presence of the stranger. Ajee Shah told him the whole tale and it took him more than half an hour. He didn't want to miss out even a tiny detail of what might have been the only story of his life. Bao Lohar very carefully listened to every word Ajee Shah said and became very concerned. He started sweating and wiped his brow many times. This was highly unusual for a blacksmith who spends all his life in front of a fire. It was late afternoon and Bao Lohar said, 'It is the declining time. We shouldn't talk any further on this subject. You should come tomorrow before noon and we will sort out everything. But don't worry. You have a lot of protection. Your ancestors in the next world are very powerful people, and I, a humble blacksmith, am also not so powerless, too. Rest assured that you have many friends around.' The stranger in the shop who had appeared to be uninterested in the conversation, suddenly said, 'Of course, you are not alone.' Ajee Shah felt a surge of unfamiliar energy entering his body when he heard the voice of the stranger. Ajee Shah didn't mind the stranger's interference as he felt that his voice came from another world, from another dimension, which posed no threat to his privacy as it was not meant for him directly. Ajee Shah stood up and shook hands with the stranger and left the shop. The stranger's hands were hot and he transferred some of this heat to Ajee Shah's hands.

On his way back home, Ajee Shah, without knowing why, smelt his hands and through his nostrils, smelt a scent unknown to his senses. It was difficult to explain that smell, but it overcame his entire being and took him far away from the street on which he was walking. Then he mixed in his mind the enchanted scent with the fragrance of his beloved *pari* and imagined it to be coming from her. In the same moment the strange smell disappeared and another distinct scent started emanating from somewhere beyond. It was definitely different in all its aspects but Ajee Shah was unable to decide which of them was more pleasing, more consuming, more absorbing, and more delightful. They were not equal in any way but were more or less parallel in their power of infinity. Ajee Shah felt that he was transformed in a mysterious way through these two fragrances. Then a very strange thought came to him, 'I would be the most blessed person if I were to leave this world just now, having the residues of these two scents on me.' With the thought of departing the world, the smells disappeared, and Ajee Shah was unable to smell, feel, or even imagine those fragrances again. He had lost both of them forever.

Ajee Shah went to bed without eating anything that night. He could not sleep for many hours and eventually fell into a half-sleep. His thoughts turned into dreams and then the dream cycle started, inviting other dream images. There was nothing abnormal, but when he suddenly awoke in the early hours of the morning, he had a feeling that he had seen something worthwhile in that dream. He didn't leave his bed and started trying very hard to remember the dream. After half an hour or so, he remembered a dream in which door after door opened for him and he was running and passing through all those doors. He had no idea why he was doing that. But somebody, a female—perhaps his beloved *pari*—was trying to stop him from going any further.

Ajee Shah didn't see her but she seemed to be holding his shirt from behind. He felt the soft grip of her hands on his back. Then she suddenly stopped at a door and he was free to go further. But the next door was closed. Ajee Shah remembered clearly that this closed door was different from the other doors he had passed through. There were many bright stones and gold metal strips fixed to the door, which made its design look so beautiful, almost belonging to the palace of a king or queen. The entity, or rather his *pari*, who was trying to stop him, was crying from behind and Ajee Shah could hear her crying. But he was scared to turn and see what was going on behind him and then suddenly he woke up.

Though there was nothing nightmarish in the dream, Ajee Shah felt a strange sort of dread in his chest. He went to the bathroom and washed his face with cold water and even drank water from the hand pump. The water felt good as it removed the dryness in his throat and the dread from his chest. Then,

Ajee Shah slept comfortably and had the deep sleep of a person who has done, in the waking hours, his duty with full diligence and has gone to bed without any guilt from neglect or fear of retribution.

God knew how Ajee Shah was convinced the closed door was not the last and that there were many doors beyond that one. Dreams always create more mysteries and solve less, sometimes none.

18

A Mercurial Inheritance

The next day Ajee Shah missed school on the fake excuse that he was not feeling well. But at ten o'clock, when he was leaving the house, his mother pointedly asked him, 'Ajee, if you are not feeling well, why are you going out?' Ajee answered, 'I am feeling too bored at home.' His mother knew that he had bunked school for some reason but she decided to ignore it. She was not in a mood to argue with him and she had a lot of work to do. Ajee Shah went straight to Bao Lohar's shop.

Bao was putting tea in his cup and, without even asking, gave the first cup to Ajee Shah, and took another cup from the kettle for himself. Ajee Shah didn't want to waste any time as he was very impatient to get the answers to all his questions. Instead of asking about his love with the *jal pari*, he asked Bao, 'Tell me truthfully how you are able to do all these unbelievable things. Where did you learn to materialise a hundred rupee note in a cigarette packet and to know something written in complete seclusion?' Bao smiled, this time not with his usual cheekiness, but with a cold seriousness.

Instead of answering his question, Bao Lohar reminded Ajee Shah about his previous request to have something from him. Ajee Shah asked, 'What is that?' Bao Lohar said, 'I can tell you only on the condition that you keep it secret, and vow that you will not reveal this to anyone in your life.' Ajee Shah promised by God not to open his mouth about the whole affair.

Then, Bao Lohar slowly put his hand under his pillow and took out two small silver balls and showed them to Ajee Shah. 'Do you recognise these balls?' Ajee Shah answered, without surprise, 'Yes, these balls are the lifetime achievement of my dearest brother Karam Shah who is now in the next world.' Ajee Shah assumed that his brother had given those solidified mercury balls to his mysterious friend Bao Lohar for some unknown reason. But he was astonished when Bao Lohar said, 'I want to have your permission to keep these two balls, and in return I will give you something that you will find very magical all your life.'

'But why do you need my permission to keep these balls with you? These were given to you by my brother and they are already in your possession,' asked Ajee Shah innocently. Bao Lohar said, in a sad voice, 'No. That is not true. Karam Shah always wanted to give these balls to you. You were the only one in his immediate family who deserved this kind of a great gift. Your brother knew this very well and was just waiting for the right moment—when you would be ready—to give you such special things. But the Divine did not give you or him that opportunity. During his sojourn on earth, Karam Shah showed me these balls many times and we had long conversations about mysteries of these balls, but he always kept them with him and the very first time I touched these balls was five days after

Karam Shah had passed away to the other side. Your brother was not a fool to give such things to an outsider and a low caste blacksmith like me at that. They always give to their family members but sometimes, because of destiny, they have to hand over all their lifetime "possessions" to an outsider. And from day one, I knew that I was an outsider but still I would be the one who would be blessed with these two balls at the end.'

Ajee Shah more or less understood Bao Lohar, but asked in awe, 'From where did you get these balls?' Bao Lohar took a deep breath and said, 'From now on I will not say a word to you that is not true as I have to deal with the truth, and I am bound to follow the fixed rules of the truth. It does not matter how powerful or weak you are, when you are in this sort of business, you have to play by the rules. There are hardly any exceptions. When I heard that your brother Karam Shah died, I sent an entity called *hamzad* to look for these balls. He searched everywhere but the balls were not in your native house in the village, and my *hamzad* came back without any clue. For years he has been serving me and it has never happened that he could not find a thing that I had asked for. He himself was in a disturbed and confused state. I told my *hamzad* that it was not his fault as the thing that he was looking for was so extraordinary that its powers were beyond any imaginable strength. Then I instructed my *hamzad* to search for the missing body of your brother Karam Shah and he found the body about thirty miles away from the bridge where he had stuck his head and died. The body was in deep water, but fully intact. Karam Shah had been holding these balls tightly in his left hand when he died. Then my *hamzad*, with great difficulty, opened the fist and recovered the balls. When I first touched the balls, a thought came into my mind that Karam Shah should be buried in the proper way. Without losing any time, I, along with my *hamzad*, went to the exact place where he had found his body. I accompanied my *hamzad* for the only reason that for a funeral prayer at least two people are needed. But the body of your brother had disappeared by the time we reached. We made frantic efforts to search for the body but could not find it.'

The explanation of Bao Lohar raised many questions in Ajee Shah's mind but he interrupted Bao and asked the most burning question, 'What is a *hamzad*?' Bao Lohar suddenly realised that he was talking to a young man who was unaware of the terminology that was taken for granted in conversations with other people like himself. 'Okay,' said Bao Lohar, with a little irritation, 'I will explain the phenomenon of *hamzad*. Every organic thing and being, whether it is hills, sea, rivers, vegetation, trees, reptiles, animals, or humans have their doubles in a parallel world. The sky is also no exception. All the stars in the sky, visible or invisible, have their parallels in another dimension called *Alame Misaal*, the parallel cosmos. It is that double that is called *hamzad*. The same term is also used, though loosely, for your aura as your etheric body holds an imprint of your *hamzad*. Sometimes it is also called *saaya*, the shadow. With various occult or spiritual practises your *hamzad* can appear in a dense body, and then, after a process of hard negotiation, it can become your helping entity, always at your disposal.'

Ajee Shah stood up and took a mug of water from the pitcher and drank it all in one go. Bao Lohar advised him always to drink water slowly and with three short intervals. Ajee Shah had had this advice so many times from so many adults that he habitually ignored it saying that, even if he tried, he could not help it. Then Ajee Shah asked, in a depressed tone, 'Why couldn't you or your *hamzad* find the body of my brother?' Bao Lohar remained silent for a while and then said, 'It is a mystery for me, and for him too. My *hamzad* is very powerful and could search every corner of the world but I suspect that the body was taken by spirits from another dimension, probably unknown to us.' There were tears in Ajee Shah's eyes. He abruptly stood up and left the place saying, 'I cannot take all this in one go. I will come again.' Bao Lohar did not stop him as he was well aware of his present state of mind.

Ajee Shah, in his heart, knew that some mysterious forces were pulling him towards themselves and creating all sorts of circumstances to get hold of him. He himself was feeling a great attraction for that unknown world but at the same time he was afraid of losing his own reality. He thought very hard about what to do. Then a thought came to his mind that made my day. If all these things were true then perhaps his notion of a djinn living within him hadn't been just a childhood notion either? Ajee Shah asked himself, 'Why don't I consult the djinn living inside me? Those invisible beings know the hidden world better than us.' I, Kabuko the djinn, laughed at his notion but it made me feel important. Then for the very first time Ajee Shah asked me my name and his voice was so loud that even a passer-by could hear it.

After checking that the human spirit no longer objected to my conversing with Ajee, I answered in my natural language, the word stretched and distorted from almost forgetting my own name through the lack of use. 'Kabuko.' He could not understand it at first because of its abnormal pronunciation and he asked me to repeat it slowly. Then I pronounced my name in the human way, which sounded weird to me, and he understood and repeated it many times, like one remembering by heart a mantra. After a while, Ajee Shah spoke to me in the same manner as he usually conversed with his close friends and I liked the easy manner in which he spoke. 'Tell me honestly, what the hell is happening to me?' I told him that as far as the *pari* is concerned, I knew more than him but that I had no clear idea about the identity of Bao Lohar's *hamzad* or those two small balls or even what exactly Bao Lohar's powers were. 'In these matters,' I said, 'your guess is as good as mine.'

Ajee Shah became silent and I knew that he was hesitant to discuss the *pari* affair with me. He repeated a popular phrase in his head, 'A dog is the enemy of other dogs.' From that I guessed that he might know intuitively that I was not the correct person to consult as I belonged to the same species. Then I took the initiative and suggested he go ahead with the deal with Bao Lohar as it sounded very lucrative to me and he should not fear the unknown as I am always within him to help. He did not say anything but I could tell he agreed with me.

Ajee Shah met Bao Lohar that same evening but with more confidence in his heart and more clarity in his head. After giving verbal permission to Bao Lohar to keep those two balls, he asked, 'What are in those two mercury balls for you if you are not an alchemist?' Bao Lohar told him in plain words, 'Those are not only solid mercury balls. In the core of both balls, there is the fifth essence of this world or cosmos. Those balls are very much alive and are a very rare commodity on this earth. They have such wonderful, magical powers that even a person like me does not know ten percent of their miraculous abilities.' Ajee Shah argued, 'But my brother Karam Shah always maintained that he only solidified mercury, so how did this thing that you are calling the fifth essence come to be in the centre? And what is the fifth essence anyway?' Bao Lohar was comfortable and relaxed and settled into the conversation. He began his explanation as though he were telling Ajee Shah a story. 'I call it the fifth *sat*, or essence, but some people prefer to call it the fifth element. Their notion is that the fifth element is subtle and thus invisible, but essentially it is like the other four known elements of fire, earth, air, and water. As nobody I have ever met has full knowledge of that most mysterious thing in the world, so everyone has made up their own theories on the basis of what little is known to them. I, without any hesitation, admit that perhaps I know even less about it, but there is one thing that I am sure about and that is that it does not fall in any way into the category of elements. All the four known elements have their elemental spirits presiding over them. But no spirit, no matter how powerful it is, could preside over that purest essence. It is itself a spirit and at the same time it can express itself in different modes. Now that I have that essence in my hands, it will hopefully reveal something more about itself to me.'

Bao Lohar took a sip of his tea and continued; 'Now you will ask how your brother got that priceless thing. It was a gift from Babaji, an old python still living in the back room of your house in the village. Karam Shah had for years regularly put milk in a bowl for Babaji every Thursday. One day, when Karam Shah was going to work, he left these balls safely in the same room but they disappeared from there. Karam Shah lost his mind and quarrelled with everyone who had access to the room. Three months later, when Karam Shah was looking for something else in the room, he found these balls in exactly the same place where he had left them. But the colour and the texture of the balls had changed. They had become shinier and their surface was softer. Then Karam Shah weighed them and was surprised to discover that they had lost much of their weight. He thought that all this happened naturally with time.

I, Kabuko the djinn, for one could not swallow the idea that an old djinn had access to such a great essence that could make a man like Bao Lohar spellbound. I hurriedly told the story of the old python djinn and suggested to Ajee Shah that he reveal it to Bao Lohar. He did it with such confidence and craftiness as if he had firsthand knowledge of it, ensuring it did not sound like hearsay at all. I was very impressed. Bao Lohar listened to the whole story patiently, showing an interest as if he believed every word of Ajee Shah. Then he asked Ajee Shah something that unnerved me and pushed me into a dreadful state.

Bao Lohar asked him in a casual way, 'Is it not Kabuko the djinn, living within you, who has told you that bizarre but perhaps true story?' Bao Lohar was the first human being to, firstly, pronounce my name as if he were a djinn of my own clan. Secondly he called my name in the manner of our elders when calling someone much younger than them. There was no escape for me. I felt naked and exposed from inside and out. After that, Ajee Shah saw many dreams in which he was naked in one or another situation, and I was the only cause of those dreams. I did not know what to do so I did nothing and left everything in the hands of my destiny. Ajee Shah had no need to lie so he admitted that it was me, Kabuko the djinn, who had told him all that about Babaji, the python.

Then Bao Lohar explained to Ajee Shah that the old python was of course a djinn, but it was with the blessings of Ajee's ancestor, Pir Shah, that the python djinn had collected this essence from thin air and then delivered it to Karam Shah. At first, Karam Shah had had no idea of the essence lying within the mercury balls. But next Thursday, when he was putting the milk in the bowl that lay permanently in the back room, Babaji appeared in the shape of an old dervish. He told Karam Shah that he had put his gift in these mercury balls. And, as he now had such a possession, he no longer needed *Kimiya,* alchemy. With the blessing of that fifth essence he could go for the magical knowledge of *Simiya.*' Bao Lohar explained, 'The person who knows *Simiya* can change any matter into another matter along with its spirit and does not need any of the paraphernalia of alchemists. He could even change the souls of beings. As far as I know, it is the highest magic in the world, if one can even call it magic. For me it is a branch of spiritual knowledge, and many Sufis had it, though they hardly used it.'

A person came into the shop to buy two steel mugs from Bao Lohar and he sold them and put the coins, without counting them, in another steel mug. Bao Lohar never counted any of his sales but that day he made the sale so quickly that it clearly showed his eagerness to get back to the interrupted conversation. Then Bao Lohar told Ajee Shah, 'Your brother Karam Shah tried to have the knowledge of *Simiya* but then for some reason known only to him he lost his interest and went back to alchemy again.' Ajee Shah asked Bao Lohar, 'Have you seen with your own eyes somebody doing wonders by using *Simiya* ?' Bao replied, 'Do you remember Yousaf fakir who used to wander around the streets of our town?' Not only Ajee Shah but the whole town remembered him.

There had been a great to-do when Yousaf fakir arrived one night out of nowhere and stood in silent vigil on the main road of the town for five straight days. He hadn't spoken, eaten, or moved from that spot all that time, causing much speculation among the town's residents. Bao Lohar said, 'Yousaf fakir was the only one in our town who knew the great knowledge of *Simiya*.' He never asked anything from anyone. If somebody gave him something to eat, sometimes he used to accept it and at other times he flatly refused with a gesture of his hand. And the refusal gesture was not always polite. He usually spent his days wandering around the locality and his nights on the front platforms of closed shops. He had no fixed place to spend the night but the platform of a herbalist's shop seemed to be his favourite because he did not have to pack up his dirty sleeping quilts early in the morning. Most shopkeepers opened their shutters in the morning, but milk, yoghurt, and yoghurt drink shops, along with the traditional breakfast serving shops, opened very early, even before sunrise. The herbalist's shop always remained closed until late mornings or the afternoon. Sometimes the herbalist did not open it for days as he had no competitors in the whole area. Most of the time Yousaf fakir lived in a trance-like state but sometimes he chanted a slogan in his excitement. He had only one slogan and he never changed, amended, or inflated it. He used to shout *"Ik ho ja!"* (Become one!) It was not clear whether he was suggesting this to himself, the listeners, or both. For years people saw him and heard his only slogan, but then, a couple of years ago, he vanished from the town and nobody knew his forwarding address.

'When Yousaf fakir arrived in town I intuitively knew that he was not an ordinary dervish simply absorbed in ecstasy,' continued Bao Lohar. 'In those days I used to observe and follow him often in the hope that he would impart something to me in due course. But he never spoke to me even once. He was deeply involved in his own game, and I knew that I was not a part of it. One day I was following him and he was in a different mood, laughing at each thing and person he came across. Then he stood near the potter's dump, where the potters throw all the things, broken or burned in their ovens, which were not saleable. Yousaf fakir stood there for a while and then picked up a clay toy of a small bird, completely burned, and turned into a black colour. He was looking at the toy and knew that I was watching his every move as I was only a few feet away from him. Then he laughed and recited something in a very low voice that I could not make out. He blew on the toy three times and raised his slogan, *"Ja, Ik Ho Ja"*—go and become one— and the toy became a living black bird in his hand and he released it into the air. The bird circled over his head three times and then flew away. Yousaf Fakir was laughing like a crazy person, and I ran away as I knew it was not the act of a conjurer but of a powerful fakir, who must have a great knowledge of *Simiya*. I have never seen any such thing before or since. But from that day on I never followed him, and whenever I saw him, I became fearful. So I always avoided him.'

Ajee Shah asked Bao Lohar why he had become fearful of Yousaf fakir as he had only shown him his spiritual power for some strange reason. Bao Lohar laughed and replied, 'I know my worth. If a holy person in his jolly mood could put life into a clay toy, he could definitely, in his wrathful moments, take the life out of a clay puppet like me. I have never taken those kinds of risks in my life.' With that, Bao Lohar poured another cup of tea, leaving his audience—both human and djinn—bewildered and thrilled.

19

Renewed Faith

It was Thursday evening and the small shop that also doubled as Bao Lohar's residence was full of people. Many people were even standing outside in the street. The local barber Bashir had to perform many jobs apart from his main duties of cutting hair, doing shaves, and removing underarm hair. He was responsible for circumcisions, picking out the bad hair that were eating the roots of healthy ones and causing bald patches, and delivering marriage invitations with *gand*, a portion of dried fruits and local sweets. He had to deliver the news of deaths too, empty-handed and with a long face. Gladness and grief had extended his job further. He was responsible for cooking food at various occasions of pleasure and pain in his catchment area. On top of all that, people traditionally expected him to talk all the time while he was carrying out his various duties. If a barber was not well-informed about his surroundings and local scandals, he was worthless. Bashir was proficient in all of his jobs and people liked him.

Today, Bashir was busy but still chatting away, non-stop, outside Bao Lohar's shop. He was preparing two medium-sized cauldrons, one of sweet rice and the other of hot mutton curry. It was a strange combination but when the two dishes were mixed together on a plate, they somehow had a fairly enjoyable effect on the taste bud. The people who had gathered there were common folk with no choices. They would eat whatever was available to them, if not always with gratitude but at least never with any complaint. The taste of the food never stopped them belching their appreciation. Any food, good or bad, elicited a belch immediately after settling in their stomachs. Every year, Bao Lohar arranged that little ceremony on the death anniversary of his *murshid*, or guru, who had lived in the remotest corner of the country, in the middle of a jungle, and who had passed away before Ajee Shah's family moved into that neighbourhood. The term for such a ceremony is *Urs* and it is understood widely to mean the death of a "friend of God", which means ultimate union with the Divine. As such it was always considered a happy occasion and the best possible conclusion to a human life. Each year the day of the *Urs* would somehow always fall on a Thursday, refuting all calendars and all numerical calculations man had yet made. That was the only Thursday in the whole year when the otherwise lazy looking Bao Lohar never showed any sign of lethargy. He was always active and excited and running around without any justifiable reason.

When Bashir announced the food was ready, Bao Lohar took charge of both cauldrons and started distributing the food with both hands. Distribution of the food was a very tricky job that only a professional like Bashir could handle, but Bao Lohar refused to take any help from anyone, professional or otherwise. That was his day and he did not want to share the labour of his spiritual love with anyone. The uncouth invitees ate too much and by the time Ajee Shah approached Bao Lohar, who was standing in the centre with the two cauldrons, Bao could only offer him the dregs of the two pots. Ajee Shah was never interested in food or eating, anyway, but I, Kabuko the djinn, was very hungry as I had not taken my share of food after the day Bao Lohar had exposed me. I ate almost all that Ajee Shah ate in that meal. There was no belching at the end as the humiliation of being exposed was still acute. A male animal spirit in Ajee Shah's being came out to sympathise with me and showed me his erect genitals. I could not understand the masculine spirit's gesture of sympathising in that peculiar way but could only guess that the gesture was telling me to "screw it all" and not give a damn.

People had eaten, belched, and left. Only a few were left in Bao Lohar's shop and all but one were regular visitors. Then Bao Lohar made tea and announced that it was a very special tea. Ajee Shah asked what was special about it and Bao Lohar laughingly answered that he had put some intoxicating stuff in it. Ajee Shah noticed that the taste of the tea was certainly different but could not discern any intoxication from imbibing it; perhaps some harmless herbs had been included just to make the tea special for the occasion.

Then Bao Lohar started praising the spirituality of his late guru. He said, 'It was the day of Sweet Eid, I was sitting outside in the wilderness along with many other disciples of my *murshid* and a thought came to my mind. I said to myself, 'O Bao, if you had a family and your mother were still alive, then, today, on this happy annual occasion, you would be eating *sivaiyan*, the delicious sweet vermicelli pudding.' Just after few minutes later a disciple came out of my *murshid's* hut and handed over a big dish of *sivaiyan* to me and said, 'Sain ji has sent this dish for you.' I could not hold my emotions and started crying. Then I ate a little bit and distributed the dish among the others sitting outside my *murshid's* hut.'

Bao Lohar was not usually prone to weeping but, after telling that tale, he started crying copiously, and that changed the whole jolly atmosphere in the shop. After a while Ajee Shah made a clever move and asked Bao Lohar to tell them something about Yousaf fakir. Bao Lohar took a big mug of water from the pitcher and went outside. He washed his face and came back with a wet face. When he had settled down, he drank the last couple of sips of water left in the same mug and without any reminder or cue started talking about Yousaf fakir.

'I don't give a damn if any of you believe a word of mine about Yousaf fakir, because, to me, he was one of the most wondrous and magical beings I have ever come across. I am a worthless blacksmith but I have been lucky enough to have the company of some very worthy beings. I have no doubt in my mind that Yousaf fakir belonged to the hidden hierarchy, of spiritual beings who are running this world. In that invisible parallel government, there are promotions and demotions, there are upper ranks and there are lower ranks, there are new appointments and there are transfers. That happens all the time. I am not sure of Yousaf fakir's rank in that mysterious hierarchy but before he was transferred to our town, he was already at an advanced stage in his service. After doing his duty for many years in our town he was transferred again to some other place. He must have been promoted.'

Ajee Shah asked Bao Lohar a very intelligent question, 'If Yousaf Fakir belonged to those "hidden men of God" then why did he make his entry in the town so dramatic and pull such a crowd around him, like a film star?' Bao Lohar answered in serious tone, 'Sometimes, for reasons unknown to us, these people have to announce their arrival in a particular place. During his silent vigil, Yousaf fakir was not wasting a moment, he was taking charge of everything and every being in his new domain. We cannot know the rhyme and reason of these spiritual officials.'

As soon as the conversation was finished, Ajee Shah stood up to go home as he realised that it was already quite dark outside. He went straightaway to his bed on the rooftop and was soon asleep, still wondering about Yousaf fakir. But I, Kabuko the djinn, was very much awake. I tried my best to settle myself but my thoughts were playing havoc with me. Deep in me I felt stupid at undertaking this adventure in an alien human domain. I became fed up with myself. I rebuked myself, 'Kabuko, now you have lived in this human body for sixteen years. Though this is not a long time in a djinn's life but to waste any time is never admirable. What have you learned in these years? Basically nothing. Only a few stories, most of them unsubstantiated, much experience of pain, and a few moments of real pleasure. And there is no guarantee that even if you waste another fifty or sixty years of your life, you will get anything worthwhile. If you leave your so-called mission unfinished and go back to your own cosy world, the sky will not fall on you. You will be depressed only for a few more days and then everyone in your clan and the girls outside of the clan will accept you back and you can easily entertain them with the human stories that you have already remembered by heart.'

The thought created a nostalgia that, mixed with frustrations, made me very uncomfortable. I lost all my confidence but, at the verge of my breaking point, suddenly a strange part of myself asked for my attention. That part wanted to say something to me. The vibrations of the new thought were more commanding than my previous one. 'Kabuko, I am your non-interfering self. That is why I sound so strange to you. But I have to say something very important to you. Kabuko, you are a djinn. You are the son of fire. Whatever the circumstances, you should always remember your origin, your mother fire. You are frustrated that you could not escape the penetrating vision of a blacksmith and he told you your worth by exposing your presence in a human body. That is not a matter of shame or guilt. You think that humans, in many respects, are more powerful than you. But that does not matter at all. Reality does not count in this changing universe at all. What counts at a particular moment is just how one sees the reality. Humans may be more powerful than you are but that does not give them the slightest edge on you. The notion of the djinn's great powers is so entrenched in human beings that they fear your strength, your invisibility, your speed, even the perception of your time. Be brave and follow in the footsteps of your martyred grandfather who gave his life but left you the legacy of never submitting without a fight.' The message was so encouraging for me that I felt a strange new energy in me but it did not boost my ego at all. It only showed me the reality of the situation and gave me the perspective that I had lost in my frustration. That was the first time in my long life that I thanked my wise hidden part with real gratitude.

The next day there was the same old rusty padlock on Bao Lohar's shop and Ajee Shah was sure that Bao would be gone for many days. He was not disturbed by the unannounced departure. In fact, Ajee Shah was much relieved as his matriculation exams were near and he had to revise his coursework in order to pass them. None of his siblings had ever failed in any exam and he did not want to be the one to hurt the family's pride in that matter. Now Ajee Shah would read his books till late in the night and again his mother started giving him a glass of hot milk during the night so that his brain did not "dry up". I never disturbed him during his studies but his mind was often busy thinking about other things.

One late night when Ajee Shah was reading a book of History, and I was searching for some beautiful moments from my past life, it occurred to me that human beings are unable to travel backwards in time. They can only remember, imagine, or visualise their past but we can at will retrograde in actual time and do things as in the present. It was a discovery for me as it had never occurred to me before. I congratulated myself and my species, and thought that my discovery was more breathtaking than that of Sir Isaac Newton's discovery of gravity, on which there was a chapter in Ajee Shah's science book. Both mine and Newton's discoveries were by chance and both were made by fruit. An apple had fallen on Sir Isaac's head but I was saved from that sort of a rude shock. I had only thought of the fresh grapes that once me and my djinn girlfriend had enjoyed while having sex. I will give you a proof of our natural power that is very much "supernatural" for you. When we male or female djinn fall in love with humans and possess them, we often produce unseasonal fruits to make our human beloveds happy. And we have been doing this for centuries before cold storage was invented in your world. How did we do it? We always travelled backwards in time and checked in which past season there was a good harvest for the fruit that we were looking for and then we picked the best fruits directly from trees, plants, or vines.

I must be honest with you. There are limitations to this kind of travel. No ordinary djinn can travel back beyond the time of his first breath in the present life. I mean the date of his birth. If you travel any further back, a black tunnel starts that we call "the black womb" which is closed from the other side. The other limitation is not exactly that of the time but of direction. There are eight directions and one dimension. The eight directions are North, South, three of East-East, North-East, and South-East, and three of West-West, North-West, and South-West. The one dimension is not penetrable for ordinary folks, be they djinn, humans, or other spirits. Out of the eight open directions, on a particular day one of them is always occupied by the highly evolved spiritual beings called *Rajal-ul-Ghaib*. They are travelling in that direction and if one attempts travel in that occupied direction, the chances of a successful journey are nil. And, besides, it is dangerous, too. One must wait to travel in that direction as the highly evolved beings change their direction every day. Even some humans know this and have calculated the chart of their directions by the Moon calendar.

The third and the most unpredictable limitation of backward travel is that sometimes you reach a particular time in the past and see nothing there. The chunk of that time was eaten by those most mysterious entities that our wise called "the time eaters". In fact, they do not eat the time but whatever happened during that time. But now I, Kabuko the djinn, am only concerned with the last limitation. Travelling in the past is not ordinary travel. You have to travel with your full being intact. You cannot leave any of your parts, even the tiniest ones, behind.

When I thought about those tasty grapes during another tasty act of sex, for a moment I wished to go back to that particular time and situation. I was sure that the time would be very much there as those most mysterious entities never eat those kinds of everyday happenings. They are always after some special incidents, some special and rare experiences. Though one can make the sexual act a very special happening but mine was not. My problem was that I could not afford to leave Ajee Shah's body completely as I had no guarantee that, upon my return, I wouldn't find some other spirit occupying my place. But still I was happy and very content that we the djinn can travel back in time and humans cannot do so.

20

Birds of Prey Do Sing

The night before his matriculation exams, Ajee Shah went to bed early with the intention of waking up fresh in the morning. I, Kabuko the djinn, was also relaxed and drew back as there was nothing interesting happening in those boring times. Ajee Shah was passing through the monotonous revisions of his course books, most of which were in a fine condition, as they had not been used too extravagantly during the whole academic year. He was fearful, like other students in his class, of the exam not corresponding exactly with what they had revised. The most dreadful thing for them was what they called "out-of-course" questions. Those hated questions were still very much in the course but, sometimes, the examiners would not include the popular questions that most of the students knew and had prepared for. Ajee Shah was so occupied with those unpredictable questions that they even penetrated into his dreams, which were otherwise filled with exuberant stuff. So, for me to be dreamless was a better idea than to watch and then suffer the aftermath of those dull dreams.

In the middle of night, my boredom was at its peak and I decided to have some fresh air and go for a fly. I left myself half inside Ajee Shah and, with my other half, I projected myself out, taking the shape of a fairly big bird. Outside Ajee Shah, my strength was obviously halved, so the bulk of my body, in whatever shape I appeared, counted very much, as a predator rarely attacks any creature bigger than its size. I flew slowly but without the natural rhythm of a huge bird and went to a tower in the town.

It was a municipal building made with red bricks during the British Raj. I stuck my tongue out of my mouth and felt the breeze, which was very pleasant, and felt rejuvenated after some time. Then, I stretched my neck upwards and saw two white spots moving quite high in the sky. 'They must be crows,' I thought. The second time I stretched, I noticed the spots had gone even further up and had became even smaller. Crows can't fly so high, they must be kites but I wondered why they were flying at this odd hour of the night. Perhaps they are lovers or a newly engaged couple, I joyfully guessed. Suddenly my half-self became very uncomfortable and demanded to return. I did not resist and flew back towards my legitimate dwelling; the body of Ajee Shah. But it was so dark that I could not find my way and soon became panicked. Then, I heard somebody calling me. I opened my eyes and realised that I was dreaming. I had never gone out and was very much in my usual place.

I guessed the time was about three o clock, early in the morning. I was still drowsy when I heard someone call me again. I could have easily ignored it but the voice sounded as if it belonged to a young female and I never ignored females, even if they had reached the age of menopause. That was my principle shared with all the fornicating beings on this earth, whether they be djinn, human, spirit, or animal. An egoist can never become a real sexual being. And my own experience was that some older females performed much better in bed than their younger counterparts. In any case, age has nothing to do with sexual desire and diversity.

When she called again I realised the female voice was not only young but also very pleasing. I allowed my half-self to go out and see who was there. To my surprise a *pari* was standing at the left side of Ajee Shah's bed. I recognised her immediately. She was the same one with whom Ajee Shah had fallen in love at first sight, the one who had created that glamour at the well early one morning, to trap him in her game. Though I was not certain what her game was but, since her older sister had killed Ajee Shah in his previous life, I was not easy about seeing her again. Her presence beside Ajee Shah's bed sent shockwaves to my mind and though I still held at least half of the powers I was born with as a djinn, I was somehow still scared. Did she want to take my place? I did not want to share Ajee Shah with anyone, apart from the natural inhabitant spirits that were born within him. Now both my parts were fully awake and alert but I kept silent. She asked me my name in a voice that was even more melodious than before. I had already revealed my name when she was hovering over the old twisted tree with her parents. Perhaps she was not interested in Ajee Shah or me at that time. I didn't reply and stared at her to make her nervous. She, perhaps, judged my intention and produced a whistle-like sound, just to tell me that she even knew that my clan spoke like birds.

For me she was a bird of prey, and as the saying goes "prey birds never sing". But she was singing in her whistle. In normal circumstances, I would be the first to appreciate her charming tactics but I knew that she was not after me. Her charming gestures were only for Ajee Shah, and I happened to be between her and him. Then a thought came to my mind. Perhaps her old father had died and the clan had made her the chief and she was attempting to erase the bad karma on her ruling family. If that was so, then I was in real trouble. In the djinn world, there is no gender discrimination as many of our clans have female chiefs. And a chief of either gender is always much more powerful than an ordinary individual. The reason being that every member of the clan, including children, give a part of their pure life force energy and any sort of special knowledge or information to the chief and make him or her very powerful. That was imperative for survival as only the chief was responsible for appearing and negotiating on behalf of the whole clan in the djinn and alien realms. So an individual's protection and growth depended on the strength of the chief. Our chiefs never interfere in our individual matters unless they could possibly ruin our collective interests.

She was constantly whistling. After a while she stopped and became silent. Then her tone changed and, in a stern voice, she warned me, 'Look, tell me your name and talk to me. I am no threat to you, and I only come with an offer that you possibly cannot refuse. If you will not speak to me, I will use my index finger and wrap you around it. Then you should not blame me.'

I became frightened as I knew that nobody other than someone very powerful could speak to me in such a way. She must be a chief. Instead of giving her my name, I asked her for hers first. She said with a smile, 'Tarru.' I was impressed with her beauty and the colourful outfit she was wearing. Our girls only wear those kinds of outfits when they want to impress somebody. I told her my name and asked what she wanted from me. She said in a low voice, 'Listen, Kabuko, you know what I want. I want this handsome boy whom you are possessing. If you leave him for me, I will arrange your marriage with the most beautiful girl of my clan. She is much younger than you but she is my best friend and has agreed to do whatever I instruct her to do.' Instead of answering her question, I asked her, 'Are you the new chief of your clan? Has your father passed away or has he given you that distinguished seat because of his old age?'

She replied, without showing any emotion, 'Yes, I am the new chief of my clan after my father died, but that has nothing to do with you. You should only answer my question and not try to tarry me.' I gathered all my courage and boosted my ego to its extreme and laughed. I wanted to give her the impression that her powers as a chief of a particular clan did not have any effect on me as I had enough power to deal with her. But she was not impressed at all and showed me her index finger, which meant, in human terms, "fuck you". Then I apologetically said, 'I do not possess this boy. I am just living with him. And even if you offer me all the beautiful girls of your clan, I will still not leave him.' She became confused at my statement and said, 'I wasn't aware that any djinn could live within a human body without possessing the human. You should not lie to me as I belong to your own realm.' I tried to explain it to her but she was not convinced that I was telling the truth. She said, 'Kabuko, though I cannot fully understand what you are doing here but I can see that you are wasting your life. It is high time that you got married and settle down.'

I laughed, again, and told her that she should leave the boy alone as he had already suffered much in his previous incarnation. She said, 'But I am in love with him. I do not want to hurt him. I want to give him so much love that it will heal all the scars of his past lives.' I was irritated and said, 'Then what is your problem? Go and love him.' She, again smilingly said, 'My dear Kabuko, you are the problem. You are the only problem. How can I love him while you are always there within him?' With no answer to that, I just told her that this was not a good time as Ajee Shah had his exams tomorrow. 'You should come some other time and we will discuss this matter in detail,' I added. I wanted to get rid of her to gain some time to think about all this. She said, 'I am going now, not for you but for the sake of my beloved. I will come back after the exams.' Before leaving, she said, 'Kabuko, the waiting is the most painful thing about love.'

I pitied her and myself. She was in love, and I had never really loved anyone, not even myself. An animal spirit, that had watched and listened to our conversation, also read my thoughts. It patted me on the back and said, 'These are only words. Don't you heed them. You are all right, nothing is wrong with you. You are a sensual being and sensuality is what matters in the end. Think, if creatures of any kind had no sexual organs, no sexual desire, then what they feel for each other would not be love as we all know it. So don't worry, if you cannot love in the lover's way, you are still not missing anything as you are dealing with the articulation of love; sex.' Living with humans makes even animals philosophical. See how cleverly the animal spirit was defending its own nature.

The first paper of the exams went fine, though afterwards, when Ajee Shah compared his answers with his mates, he realised that he had gotten one out of the seven questions wrong. But that was not a matter of any consequence.

During the whole exam period, Ajee Shah worked very hard. He worked relentlessly, and so did I. I was busy thinking up a strategy to deal with Tarru, the *pari*. I decided that, whatever happened to me, I would not leave Ajee Shah. The exams finished and though Ajee was not completely satisfied with his performance, he was confident that he would pass the exams with reasonably good marks. He was excited as now he had three months of holidays without any homework and nobody on earth would ask him to study anything.

He wanted to enjoy himself as much as he possibly could. But Tarru, Ajee Shah's self-professed lover, was so desperate that she did not waste even a day and came back the very next day after the exams ended. Again, it was early morning and she called my name in a whistle, 'Kaabbbookooo' and I projected myself in my real shape. This time she was not alone. A beautiful young girl was with her. With a lovely and somewhat naughty gesture, she told the young girl, 'Go and kiss your groom.' The girl blushed and I leaned a little bit backwards. Tarru explained, 'Our beauty is too young to take such initiative. She is shy but you can come forward and kiss her. You know how to kiss, don't you?' I was confused as to how to deal with the situation but, before I could say anything, the young girl suddenly hugged me and kissed me on my lips. I felt two rose petals touch my lips and leave all their softness and indulgent fragrance with me to enjoy ever after. I was thrown off balance. Tarru, the clever lover, could see the lustful delight her little friend had thrown me into. She said proudly, 'Didn't I tell you that she is the loveliest *pari* of our clan? No djinn can resist her. Kabuko, you are lucky. Say yes, here and now, and she is all yours. My clan will look after both of you very well. That is my promise.' I was silent and she had the wrong impression that I was thinking carefully about her offer. I was utterly lost and had no idea what to say or how to deal with her.

As we were standing there, something happened in the clear skies above our heads. The whole atmosphere suddenly became very heavy. Then something sparkled, and I realised that were many small round-shaped flashes happening in the sky. It looked purely magical. Whatever we were arguing about, the fact remained that all three of us were not human beings but djinn.

We knew that it was not a good sign. Something much more powerful had entered into the sphere where we were playing our little games. Then the aura around us turned so dense that we became very uncomfortable. All three of us were frightened, but Tarru and I were trying to save face. However, the girl who had kissed me was utterly disorientated and showed her terror. She started crying and screaming as her present blurred and she started seeing images from the near future.

Then there appeared a flock of male and female djinn of many different clans. Most of them I, Kabuko the djinn, had never heard of nor come across before. Some of them were so ugly looking that I was ashamed of my species. They did not come down to our level but stayed a little above our heads. Why they stayed to the left of us, we had no idea. Then their flock-master appeared from the midst of the crowd and distinguished herself, so that we could recognise her. I recognised her instantly. She was my old benefactress, though she looked much younger than her age. I was overwhelmed with joy but didn't know how to respond. Tarru saw her, too, and waved her upper body to say hello to her. It seemed she also knew her well.

The young girl with Tarru was now even more fearful, and, holding the long colourful dress of her friend, she tried to hide behind her to escape the vision of the old lady. My old teacher soon addressed the whole flock and told them to withdraw, as they were not needed any more and she could alone handle the situation easily. All flew back but made no sound or flash. I was now fully confident as my saviour was there and I started preening. I showed my index finger to Tarru and challenged her to come forward and face the music. But she stayed calm and didn't react to my childish gesture.

Just as I was going to say something very nasty to Tarru, my old teacher stopped me, and said, 'Let me deal with her.'

Addressing Tarru, her eyes never leaving hers for even a second, she said, 'O stupid child, come and hug me. I want to kiss your beautiful belly button.' The *pari* didn't move an inch. My master lady recited in her own old voice something resembling a lineage song with different sounding names, cleverly maintaining the rhythm with the natural exaggerated sound of her deep breaths at all times.

The song was filled with the events when my old teacher had helped the ancestors of Tarru. Tarru listened to her carefully and with the grace of the chief of a clan, no matter how small that clan was. Then she confidently approached my master lady as she had been convinced that she would not harm her. When she was near enough, my master lady took Tarru into her arms and lifted her up as if she were a little girl. She kissed her belly button and then hugged her. When she freed her from her embrace, Tarru kissed the feet of my master lady, and stood up and moved to the right side of her. 'What do you want from my boy Kabuko?' the old woman asked. 'Nothing, really nothing. I did not know that Kabuko belonged to you. I was just suggesting to him that he marry my friend. She likes him very much.' The old lady smiled and said, 'Why are you youngsters always looking for trouble? And you, Tarru, you are the head of your clan now. These adventures do not suit you any longer. Now you should be more responsible.'

I felt relieved. Suddenly Tarru started crying and tears were falling on her cheeks. It was out of character, but then I didn't know her that well. She said, sobbingly, 'O my great, great ma, you helped our clan many times. I acknowledge that but we have nothing in this world that could return your favours to us. Do our clan another great favour, I beg you. You know that I am in love with this boy. I have nothing to do with your Kabuko but I will die without Ajee Shah.' The old woman was not impressed by her crying or begging, and asked in her usual stern way, 'You want to seize this human boy. I will break your skull in which these sorts of intentions grow.' Tarru immediately explained, 'No ma, I never thought of this evil act. I just want to love him without any possession, without any intrusion, or any compulsion on his part. I promise you that I will never do anything that will even slightly hurt the boy. If I do, then you are free to punish me as you would like.' To my surprise, my master lady seemed to melt as her tone again became mild and sympathetic. She said, 'Okay, if your intention is just to love, I will not stop you. But there are two conditions. First, you will never interfere with Kabuko. He will remain as he is and accompany the boy wherever he goes. The second condition is that if you do eventually indulge yourself physically with the boy, Kabuko will also participate in the activity.'

Tarru was ready to accept the first condition, but she was reluctant to make love with a djinn and a man at the same time. She said, 'Ma, you know I am now head of the clan that is burdened with your past kindnesses. How can I sleep with Kabuko, a djinn from another clan, without a public announcement and without a proper ceremony of "locking together"? You know much better than I do that if any illicit relationship with a djinn from a different clan results in me having a baby, then I will be stripped of my status without any delay, and, if the elders aren't lenient, they will send me into exile. On other hand, if I became pregnant by Ajee Shah, I am permitted to have a child of mixed human and *pari* blood. You know that is allowed to the ordinary folk and to royalty as the mixed ones always enhance the survival of our seed. Now dear old mother, what do you say?'

The old woman was lost in her thoughts. After a while she said, 'Tarru, I see you have a valid point. In that case, when you come for the love making, always bring some girl of your own clan with you for Kabuko. She should be of pure djinn blood and not of any mixed race. He is in the middle of his mission and has done so much hard work to achieve his goal that I do not want any sexual trouble for him.' Tarru instantly agreed and kissed the feet of my old lady. The old woman did not kiss her in return, but she kissed me on my forehead and departed. We three remained silent for a while. Then Tarru asked me when she could return. 'Any time,' I replied and withdrew into Ajee Shah's body. The remaining part of that night I had a deep sleep and saw many sweet dreams after many days of suffering terrible anxiety. In one of the dreams I slept with the young friend of Tarru. Believe me, she was quite wonderful!

21

At The Dervish's Fireplace

Ajee Shah had three months of holiday, and I, Kabuko the djinn, hadn't even had a short break for the last sixteen years. Now I was looking forward to spending some time with the beautiful friend of Tarru to unwind myself. Last night's dreams had awakened my sexual desires, and now they were playing havoc with my thoughts. In just one night I had changed a lot. Before I was escaping from Tarru, the *pari*, but now I eagerly awaited those daughters of fire. Two whole days passed, a long time for me, but there was no sign of Tarru along with her sweet friend. What happened to the impatient lover of Ajee Shah who was more involved in her love affair than her new exalted status as head of a djinn clan? I was asking myself questions and making myself more anxious. Tarru didn't turn up even on the third day but Bao Lohar came back with "good news" for Ajee Shah, news that made me even more nervous than the thought of confronting Tarru had made me a few days back.

Ajee Shah had not been expecting Bao Lohar to return so soon. He knew, through his intuition, that this time Bao had left with the two magical mercury balls to explore their powers, and that these things take time, in some cases, a whole lifetime. However, just as Bao Lohar was trying to pull the big key out of the rusty padlock on his shop door, Ajee Shah happened to walk by that street and sighted him. Bao was such an unpredictable person that no one, no matter how close one was to him, could figure out his schedule, perhaps not even himself. The men around him were convinced that he was a *sailani*, a wanderer, by nature, and wondered why he still had a base camp in a rented shop, with the free distribution of strong but tasty tea. Only his old astrologer friend had an explanation. If his initial premise that Bao Lohar was an Aries was correct then his explanation made some sense. 'A person born under the influence of Aries wanders around and can even go to the other side of the world, but, at the end of the day, he always returns to his base, to the place where he really belongs.' The astrologer always said this in such an authoritative way that he left no room for further argument. But even he could not figure out exactly which planetary position made Bao Lohar so unpredictable. As no one knew Bao Lohar's date of birth, the astrologer's best guess was to suspect the planet Mercury as the real culprit.

Ajee Shah excitedly greeted Bao Lohar, and said, 'What a pleasant coincidence.' Bao Lohar didn't return Ajee Shah's greeting and looked at him as if he were a complete stranger and they were meeting for the first time. Then, Bao, with a fixed stare upon Ajee, declared in a commanding voice, 'It is not a coincidence. Not at all. It is an omen, a very good omen, clearly indicating that your path is clear now.' Ajee Shah did not understand what he meant by that. Seeing surprise on his face, Bao Lohar explained, 'This time my journey was just for your sake, and you are the first to meet me on my return. As soon as the lock opened, you greeted me. I am very happy at this synchronisation. It speaks for itself.'

Bao Lohar's eyes were now glowing as usual, a trademark of his residual excitement at being away from the mundane business of melting, twisting, and turning iron into useful commodities. But, he still did not return Ajee Shah's greetings. If that had happened with anybody else, Ajee Shah would have never greeted that person again in his life, and justifiably so. The act of not returning greetings was considered so humiliating that hardly anyone could tolerate it. But here things were different. There was no reaction but a pleasant ignoring of that gross misconduct of Bao Lohar.

Ajee Shah noticed that Bao Lohar was frenetically excited and his tongue was trying in vain to catch up with his thoughts. There were some emotions creating an overwhelming commotion in his being. It took Bao Lohar and Ajee Shah almost half an hour to settle down in the shop. The strong tea was ready with the little milk that Ajee Shah had brought from the corner shop with his own money. During the whole time Bao Lohar was talking to himself, sometimes in a low voice, as if conspiring with someone, and sometimes loudly, as if arguing with someone. After having half his tea, he became a little bit calmer and it seemed to Ajee Shah that Bao was trying to return to normality. Ajee Shah had either learned the art of being silent or he had no urge to speak at that time. Then Bao Lohar took out a foul-smelling herbal paste out of a battered small tin can that had clearly not been made by him. With his index finger, he ate all the paste and threw the tin can into a messy corner in the shop. That must have been some intoxicating stuff as, after some time, Bao Lohar's voice seemed to be coming from far away. He had stepped out of normal time and space. 'Listen to me carefully, you, a son of Mola Ali. Mola Ali, from whom stems the whole spirituality of Sufism. This is something serious, very serious. From now on you have to keep everything secret. Make your heart as deep as the ocean. Secrecy will protect you, revealing will destroy you. That is the law and you and I are not above the law.'

Bao Lohar stopped and it seemed as if he were trying to articulate his revelation. Then he said, 'You remember we often talked about Yousaf fakir, the former spiritual guardian of our area. When he disappeared, I knew someone else had taken charge of our area. But I did not know who. I suspected every new dervish that appeared around here but was always disappointed in the end. A couple of months ago, a friend of mine told me that a dervish had come and sat in the middle of dense woods on the bank of the Chenab. The timing of his arrival more or less tied in with the disappearance of Yousaf fakir. This time I went to visit him and found that he was indeed the one who is the new spiritual guardian of our area. People call him Sidho Sain. He will not come into our town but will guard us from the banks of the River Chenab. He is a residing dervish, not a wanderer like his predecessor Yousaf fakir.'

Bao Lohar took another mug of tea from the kettle and started speaking again, 'I went to Sidho Sain and stayed with him all the time. As I promised you that I would give you gift of a lifetime in return for those mercury balls of your brother Karam Shah, God bless his soul. That gift is your own *hamzad*, that, with my help and guidance, will become your faithful ally and serve you at your will. But for that we need the protection of the spiritual guardian of the area belonging to the hidden hierarchy. That protection is imperative for two reasons; the first is that I am an extra careful person in these matters, and the other is that you are still young and inexperienced. Sidho

Sain, though he did not admit that he belonged to the "official spiritual hierarchy" —which is very much understandable— allowed me to go ahead. He was happy that I am helping a Syed. At my repeated requests, Sidho Sain penetrated into the parallel world and saw that your *hamzad* is ready to come and serve you. So half of the job is done and for the other half, Sidho Sain and this humble blacksmith have to take care of you.'

Although Ajee Shah didn't understand Bao Lohar's excitedly narrated "good news" fully, he knew in his heart that something very important was going to happen to him very soon. That made him excited, too. Ajee Shah told Bao Lohar that he was free of any real engagement for almost three months. After that he had to join the college and if everything could happen in this free time, he would be very happy. Bao Lohar smiled and said, 'You are too inexperienced. These things set their own schedule, not a moment earlier and not a moment later. We all have to follow their speed and one can only succeed in these matters by exercising great patience and courage. But before we go any further, you must visit Sidho Sain so that we can proceed under his protection.' Ajee Shah said, 'That is no problem for me. Whenever you are ready we can go to Sidho Sain.'

'Next Thursday,' replied Bao Lohar.

Ajee Shah's parents had no objection to him visiting a dervish. His mother was so happy that she gave him two rupees, one for him and one for Sidho Sain as supplication before asking for his blessings. His mother even ordered Ajee Shah's older brother to lend him his bicycle for the journey. His brother initially protested but then agreed with the condition that if anything happened to his bicycle, their mother would pay all the costs for its repair.

The river was about nine miles from their neighbourhood

and according to Bao Lohar they would have to go more than three miles on the other side of the bank to reach Sidho Sain's dwelling. That much distance posed no challenge to the young and energetic Ajee Shah. He pedalled the cycle, and Bao Lohar, despite his not inconsiderable bulk, rode on the rod. They soon reached the Grand Track Road, where they shared the road with buses, trucks, cars, horses, oxen carts, and other traffic. They stopped three times at roadside shops and drank tea. On their last stop, they bought sweets to present to the dervish. After crossing the bridge they left the GT Road and went down to the path leading towards the woods. It was lush green everywhere and Ajee Shah suddenly felt that they had entered wilderness. The trails were so uneven that at times it was better to walk than cycle.

At last they reached the dwelling of the dervish. This consisted of three small straw and mud huts and a round platform under an old tree. Flags of different colours were tied to the tree and one could see them from far away. There were three mats under another tree where the dervish and other people were sitting. Bao Lohar and Ajee Shah greeted the dervish and shook his right hand with both hands, a gesture of respect. The dervish indicated with his hand and the people already sitting with him made space for Bao and Ajee. Bao sat on the right side and Ajee Shah on the left of the dervish. It was evening and a couple of long-haired *malangs* were preparing *bhang*, the Indian hemp drink. There was silence as if everyone were waiting for something.

A small fire burned in front of the dervish and a few damp pieces of wood produced a lot of bitter smoke. The tears in Ajee Shah's eyes blurred his whole view. The dervish was fully absorbed and didn't seem concerned by his surroundings. It seemed as if he were taking some sort of pride in that bitingly smoky atmosphere. Every few moments he stoked the fire with his bare hands. His hands were dirty but much less than his mat. The aura of his presence was neither light nor heavy. Then the *malangs* brought that hemp drink in bowls and served everyone with one. Ajee Shah took the bowl and looked towards Bao Lohar. The dervish opened his mouth for the first time and said to Ajee Shah, 'Drink it. This hemp is so weak, it is just like *sardai*.' *Sardai* is a light drink made from almonds and other nuts and seeds.

Ajee Shah was still a little bit hesitant as he had never drunk any hemp before, whether weak or strong, but he started taking it slowly. By the time Ajee Shah had finished his bowl, the others had already had three or four bowls of the hemp. Soon, Ajee felt a strange change in him and he entered into another realm, a realm that bore a faithful resemblance to his present reality but which was completely different in its texture and feel.

He saw the dervish and felt the shocking redness of his eyes. Those red eyes were unsettled, moving in various directions all the time. The movement of his eyes and the angular shifting of his pupils were too swift to follow. Apparently his eyes were directionless. But there was an ogling quality in his looks. Then suddenly a picture emerged in Ajee Shah's mind. He saw him as a conductor of an orchestra whose eyes were not eyes but hands, holding beams of light as two sticks. And with the sticks he was directing all the players in the surrounding universe to follow his composition. The composition was one that he had created long ago, putting in much effort of his body and soul. Ajee Shah felt as if he was trying to play all the complex notes of his archaic music and was anxious not to miss even a single note.

Ajee Shah could only see his gestures but was unable to hear his music. In spite of that, he was so sure in the depth of his heart that the whole piece of his music had entered into his memory forever. He could replay it with ease at any time. But instead of hearing it, he was still only seeing his music. It was in layers. It was triangular. It was moving in circles. It took all the possible shapes and all the geometrical angles he had ever perceived. The dervish's music had a vertigo effect on me, Kabuko the djinn. The dervish's strategy to avoid direct eye contact with Ajee Shah was superb. But after some time that had produced an uncomfortable arrhythmia in me.

The dervish had a strong but strange smell. It had an intriguing freshness in it. Perhaps that was the only quality of the smell that differentiated itself from the body smell of other dervishes. Ajee Shah had never smelled that kind of mysterious smell before. In one moment he could feel it in his nostrils, in his whole body, and in the very next moment it roamed away, centuries away, galaxies away. Ajee Shah had no power in him to hold it constantly. Whenever it went away, it went out of the reach of all of his senses, leaving no residues at all. He felt estranged. He felt worthless. He felt helpless. He thought, 'I have spent all my life on residues that my past had left on me. I played with them. I rubbed them to get rid of pain. I scratched them to escape irritation. But these present remedies never deprived me of the original taste of a residual memory.'

A feeling of deprivation was encompassing Ajee Shah totally. But it never completely happened. Moments before he sunk into depression, the smell would always come back. It was playing a game or a joke with him. Not a joyful play at all. He became confused, not at the mercurial play of the smell but for another reason; a reason that lay in the depths of his own being. Something or somebody in Ajee Shah was insisting that he must have smelt it before and he must have forgotten it. If he tried hard, he might be capable of remembering it once again. To that part of him, the smell was very familiar. But the nostalgia of the smell was as real as the conscious awareness of its novelty. He was caught between the two. Who to listen to and who to ally oneself with? Maybe both were true, maybe both were false. Maybe both were not his selves but belonged to someone else. And that someone was playing this mysterious game with him.

The dervish was now talking but not to anyone in particular. He was either unaware of Ajee Shah's inner conflict or was so absorbed in his own flow of deliverance that he ignored it completely. He was still talking; talking through his tongue, through his evasive eyes, through his nostrils, through his hands, and sometimes through the spontaneous shivers in his body. His vocabulary was exuberant but not easily understandable. He was in the habit of repeating himself. But then Ajee Shah realised that he was using his pet words and his favourite Sufi terminology in such a way that almost every time those implied different, and sometimes even contradictory, meanings. It was hard to concentrate on his conversation and at the same time grasp what exactly he meant of a particular word or a term. The word yaar, meaning "friend", was one of his pet words which he used for himself, for the carnal self, for spiritual masters, for the beloved, for lovers, for the Divine, and, of course, for a friend. He used it so many times that Ajee Shah was sure he missed many of its other more arcane meanings. He had coined his own vocabulary, perhaps only to converse with his friends—yaar—and not a stranger like Ajee Shah and Kabuko, a djinn, who both were habitual of understanding only the established meanings of words.

Then a man came down the same path that we had taken to reach there. The dervish must have seen him. He called to him loudly, 'O friend, where have you been lost?' His calling was so intense that I felt as if he had raised a slogan with all the strength of his fragile body. Ajee Shah did not see the man and asked the dervish, 'Sain ji, who are you calling to?' 'I am calling myself. Nobody has ever been able to call another. Because there is no other. Neither here nor out there.' Before Ajee Shah could think on this obscure statement, a man came and sat on the ground in front of the fire, facing the dervish. The dervish repeated his sentence. 'O friend, where have you been lost?' But this time his voice was so low as if he were sharing a secret with the newcomer. The man explained in the same low tone that he could not find *shamama* in the vicinity and he had to go far away to get it.

Initially Ajee Shah thought he might be talking about some cloth or perhaps some woman by the name of *shamama,* but soon he learnt that *shamama* was the best quality of cannabis available in the country. As the man started emptying his cigarettes to mix the tobacco with *shamama*, the dervish concluded his conversation. He said, 'There are only two things in this transitory world; fear and love. Either you live in fear or you live in love. There is no third choice. And the choice between the two is not even always in your hands. But one should always crave for love. This longing helps the person all the way along. Sometimes, if you are lucky, your fate will push you into the infinite sea of love. All your fears are washed away and you become a lover.' As soon as he finished talking, the man lit a cannabis-filled cigarette and presented it to the dervish. His style was in the manner of someone presenting something very sacred. It appeared to be a supplication. Ajee Shah remembered the one rupee coin in his pocket, took it out, and presented it in the same way to the dervish. The dervish took it and gave it to a man whose duty it was to prepare the food. The dervish held the cigarette upright in the typical style of hashish smokers to avoid the ash falling down. He took a few deep puffs, and said to himself, 'Oh you forgetful man, be grateful for this smoke. If it won't bring out some of your inner fire, that fire will burn you alive. It will definitely burn you alive.'

I, Kabuko, the son of fire, thought, 'Whoa, how fiery some human beings are! What would they do if they were made of fire, instead of clay?'

22

Among The Log Thieves

Ajee Shah became intoxicated with a blessed potion of hemp drink. For the spirit of hemp, his body was a virgin, and even the mild piercing of it had its indulgent enticement. He was lying on a straw mat on the platform built around the big tree trunk. Bao lohar and about a dozen other men were also sleeping on the same platform. Almost all of them were accustomed to the hemp drink and its flighty green spirit. Sian Sidho, the dervish, never left his seat in front of the fire though now the smoke had lost its bite as the fire was dying down. He was not stroking his *mach*, fire place, and was lying down on the same mat. He was very much awake as he periodically recited a couplet of the famous Sufi saint Sultan Bahoo.

'Within I am filled with the fragrance of the intoxicating plant
And my soul is about to burst into bloom.'

There were no pillows under any head, but Bao Lohar gave Ajee Shah his thick cotton shawl to roll and put under his. But that was not much comfort as I, Kabuko the djinn, could not remember a time Ajee Shah had slept so rough. But the inertia, created by his debut with the hemp, was overwhelming enough to conveniently forget his present discomfort. I could see without any difficulty that Ajee Shah's mind was floating here and there, like a small boat on the waters of River Chenab. The Chenab had flowed for centuries. Rivers have a very long age and no djinn could ever compete with them, even having the longest djinn life.

There was nothing shiny on the ground, no lantern, no visible light from the dervish's supposedly illuminated being, and straw never shines in the darkness. But above, the sky was clear and filled with stars and constellations. You had to search for black patches between them. And strangely there were more fireflies moving around that night than I had ever seen in my long life, even though I had spent many nights with illuminated girls in the wilderness. But then again who cares to look for the tiny lights of fireflies when you have such glowing girls in your arms?

The aroma of the jungle-like woods was also showing off its wild intoxicating presence. Now Ajee Shah was recalling what the dervish had said earlier, 'Intoxication is the only blessing that holds this cosmos together. No intoxication, no togetherness. No togetherness, no chance of embodiment or mergence or unity, and love is the most intoxicating stuff in this cosmos.' It was difficult for Ajee Shah to understand the imperative role of intoxication described by the dervish in his own exclusive terminology. But he was content as he believed that a deeper part of him knew exactly what the dervish meant by his metaphors.

Ajee Shah must have been in the grip of the hemp drink as he started seeing the colour green everywhere. Whether he opened his eyes or closed them, the green did not disappear but became more and more bright. 'That is why they call the hemp *savi* which literally means green in Punjabi.' Ajee Shah thought in a dream-like state while his mind continued to flow in overlapping numerous shades of bright green. It was a joyous experience for him. Then he saw himself floating in the green cloudy atmosphere and following a most illuminated entity. The entity merged with the cloud and all became green. Sea or space, whatever that was, became nothing but a singularity. Then a gravitational force sucked Ajee Shah into that "greenish realm" and absorbed him in its mass. Ajee Shah suddenly realised that he had lost all of himself and he no longer existed as the Ajee Shah as he knew himself to be.

But on another level his individuality was still intact as there was some other Ajee Shah existing in another unseen world. Then he was shocked to realise that he was not thinking all that, but had become the singularity, outside of which nothing existed. And the other Ajee Shah was also the same entity that he had turned into. But there was no remorse or regret, no fear, no guilt, no desire, nothing. Then, with no effort on his part, Ajee Shah felt that every time he breathed in, the singularity expanded into a whole cosmos, and when he breathed out, the cosmos and the singularity both disappeared mysteriously.

I, Kabuko the djinn was also more or less experiencing the same phenomenon but I think I was not as high as Ajee Shah was. Suddenly a hand came from somewhere and shook Ajee Shah with full force and at the same time Ajee Shah heard the loud voice of the dervish, 'Wake up! Wake up! Wake up! You have gone too far! You have gone too far. Wake up, wake up!' And Ajee Shah suddenly woke up and sat down on his mat. He was utterly bewildered and did not know what had happened to him and where he had been just a moment ago but he felt terrible coming back into his normal senses. He started crying as his whole being was still filled with the residues of his joyous experience.

The dervish also stood up once and recited again his favourite couplet.

> 'Within I am filled with the fragrance of the intoxicating plant
> And my soul is about to burst into bloom.'

But this time his voice was more excited and heavy. He, then, sat down on his mat and stoked the fire. 'You do not have to die yet. Your time of departure has passed and you missed the train. Now wait here with me and some day we will catch the train together.' The dervish was apparently talking to the fire as there was nobody near him. He put a couple of pieces of wood into it and stoked it with his hands. In few moments the fire was again releasing a lot of smoke. Then the dervish shouted, 'O, youngster, come here,' and Ajee Shah knew that he was calling him as there was no youngsters present there. He went to the dervish and sat down in front of him on the ground. The fire was exactly between them but Ajee Shah was no longer concerned about the biting smoke as his eyes were already running with tears. The dervish turned his face as if he didn't want to look at Ajee Shah directly. He whispered, 'Where did the *savi* take you?' Ajee Shah answered in an equally low voice, 'Sain ji, I have no idea. But I was somewhere out of this world. I saw something but now it has been erased from my memory. Now only the residual feeling is left in me.' The dervish, still facing away, came back to his normal voice. 'You were taken into the domain of Hazrat Khidr, the immortal prophet. It is he who rules the realm of *savi*. You were shown what was appropriate for you and don't worry about forgetting it. You have forgotten it and it

206

is good for you. But whatever you went through is permanently imprinted on your soul. Your soul will always have access to it as the experience has become an integral part of you.' The dervish abruptly stopped and asked Ajee Shah to go and wake up the "log thief" snoring out there on the platform.

Ajee Shah stood up without knowing which of the dozen sleeping men he had to summon. Instantly he recalled what Bao Lohar had told him when they were coming here and they saw a couple of logs flowing in the river. 'In every village, near the banks of the river, there are two or three people whose only real occupation is to steal these logs.' Bao told him. Ajee Shah asked where the logs came from and who owned them. 'When they cut the wood up in the forests, they cut it into logs and number them individually and throw them into the river to be collected at many different points down the river. This is a free mode of transporting such heavy timber by the government forestry department. But these thieves operate during the night and steal a few of these logs. They sell them to the people cheaply who use them to build the roofs of their houses and thus make their living. But this is not the cup of tea for every Tom, Dick, and Harry. It is an art. It requires physical strength, courage, bravery, swimming techniques, knowledge of all types of whirls and water levels in the operating area, and, above all, the blessing of someone spiritually powerful on your back. So many of these logs thieves of the surrounding villages come and serve Sian Sidho and became his disciples. But these logs thieves are very dignified people, enjoying a great respect for their unusual profession in their respective communities. No one would dare report them to the authorities. And the young girls dream of marrying one of them. They are the men of night, the men of dreams.' Ajee Shah had asked Bao Lohar a very unexpected question at that, 'Are the log thieves more popular among the village girls than the Heer singers?' Heer was the most famous love story of Punjab and people sang it in a traditional way. Bao was confused by this unexpected question and didn't answer it.

Now, Ajee Shah was standing near the platform and didn't know whom to wake up. Using his rustic wisdom, he shouted, '*Uthh gaili chor, Sain bolanda aee.*' Wake up, O Log Thief, the Sain is calling you.

On his third loud shout three men woke up and ignoring Ajee Shah went straight towards Sain Sidho. They stood in front of him, eyes lowered and both hands capping their stomachs. 'What is your order, Sain?' 'Make a strong tea for this young man and also a bowl for me.' All three of them went away. Two of them again went to their mats and lay down but one of them who must have been about six and a half-feet-tall, robust, with the looks of a *mafroor,* an absconded outlaw, went into the mud hut and brought out a pan, tea, sugar, and milk in a bowl. He poured the water from a pitcher into a pan and put it on the fire in front of the dervish. Then he started blowing on the fire. He made three bowls of tea, including one for himself. The tea was too sweet and didn't have any match to the tea served in Bao Lohar's shop. The man finished his tea, collected the bowls and went away.

Once he left, the dervish turned his face and looked directly at Ajee Shah. After a while he became curious and started staring at him. Then he went into some kind of trance and asked, 'What are you doing here?' Ajee Shah was puzzled and stood up, thinking that the dervish wanted him to go back to the platform. 'You sit down and do not move. I am asking you.' Ajee Shah sat back down at the instruction of the dervish.

The dervish had fixed his eyes on Ajee Shah's belly button where inside the body, I, Kabuko the djinn, was residing at the time. I felt a shrug of energy like an electric current in me.

The dervish repeated his question, 'What brought you here? I was not expecting you. Why did you come here?' Ajee Shah remained silent but I knew without any doubt that the dervish was addressing me. But somehow I did not feel threatened, as the dervish, with all his unpredictability, still looked harmless to me. Still I did not answer his question and went deeper into the body. In the years of my sojourn in Ajee's body, I had created a cave-like space where I felt very safe and relaxed. All the other spirits living with me had long ago accepted my exclusive rights to that cave. I moved to that place to get rid of the uncomfortable energy coming out of the dervish's stare. As I told you I was not scared of him but I did not want to get involved unwillingly and unnecessarily in situations that did not concern me and which were not facilitating my purpose in the human world.

I tried to pretend that I was not there and that had never heard a word. Then the dervish called somebody in a low voice by a nickname that I could not pick up, and stretched his right arm to the extent that it touched the person sleeping on the platform about twenty feet away. His outstretched arm shook the person only once, but a little forcefully. The person woke up and said, 'Sain ji, what is your order?' Sain Sidho, while not having moved an inch from his place, ordered him to bring his staff. In the darkness he went inside one of the mud huts and brought out about a three feet long staff. I was apprehensive and remembered the Muslim occultist who had used his staff to extract a djinn from Nasreen, the girl from Ajee Shah's neighbourhood. I said to myself, 'O Kabuko, be ready for a beating' and suddenly I felt the very first real human experience of anticipating pain and torture. It was more dreadful to expect something bad than to bear it. The present moment spread out before me into a much longer time, giving me the opportunity to recall all those times in Ajee Shah's life when he had been anticipating pain. I saw many hands and many staffs coming to hit him on the head, face, hands, arms, bottom, legs, and feet. Every part of the body was vulnerable and fearful. But the most agonising part of the experience was that those hands included Ajee Shah's mother, father, teachers, mates, and other siblings, with whom he was bonded in a reciprocal love. Love and pain always had an incompatible combination that was hard for me to swallow. Like sugar mixed with chilli.

I was busy in my thoughts and Ajee Shah was not at all concerned by what was happening around or inside him as he remembered, again, being submerged in his greenish mystery and enjoying the fragrance of that. The dervish's staff hit me on my abdominal area as he slightly pushed Ajee Shah's belly button. That stroke did not hurt me but I felt very vulnerable as I was sitting in the securest place I could ever imagine in the human world. The dervish again addressed me but this time he seemed irritated, 'I asked you what the hell you are doing here?' I left the cave but did not project myself outside Ajee Shah's body. Instead, for the very first time, I used the tongue and mouth of Ajee Shah without changing my original voice.

For half an hour, the dervish asked me questions and I answered them. During the whole interview, at no point did I show any irritation or disrespect for the dervish, and I tried answering him as honestly as I could. The dervish was also not hostile towards me but he looked unhappy at my being in Ajee Shah's body. He did not say anything but I could sense that he was serious and careful in his conversation. At last, the dervish said to me, 'You have no need to learn in this hard way but now stay where you are. Perhaps that is what your destiny is. Only God knows best.'

Then the dervish instructed Ajee Shah to sleep on the mat

next to his. When Ajee Shah lay down, the dervish put his right hand on his forehead and in a few seconds both of us were in deep sleep. When Ajee Shah woke up the next morning, the sun was quite high and the atmosphere was becoming humid. The same man who had brought the dervish's staff last night was serving tea in the same bowls in which the hemp had been served. He also distributed two rusks, unsweetened cookies, with each bowl of tea. Now, most of the people present were sitting around the dervish. The dervish joked with Bao Lohar and said, 'O Bao, you asked my permission to bring one young man here but you have brought two.' Bao Lohar took some time to understand the joke, then he said smilingly, 'O Sain, does it make any difference to you? You have enslaved many log thieves and this poor djinn is of no worth in front of you.' Then they both laughed and I, Kabuko the djinn, became very relaxed and felt at home. I did not mind Bao Lohar calling me the 'poor djinn' as I was sure he knew us djinn well. Perhaps, too well.

At about eleven o'clock, Bao Lohar asked the dervish for permission to leave. Bao Lohar and Ajee Shah shook hands with the dervish and when they were leaving, the robust log thief also accompanied them. He was going to his village that was about six miles away. They were walking in the woods when Bao Lohar said to the log thief, 'Talk about something. It will make the walk easy if we talk.' As he was thinking of something to say, Ajee Shah who was holding the handle of his bicycle, asked him to tell them something about his strange profession. The man took pride in Ajee Shah's request and said that he would tell them the strangest story of his life.

'I started stealing logs when I was only fourteen years old. My uncle taught me this "business" and now everyone accepts that I am the best log thief in the whole area. Now most of the time my pupils work for me and I only intervene when they have some difficulty in handling a log. I know every inch of the river over a twenty mile stretch. In all these years, I have stolen thousands of logs and was caught only once when there was a special raid by police and the forestry department. They could not have caught me if I had been alone but I was with an inexperienced pupil and, in helping him to escape, I was trapped. But he got away.' Ajee Shah was not interested in his boastful conversation and interrupted him to get to the strange story he had promised to tell.

The log thief, somewhat embarrassed, said, 'Oh, yes. That was early in the morning and I was very young in those days and always worked alone. I saw three logs coming down the river and jumped into the water. I checked two of the logs but those were very heavy and I could not carry them for miles on the ground. So I left them in the water and cursed the arrogance that made me work alone. The third one was of the perfect size. I had seen a big snake sitting on one side of the log. That was no problem for me as there is a time-tested procedure to get rid of a snake. I went to the other side of the log and turned it slowly and now the snake was sitting on the side where the water was flowing. Then I rolled the log to throw the snake into the water. I held the log in that position for a couple of minutes so that the pressure of the water would push the snake further away. Most of the water snakes are harmless but the snakes often found sitting on logs are not water snakes. They are ground snakes and somehow end up on the logs and there is no way to tell whether they are poisonous or not so we have to be very careful with them. After I had gotten rid of the snake, I pushed the log towards the bank and then onto the ground. After that I sat on the ground and took a few minutes to rest, as I would have to carry the log for many miles. When I put the log on my shoulder, everything was normal and even the wet log's weight was exactly to my expectations. After walking about a hundred yards, I noticed that something was pulling the log from behind. I turned my face to see what it was and what I saw was unbelievable. The other end of the log was still in the river and suddenly I realised that what I was carrying on my shoulder was not a log at all but a big snake's tale! I threw it instantly on the ground and moved away from that thing, about ten yards or so. Then, I saw the whole thing start moving towards the river. I followed it until it went into the river completely.

I was scared as I had never heard of this sort of thing in my life. I ran towards a nearby temporary dwelling of Gujjars, who used to feed their cattle in the woods. One of them was a friend of mine and I woke him up and told him the whole story. He gave me milk and called his grandfather, who was sleeping near the cattle. The old man listened to the story and said, 'Oh, that was nothing. That must be a *chhaleda*, a shape-changer. They often do those sorts of mischievous things. Get some protective talisman and tie it on your right arm and you will be saved from these windy creatures.'" The log man finished his story which had been very exciting for Ajee Shah but not for me as I, Kabuko the djinn, knew that what they call *chhaleda* are our low-ranking djinn. They can only take the shape of various animals and reptiles. We call them the shape-changing imitators and sometimes call them to entertain our children at various ceremonies. But the old man was right that they are basically harmless. Though sometimes, the faint-hearted get so frightened by them that it takes away their life.

They came to the GT Road and the log thief bid them farewell. Bao Lohar then sat on the rod of the bicycle and Ajee Shah started pedalling them home.

23

A Negotiated Love

Another week had passed, and Princess Tarru and her adolescent friend had still not shown their faces. I, Kabuko the djinn, was anxiously waiting for the pair, or perhaps, only for Tarru's friend. Lovers are very unpredictable, I thought in awe. Last time Tarru had been so desperate to make love to Ajee Shah, that had I encouraged her, she wouldn't have waited for another moment. But now she was nowhere to be found. Since visiting the dervish in the woods and encountering the spirit of hemp, Ajee Shah was still under the spell of the biting smoke from the dervish's fire and the hemp's floating spirit in green clouds. He was not thinking about Tarru, the *pari*, his first love, and was not even concerned about the forthcoming event of invoking his *hamzad* with the help of Bao Lohar. He had met Bao Lohar three or four times since then but the *hamzad* hadn't entered his mind or their conversation.

Ajee Shah was obviously unaware about the deal my benefactress had struck with Tarru, which was perhaps more promising for me, Kabuko the djinn, than for him. But ignorance is a blessing sometimes. You don't have to worry about the unknown. For me, Tarru's future visits held many expectations, and I was becoming more and more desperate to make love with the promised beauty. Her name had yet to be revealed to me but I could already feel her seductive tongue moving with circular perfection in my mouth. My mind was busy creating all sorts of projections involving her lovely body indulgently making love with mine, in all possible positions.

I am not a pervert, only a sexual being. And you should have compassion for my situation as I hadn't had sex for the last seventeen years. Now, I had started paying for my long abstinence. All my ignored sexual energies had turned into a hungry lioness, ready to tear apart every bit of my being. If Tarru and her young friend did not turn up soon, I might have to masturbate to get rid of that beast. For me it was such an odious act that I could not bear to think of it. You may not believe me but I swear by the name of Abu ul Djinnat, the forefather of the djinn, that I have never masturbated in my whole life. This was not due to austerity on my part but because I was so darned lucky in sexual matters that whenever I felt the urge I found someone with whom to copulate. When it came to screwing, I was unscrupulous. I am neither ashamed nor do I have any feelings of guilt, unlike you humans, to reveal that on the occasions when I couldn't find any suitable partner, I slept with the female species of djinn animals and even the lower classes. It might be repulsive to you but for me, in pure sex, what mattered was only the joy of the experience and the immediate after-effects. If both were fine then there was no problem. But, I Kabuko the djinn, now understand that you human beings are very different from us. You carry too many thoughts all the time and that is your problem.

Three more days passed and nothing happened to give me solace. During the night I was watching Ajee Shah as well as the sky above to look for Tarru and her friend. Ajee Shah was half asleep when he felt the need to masturbate and he covered himself with the sheet at the foot of his bed. He masturbated for quite some time, and then put his white cotton handkerchief, wet with semen, under his pillow and went into a relaxed deep sleep. A cheeky thought came to my mind. 'That is why white handkerchiefs are so popular here among the people. They conceal the whiteness of their semen.'

Strangely, that night I was not tired but was feeling very energetic for no apparent reason. I was observing everything inside and outside Ajee Shah with a great deal of curiosity, amicably switching between the two. It was the third and final part of the night—the most powerful and magical time before the first ray is born out of the womb of the ever burning sun— and I watched Ajee Shah dreaming the usual things in his sleep. Suddenly, his body jerked as if he were having an epileptic fit. It even caused me to shudder within him.

Ajee Shah, in his dream, slipped into a region that I can only describe as most fanciful and unusual. It was definitely not the day-to-day stuff that his dreams were usually made of. Moments before the jerk, Ajee Shah was dreaming of clouds of green hues—floating in it and thinking how easy it was to fly in the air. He was wondering why on Earth people couldn't fly. Those were, more or less, the sorts of thoughts that were passing through his dreaming mind. After meeting with the dervish and having the hemp drink, his experience of encountering the spirit of hemp had moved his dreams beyond previous invisible boundaries. This unknown region in his dream was breathtaking. I had never seen that kind of natural or man- or djinn-made beauty blooming in all sorts of shining colours. But

216

then those were not earthly colours as I could not discern any similarity to the colours I had seen in my long life in the djinn or human world.

A big silver tree appeared; it was a translucent tree moving between having leaves and branches and not having leaves and branches. It was hard to even perceive it. Then the whole landscape became naked, unhidden, showing itself off. At that point, I thought that I, Kabuko the djinn, was the only one for whom this whole scene had been created. I do not know why I thought that. On another level I knew that the dream, or whatever it was, was in Ajee Shah's mind, and that I was only an observer, an additional observer. But, somehow, the situation did not allow me to think rationally any further. I was not confused but in another state of being. Many birds came and sat down cheerfully on the tree. I can't describe their colour but can only say that they were of some kind of dark colour. Maybe they were not originally dark but the shining background of the silvery tree was presenting them in such a shade. Two white birds came and sat on the same tree. They started singing and after a while all the coloured birds followed their course. I could hear their singing—they were fully in tune, the white pair and the many coloured ones—and I could vaguely differentiate between them, too. Then I remembered my mother, who used to say, 'Kabuko, you are blessed with very sharp ears.' I started crying. I had no idea why I was crying but I wanted to cry till my death. Tears covered my face. With blurred vision, I again watched that extraordinary dream.

The scene had changed and a shiny white palace on a hilltop appeared and now dominated the whole view. But the magical tree was also there; this time without the birds and without any songs. A strange calmness vibrated everywhere. Then I saw Ajee Shah going towards that white palace. Two other entities in white silk, loose and waving in the wind, joined him. One to the right and the other to the left. Although I was still very much inside Ajee Shah, I could only see him and the accompanying entities from behind and, with every step, the distance was increasing between them and me.

When they reached the door, suddenly the distance compressed and I could clearly see the amazing patterns of stones and pearls on the white marble door. Somebody called me by my name and I felt, again, a jerk in my body. 'Come out, Kabuko, it is the time for you to leave.' The female voice ordered me. I had no resistance left in me and I obeyed the order as if it were a royal decree. I came out of Ajee Shah's body but felt that there were many parts of me still inside him. I tried to collect them but couldn't. Then the same voice said, 'Kabuko, leave them there. They are no problem. Do not waste any time. You are in a realm where time moves very fast.' I gave up immediately. In a split second, the two entities took physical shape. One was Tarru and the other her beautiful friend. I was so bewildered by the experience that I couldn't speak a word. Tarru held the hand of her friend and put that fair wrist in my hands and said, 'Kabuko, you are very lucky. Take Nirva with you and do not show me your face until I call you. She will take you to paradise.'

Tarru didn't waste a moment; she kissed Nirva farewell and then kissed Ajee Shah, took him into her arms, and went inside the palace. Neither of them turned back to give us a departing look.

As soon as the door closed, I divided into two. The nearest analogy that came to mind was that I am a river, whose main stream is here, where I am standing with Nirva, and a side stream from my body went inside the palace with Ajee Shah. It was difficult to explain. I was conscious of both my selves but my main self felt more real to me and the side self felt dreamier. I was in a magical world that I am unable to narrate even metaphorically, not in human terms and certainly not in djinn terms. But, most strangely, I was not confused at all. I knew that I would not have to account for all this at any future time as the whole experience would, at the end, consume itself and become only a forgotten rich nothingness that remains within me for all the time to come.

I kissed Nirva while still standing outside the closed marble door. Her tongue moved in my mouth with the same circular perfection as I had fancied in my daydreams many times, but there was another element, almost alien to me. She was kissing me not as a sexual partner but as a beloved. I had kissed hundreds of girls from the djinn and human domain but had never felt anything like that. I was certain that it was not that she was new to me or her tenderness or her kissing technique but something beyond that, which I, Kabuko the djinn, was not acquainted with. Nirva uttered a magical word that included a lot of vowels and we both ended up in the bed of Ajee Shah, holding each other.

Then she started making love to me, as if I were a boy of twelve or thirteen and she more mature. Fully experienced. Fully commanding. I felt I was a young virgin boy and somebody had picked me up from the playground and was now seducing me with the fullness of her gender's strength. I surrendered myself to Nirva and her protective covering of my being expanded. When the moment of climax came, she kissed me, and with the speed of lightning turning back to the sky from the earth, she disappeared.

The rays of the sun woke me up, and I found myself in bed, hugging Ajee Shah, who was still in a deep sleep. I entered into his body and embraced the parts of myself that went with him.

They were filled with some kind of experience, perhaps more rich and abundant than mine. I tried to penetrate in the parts of myself to get some clues about what had happened to him but there was no specific memory of the night, only the residues of some most pleasant feelings.

Ajee Shah woke up with a start. That was unusual as before that night, he had never had fits and starts like this. I became worried but then I looked at him more closely and I became at ease. I had never seen him so happy and contended in his whole life. He was whistling and I knew that he couldn't whistle in that way before. A few of his friends knew the art and had the physical ability to produce long, slow whistling but Ajee Shah had always failed to whistle. His mouth only produced the unsweetened sound of blowing breath but without any warbling. 'It must be the kisses of Tarru during the night,' I guessed, 'and our nightingale has changed the whole anatomy of his tongue and made it free for all the twists and turns.' Then I remembered that old tree, with its twists and turns, where Tarru's older sister had sat for years to mourn her beloved, the same Ajee Shah but in a previous incarnation.

I, Kabuko the djinn, was now convinced that Tarru and her friend Nirva were not ordinary creatures from the djinn realm. They were top-class magicians, practising the highest forms of magic. First, Tarru had conjured the scene at the well to attract Ajee Shah, and that was too impressive even for me to absorb. And now, the pair had created a perfect dream world and pulled Ajee Shah and me into it. I remembered my grandmother and other elders and even my magician benefactress. All of them at some point had advised me not to go into the human world but I had never listened to them. If I had explored my own djinn world, I would have been much better off, I thought with regret. My vibrations must have changed with the thought as a friendly animal spirit, the same who had once shown me his phallus as gesture of sympathy, came out of hiding and stood in front of me. He remained silent for some time, but when I asked 'What is the matter with you?' he gave me a strange look and said, 'Kabuko, are you sure that if you had not entered into the human body you would have had this type of experience? These experiences are meant for humans, and you and I are having a free ride.' I ignored his wise words and asked him, 'Did you enter with Ajee Shah into the white palace when Tarru took him there?' 'Of course, everyone was there. Only a fool would miss that sort of a chance.' 'Tell me what happened there?' I asked excitedly. 'No, Kabuko, I cannot tell you anything. It is a secret. Before participation in whatever it was, we all had to take an oath, one by one, according to our respective customs, that we would not reveal anything.' He paused and then said something really hurtful. 'Kabuko, you and your benefactress were so foolish to make a deal with Tarru. She tried to persuade everyone inside Ajee Shah to make a similar deal but no one fell into her trap. No one made a deal with her. Only you did this stupid thing. Kabuko, you do not know what you have missed.' After saying that, the animal spirit left me alone to swallow his most distasteful verdict on me.

24
The Miracle of Love

In just one night, the love magic of the fairy princess Tarru had worked wonders. Her sensual charisma in that makeshift magical setting was so powerful and consequential that it had changed Ajee Shah's entire being. During the breathtaking spell of intimate moments, every part of Tarru and Ajee Shah's bodies, sensitive or otherwise, had lost their identities voluntarily—and effortlessly—and played their roles in a blessed unity with precision and perfection. I, Kabuko the djinn, was convinced that somehow the change in Ajee Shah was not intentional but was the peripheral impact of that magical night. The magic didn't transform Ajee Shah into a ringed-neck speaking parrot or a hugging puppy with blind affection. He remained the same old handsome guy with dimples on both cheeks. Those same deep and visible dimples that never needed a helping laugh to manifest themselves. Yet, still, a change had occurred, inside and outside. An immense change. He was aglow from every angle. I, Kabuko the djinn, had witnessed the change from all the different angles my two eyes could perceive in their incarnated intimacy with Ajee Shah. There were many lessons for me to learn as a non-human just by observing the changing process in the being of Ajee Shah.

As I was now one of the oldest inhabitants of that human body, I could say with some authority that the most amazing process of change in the body was always at the cellular level. Before the magic of Tarru happened, cells died and new cells emerged all the time. But with the magic, that natural process of cellular shift had changed. Before, when a cell died, the tiny spirit residing in the cell often jumped into the new born cell and occupied it, though some tiny spirits that were too attached or deeply imbedded in the cell could not escape the natural death of the cell and died with the body of the cell. That was why I called these tiny little spirits "the soul" of the cell. But now, with the magical impact, thousands and thousands of cells in the body died and not even a single tiny spirit had the opportunity or even the wish to escape death. With the birth of each replacing cell, a new tiny spirit with its fresh breath entered the body of Ajee Shah. These new spirits were different in mood, appearance, and characteristics. They were exuberant, carefree, and happy-go-lucky types. They didn't care for anything that was heavy in any way, in contrast to their predecessors who always clung to weighty things. They were both petite, yet these new "cell souls" were a breed apart from the old ones. Their arrival in the thousands changed the whole inner atmosphere, which instantly manifested outside. All sorts of intense feelings, emotions, and actions left Ajee Shah, and he was transformed into an unbelievably joyful and content person. There were no more biting chillies in his heart, no more burning desires, no more desperation of any kind; there was only a naturally-refined sense of fondness, liking, and preference, appearing voluntarily with a peculiar manner embodied in humility and patience. It was like the inner life of a mystic. An inexplicable calmness was reflected in all his manners. Now Ajee Shah talked smoothly and gently even to himself and, instead of running around all the time, walked with the dignity of a fulfilled person. What kind of fulfilment was that? Of course, it was not exclusively sexual. The magic of Tarru was a piece of impregnated art, a cocktail of many different fragrances that would intoxicate Ajee Shah for a long time to come.

After the experience, I, Kabuko the djinn, was keenly watching Ajee Shah's thoughts and noticed that the dream-like encounter with Tarru was sitting comfortably at the bottom of his mind and never expressed any urge to come to the surface. It was a permanent remembrance that didn't require recalling or sharing with anyone else. It was present all the time, making its existence noticeable not in the shape of thought forms but as an illumination to brighten his mind and make it very optimistic. I could clearly see that now Ajee Shah's orientation had changed and, instead of dwelling on his past memories, he was very much living in his present as a person who is convinced of a bright future. Future scenarios, real or imagined, were providing him with a full energy diet for the body and soul. The new mood of Ajee Shah also made everyone inside him more happy and exuberant. Even I forgot the remarks of the animal spirit and enjoyed the memories of the time I had spent with Tarru's friend Nirva. I think that was the happiest time for all of us.

Like everyone else, Bao Lohar also noticed the dramatic change in Ajee Shah's behaviour. But he didn't for a moment suspect the magical experience that Ajee Shah had gone through. It never occurred to him as his clairvoyant faculties were unable to trace any thought of the experience in Ajee Shah's mind. He was amazed and fairly certain that the transformation was the result of Ajee Shah's encounter with the hemp spirit. Bao Lohar had heard from dervishes that sometimes the green spirit of hemp left such an impact on the person, who drinks it for the first time, in order to make itself attractive to him and to pull him towards hemp intoxication. It was almost impossible to ignore the call of the powerful hemp spirit. Bao Lohar's conclusion about the source of Ajee Shah's transformation at first made him happy and then left him saddened. He was happy that the hemp spirit had been so kind to Ajee Shah that only one little dose had changed him so much but he was sad too as he knew that now Ajee Shah could not for a long time depart with the spirit and would become addicted to the hemp drink.

Bao Lohar was a wise man and wanted to check his notions about the encounter, so he invited Ajee Shah to visit Sian Sidho's dwelling in the woods again. But to his utter surprise, Ajee Shah declined the invitation politely and said that he needed time and was not yet ready to take hemp drink again so soon. Bao Lohar did not mind Ajee Shah's declining the invitation and left him alone.

Ajee Shah passed his matriculation examinations with such high marks that no one in his family had ever dreamt of that level of success considering Ajee's elaborate non-academic activities. He got admission to college, the only one in his area that was run by a local trust. The college had quite a good reputation and many of its students went into the country's civil service. The college was about six miles away from Ajee Shah's house and his father bought him a locally-made new bicycle. Now Ajee Shah was very happy with his new college student life as there was no physical punishment, no homework, and no packed study periods. On some days he had only one or two lessons. He made many new friends and among those were some typical village boys belonging to those well-to-do families who can afford to send their sons to college. Though their villages were only a few miles away from the city, their rural ethos was present in all their manners and actions, and they were differentiable from Ajee Shah at first sight. They always took greater pride in their physical strength than their mental abilities. They never liked those games that required non-physical skills. Ajee Shah had an edge vis-à-vis this lot as he had both physical and mental capabilities. His physical charisma was obvious but then he was also in the first two years of college nominated assistant editor of the college magazine, before making it to editor in his final year. The village boys would often invite Ajee Shah to their villages to stay over the weekend and such visits always brought a different taste to life.

Together they would go to the fields and eat fresh raw vegetables and fruits and swim in the deep wells when they were not being run by oxen to water the fields. There Ajee Shah learnt a swimming technique called "cycling", which was necessary to keep your head above the water. Ajee Shah always shouted out his own name in the well and then listened for the echo. He had a kind of excitement in this activity. Twice they went out to the swamps with double-barrel rifles to hunt doves but it was unbearable to Ajee Shah to kill such a beautiful flying creature. There was another thing even more excruciating for him. When the bird fell down after being shot, someone had to catch it immediately and cut its throat half way with a sharp knife to make it *halal* for Muslim consumption. If the bird died before you could reach it then it was useless and had to be left there. But with all his feelings of sympathy with the bird and other living creatures I, Kabuko the djinn, must admit that Ajee Shah and I both enjoyed tremendously the dishes made with freshly-hunted doves.

Our nights were also not without excitement as Ajee Shah

and I, Kabuko the djinn, now had girlfriends. Tarru and Nirva would come regularly and take us to their magical world. Then both Ajee and Tarru would disappear in an exclusive world of their own and leave me with Nirva. Nirva was now so much attached to me that if I ever jokingly said something insensitive she reacted with tears in her eyes. One day she smilingly said, 'Kabuko, let us marry.' I replied, 'No, you are no longer a virgin, and I will only marry a virgin.' She burst into tears and it took a lot of effort to convince her that I was just joking. In the end my sweetheart smiled again and said, 'Do you think I will leave you with any potency or stamina to face a virgin? You are a bloody fool, Kabuko, you do not know about us, the female kind.'

Time passed quickly and with ease. Ajee Shah was now in the fourth year of college and was blooming in his youth. At that age almost everyone fell in love with some girl or other. But Ajee was no longer interested in the opposite sex. Though his was a boys-only college, there were many girls of his age in the neighbourhood and all were prone towards falling in love. Even in his own extended family there were a few mothers with young girls who looked upon Ajee Shah as their potential son-in-law. Whenever they visited his house, they made sure they brought their daughters along and, between the lines, revealed their intentions. Although Ajee Shah was friendly enough towards those girls, he always avoided the opportunity to be alone with any of them. One of the girls, who lived on the same street as him, was a childhood friend of his. She kissed him once in a secluded corner of his home and expressed her love but Ajee Shah told her point-blank that they were only friends. I, Kabuko the djinn, could safely assume that Tarru had not only sexually but also emotionally fulfilled him.

Bao Lohar was now hardly seen in his shop. A young man distantly related to Bao, whom he always called "nephew", came from the village after learning the family trade of ironsmith and ran Bao Lohar's shop. That gave Bao the opportunity to explore his other activities which were shrouded in mystery. During the last three years Ajee Shah had visited the dwelling of Sian Sidho with Bao Lohar more than a dozen times and on each occasion he had the hemp drink in such quantity and with such self-possession that he could match any mature hemp drinker. I, Kabuko the djinn, was surprised that the trance experience of hemp remained more or less the same as it was the very first time. But every time, despite its identical nature, the experience was enriched somehow. It was like a human friendship or a love affair in which you have the same conversations and the same activities but the bond between you becomes so solid that one day you cannot imagine yourself without each other.

Then one day Bao Lohar went away as usual and did not show his face for six months or so. His nephew became very concerned and so did Ajee Shah. Both went to Sian Sidho's dwelling but even there nobody knew Bao Lohar's whereabouts. Sian Sidho was calm, as he always was, and said that one day Bao Lohar would come back on his own. Ajee Shah and Bao's nephew had only one clue as the log thief told them that Bao Lohar might have gone to visit the shrine of a famous Kalander Lal Shahbaz in Sindh. The log thief said that Bao in his hemp drunkenness often expressed his desire to go to the shrine and said that Lal Shahbaz was calling him.

Another six months passed and Ajee Shah graduated and started looking for a job in one of the local newspapers. Suddenly, in the dark of night, Bao Lohar reappeared in a shining red cloak and settled on his bed in the shop. Early the next morning the nephew informed Ajee Shah with great concern that Bao Lohar had come back but had lost his voice. Ajee Shah straightaway went to the shop and was shocked when Bao Lohar looked at him with blank eyes, showing no reaction at all. The first thing he noticed was that Bao looked visibly years older and that he was in a state of complete silence. He did not answer any of the probing questions that Ajee Shah asked in excitement. It was obvious that although Bao was physically there, in reality he was completely unconnected with his environment. He did not even bother to look at the world around him and closed his eyes to escape any encounter with anyone, including Ajee Shah. Ajee Shah decided then and there that he would now serve Bao Lohar until he returned to his normal state.

I, Kabuko the djinn, could not understand this mysterious human faculty to make such urgent decisions and to differentiate so quickly between the time to serve and the time to be served. The only indication that I gathered in those days while picking Ajee Shah's thoughts was that he was convinced that something extraordinary but very powerful had happened to Bao Lohar which had pushed him into an alternative state. He was also convinced that the happening would eventually be of great benefit to Bao and, perhaps, even to himself. Now Bao Lohar was either lying down or sitting on his bed. He stopped talking to anyone and if somebody tried to speak to him, he just received the same blank look in Bao Lohar's eyes. It was almost impossible to imagine Bao Lohar without a mug of tea but for many days no one saw him drink or eat. Everyone around him was concerned about this strange condition except Ajee Shah. Although people didn't say it openly, they must have thought that Bao Lohar had experienced something terrible and not from this world. Ajee Shah's reaction was very weird. He was not concerned at all about Bao Lohar's condition and didn't even try again to speak to him or to draw his attention towards him. But at the same time he looked after him like a disciple takes care of his guru.

Each day, Ajee Shah visited him at least a dozen times, leaving all manner of edibles near him. He made three or four mugs of tea in a day and left it in the shop of Bao Lohar. Ajee Shah also made sure that nobody disturbed Bao Lohar in his enigmatic condition. But one thing was very worrying for Ajee also. Bao Lohar hadn't left his shop for many days to use the mosque toilets. How on earth could he avoid that human need? Ajee Shah thought that perhaps Bao left his shop during the night, but he knew in his heart that this was not true. Bao Lohar had not even moved from his bed. He was sitting or lying in the same place, doing nothing, not even moving his limbs for days. Sometimes he took a couple of sips of tea and on others took a bite of any edible thing left at the side of his bed.

Forty days passed like this and on the morning of the forty-first day, when Ajee Shah went to Bao Lohar's shop, he could not believe his eyes. Bao Lohar had had a perfect shave, a haircut, and was wearing a new red cloak. He was sipping tea and was talking to his nephew, giving him instructions about joining those iron cups that are used in pulling water from the well. Bao Lohar welcomed Ajee Shah in his usual way and said that his fasting was over now. He related, without any prompting from Ajee Shah, how he had spent a year at the shrine of Lal Shahbaz Kalander and had done some high spiritual practises there. He also proudly informed Ajee Shah that he was now blessed with a new uniform of red that not only would he wear all of his remaining life but also in the grave.

Life became normal. Bao Lohar often mentioned his promise to give him a special gift and settle the account of those two mercury balls of his brother Karam Shah. Bao Lohar made it clear to Ajee Shah that before he could only afford to offer him the gift of helping him to invoke his *hamzad*. But now, after having acquired the red uniform, he would present him with a much more precious gift. Before moving on to other subjects, Bao Lohar always told Ajee Shah, 'Tell me when you are ready to receive your legitimate gift from an ironsmith with a poor lineage.'

25

An Assignment For The Heart

The editor and owner of the local weekly newspaper, Tahir Zaman, was in his early fifties and had a somewhat ambiguous reputation in city circles. On one hand he was known as an old, rotten blackmailer who could snatch his living and the expenses to run the paper from the udders of a dry cow. There were many such cows in and among the local businesses, the local administration, and the local politicians who were vulnerable to that sort of mildly hurtful blackmail. But at the same time, he was known as the only journalist in the area endowed with knowledge of local history, the blood lineage of all the local important people, and many scandalous stories that other people ignored or had forgotten. The information of who was related to whom and who should be approached at what particular time of the day to get the best out of him was at his fingertips. He was pleasant enough as his conversation was never without fresh jokes. People around him often wondered from where he could always get such new jokes. Many believed he made them up by himself using his native knowledge and his creative skills.

Ajee Shah knew Tahir Zaman quite well as many of his stories and articles had been published in Tahir's newspaper. One day, as Ajee Shah was going somewhere on his bicycle, an idea came to him. He asked himself, 'Why don't I join the newspaper of Tahir Zaman?' The answer came from inside without any delay and with a shiver of excitement, 'That is really a good idea!' and Ajee Shah went straight to the office of the weekly newspaper.

Tahir Zaman's initial response was very discouraging. He went to great lengths to try to convince Ajee Shah to join some pensionable government job and not ruin his life by becoming another Tahir Zaman. But Ajee Shah was adamant and said that he had always wanted to become a journalist. At last Tahir Zaman agreed but it was very obvious from his body language that he was very unhappy about it.

Ajee Shah was the fourth person on the team. Besides Tahir Zaman, there was Mubarak, the calligrapher, and Sharif, the peon. The first assignment Ajee Shah was given was to fill three pages with local court stories, particularly of a criminal nature, and mostly consisting of murder case proceedings as their district was notorious for that, each week. Tahir Zaman believed that those pages presented the most interesting material for his newspaper readers. Before Ajee Shah was taken in, he himself was responsible for those pages. Tahir Zaman took Ajee Shah to the district courts and introduced him to all the relevant court clerks and lawyers' assistants.

In a short period of time, to the utter amazement of Tahir Zaman, Ajee Shah was not only proficient in court reporting but had also filed some very interesting stories with a pinch of human touch. Tahir Zaman always congratulated himself that he had made Ajee a good reporter in such a short time though transferring his years of experience and teaching him the ins and outs of local journalism. He refused to entertain the role that hard work and enthusiasm had played in Ajee Shah's achievements. But Ajee didn't mind at all.

Tahir Zaman had another very good quality which was a rare one. Whatever happened, he always paid salaries on the tenth day of each month. Ajee Shah got eighty rupees a month, which was not bad at all considering his age and experience and the general pay scale in such a small private business that only sold printed words on rough newsprint. Ajee Shah was very happy with his first job and eighty rupees a month gave him much respect and freedom. Now he could return home late at night and even if he did not show up for a couple of days, no one at home could ask any questions of him. And he always had a convenient lie to say that he was busy at work.

Ajee Shah's new job and new freedom didn't interfere at all in our night-time routine. We would visit Tarru and Nirva and both of them never allowed us to escape that routine; "tiredness" was not a justification they ever accepted. A number of enjoyable years passed in this fashion and I was pacified by the human stories Ajee would investigate as a journalist and did not resent the djinn intrusion in our nights with the colourful tales of his days.

One night when Ajee Shah and I, Kabuko the djinn, returned after our usual love-making trip, an animal spirit that I always called "Malhi", as she looked to me like a very tasty local river fish of the same name, came up to me and congratulated me. She was always friendly to me and we had had years of perfectly harmonious relations but I still could not understand why she had greeted me in this way. 'What is the occasion?' I asked in pleasant surprise. 'You really don't know?' Malhi asked laughingly. Then she became serious and told me that a date had been fixed for Ajee Shah's marriage.

I could not believe my ears as I was always observant and fully aware of whatever was happening around Ajee Shah. In my sheer astonishment I asked her, 'With whom?' 'Tarru, the djinn princess.' I couldn't believe my ears because, as a djinn, I knew that the Tarru's clan would never allow this to happen. I thought that Malhi must have picked up some half-baked information and interpreted it through her little and limited mind. God knows how but she read my mind and started laughing hysterically. Her laughter was very annoying to me as I took it to be racially oriented. I moved to another part of the body and started small talk with the spirit of a fallen angel that I knew somehow was on its last legs and going to leave any day now.

In the early morning, Malhi again approached me and said that not only had the marriage date been set but that Ajee Shah had agreed to many conditions of the djinn clan, which humans do not usually accept. She said this in a serious tone with a ting of concern. I asked her what had happened and requested her to tell me the whole story without any observations of her own.

Djinn pregnancies last for three human years and Tarru had been pregnant for almost a year. She had wanted to have a child with Ajee Shah from day one, Malhi told me. This special child, with all the best human and djinn qualities, would rule the clan after his mother. She expects this boy to become a great royal asset, expanding the influence of her clan after her. At first the clan elders were so against the idea that they even discussed getting Tarru to abdicate her crown. Tarru tried very hard to convince them that the great spiritual lineage of Ajee Shah was a perfect match for her own royal ancestry and that their loving relationship would create a great fusion of "homo djinn" having all the best qualities of clay and of smokeless fire. But they were not convinced even though they made enquiries about Ajee Shah's lineage and knew that Tarru was not lying about that at least.

When Tarru refused to get rid of her love child and announced that she did not care to lead a clan whose elders had more respect for their old traditions than the heartfelt wishes of their princess, the elders somehow devised another strategy. It was an open secret that the elders were afraid of Tarru's popularity. Tarru was the apple of the eye of the younger generations of the clan as she was always a liberal ruler and never insisted on the punishment of petty delinquencies, and even indulgences of the adult members of the clan. There was also a general sympathy for her as her older sister had gone through a lot of agony and had died in very miserable circumstances.

The elders did their homework and collected some old scripts that allowed Ajee Shah to have a marriage for a predetermined and fixed time. Their greatest worry was that after the boy became their ruler, his human father should not be able to interfere in any way in the matters of the court or the clan. They put many strict conditions that included that Tarru would marry Ajee Shah according to the old customs of their clan for a fixed period. That period would end sixty days after the child's birth. On the sixtieth day, Tarru would show the child to her husband for the first and last time. Tarru and Ajee Shah had to promise and swear, according to their respective traditions, during the marriage ceremony that they would never meet after that and that Ajee Shah would never try to meet or see his child for the rest of his life. The elders thought that this was such a condition that no human being would ever agree to it but they were mistaken.

When Tarru, in the middle of intercourse with Ajee,

conveyed this suggestion his thoughts went back to Janti, the prostitute who after marrying the king of snakes had become his now respected sister-in-law. Ajee Shah agreed to the conditions as he did not want any problems for his lover who had fulfilled him to an extent that no human girl could ever do.

I was lost in my thoughts, when Malhi asked me, 'Do you know why I have revealed all this to you?' I answered flippantly, 'Because your stomach is so small that you could not hold it all in.' 'Wrong, wrong, wrong!' she yelled like a child. 'I want to know something in exchange for this information,' she said seriously. 'What is that?' I asked worriedly. 'I want to know how Tarru and her clan are sure about the sex of the baby still in the womb of the mother as they always call the baby a boy.' Now it was my turn to laugh and I told the little fishy creature, 'They are djinn not a river fish like you. They can see through their own subtle bodies and know what is happening inside.'

After that conversation, Malhi suddenly departed without saying goodbye to me and I, with some effort, entered the "hiding cave" in the body where I had spent a lot of time when I first entered into the unborn Ajee Shah. I had come to this sanctuary after such a long time that I had to make sure that this was the same place that had given me security from all kinds of other inhabitants in that alien being. My mind was wrestling with many questions and many more concerns. What would happen to me? What would happen to my relationship with Nirva? Would they allow me to attend the marriage ceremony? How would Ajee Shah feel about ending his unique relationship with the djinn princess Tarru? I felt like I would go mad with all these tedious questions when I remembered a quote of Ajee Shah that was "Whatever will be, will be, so don't worry". Somehow that comforted me.

When I had become quite relaxed, a strange thought occurred

to me. Tarru's clan had a great respect for my old benefactress, the Lady Kyia, and she was equally knowledgeable about the inner lives of humans and djinn. If she led the marriage ceremony of Tarru and Ajee Shah, it would be a great honour as well a guarantee that nothing could go wrong during the ceremony. I knew that this would not be an ordinary event as the bride and groom belonged to two species that originated, lived, and went through evolutionary stages, in completely different realms and I was concerned that something might go wrong. Perhaps my worries were coming out of my insecurity about how to deal with the situation. When I had first entered the life of Ajee Shah, I had never thought for a moment that in the human world I would have to deal with djinn. At that point, I had no idea that these two worlds are intermingled to such an extent that even in a single lifetime one could not escape either of them.

Our next date came sooner than my expectations. The minute Ajee Shah and Tarru departed, I excitedly asked Nirva, 'Do you have news for me?' 'What news?' she said, casually. 'Why are you girls so secretive? I have my own spies you know. And then there is great truth in the human saying that no one can conceal love or perfume.' Nirva was still not moved and said, 'I don't have any idea what you are talking about.' Then the breeze helped me and from a nearby garden wafted the penetrating sweet smell of *Raat Ki Rani* flowers, surrounding us both. We both laughed at the same time. Nirva, after a while, blew her breath on my face and asked why I was always so edgy. 'Relax. Time is not running so fast in our djinn world and we have plenty of time to discuss these trivial things. Let us shift to our realm.' At that she embraced me with her full strength and I realised how strong she was. The age difference embarrassed me a little but I said to myself, 'Don't worry, Kabuko, you are still young.'

Nirva told me the whole story with some curious details but the basic storyline was the same as that of Malhi. When I suggested that my benefactress Kiya should lead the ceremony, Nirva suddenly became uncomfortable and tried to avoid eye contact with me. Then two tears ran down her cheeks and she said, 'Kabuko, the great Lady Kiya, the fifth pillar of our dynasty, the master of many realms and many more dimensions is no more with us. She passed away and disappeared into the world of eternal peace and bliss.'

I wanted to cry not with tears but with a penetrating sound of grief that would emerge from my heart and be heard in all eight corners of the world. I was lost and in such dread that everything, including Nirva and myself, became irrelevant to me. Nirva tried her best to console me but she was too young and had not seen enough deaths to give her consoling words the power to heal.

26

A Fated Engagement

In my sad moments I, Kabuko the djinn, always indulged in self-pity and took a subconscious pleasure in that. How could I miss this opportunity? My benefactress Kiya had left me all alone to face an unkind and volatile word, and I was genuinely feeling very insecure and vulnerable. I tried to convince myself that I was now alone and that nobody would ever care for me again. I became fearful that if I did not get true sympathy from the people and spirits around me then who knew what would happen to me. But soon I realised that my negative thoughts were baseless and only the product of my own imagination.

Ajee Shah, Tarru, Nirva, and even most of the animals, entities, and fallen angel spirits living and sharing this dwelling with me had felt and expressed their deepest compassion for me. But some of them had their own different postures, strange ways, and genetically administrated customs to express their sorrowful feelings. For example, one spirit approached me to offer its condolences, and after shaking its body with mine, it started walking upside down on its hands and moving its legs in circles. Then it showed me its hands, now red with the downwards circulation of blood, and put those hands on my face, covering it altogether. Then it made many noises that sounded as if they were coming from the remotest corner of the cosmos. I, not knowing a bit of what and why it was doing all that gimmickry nevertheless accepted its condolences with all my appreciation. In these matters one should always deal with the logic of the heart and not of the mind.

But the biggest solace for me came from Ajee Shah and Tarru. They had postponed their wedding; both leaving it to me to inform them when I was done with mourning and ready for the occasion. They even decided that I would be the best man for the ceremony and it was entirely up to me if I wanted to perform that role in a human costume or in my original djinn form. All this was very comforting for me. It left very positive effects on my whole being.

Along with the great healing power of true affection flowing out of many hearts and the natural process of the time in which layers upon layers of soothing medicinal bandages are neatly and modestly placed on the wounded part of the being, it took only a few weeks to recover my usual composure. I became normal, although from time to time I still had to conceal my real emotions and tears but such residues were not too painful to hide. I declared myself out of crisis and fit to face the normal world with its all unpredictability and random shocks. To prove my condition to others, I even took the lengthy and enjoyable bath that some humans take after a disease or illness. They celebrate their recovery with this water ritual known as a "health bath". Everyone was convinced of my improved spirits.

Soon after that the marriage date, place, and other necessary details were agreed among the elders of Tarru's clan. Many years ago, when Tarru's clan had its last royal wedding, more than three thousand guests were invited from many djinn clans around the world, and for a whole seven days and nights the ceremony had continued with only a few intervals for guests to freshen up and get dressed for the next part of the ceremony. But this time it was quite different, because the princess was not marrying a djinn but a human being. There weren't even any rehearsals and, only the day before the wedding, the master of the ceremony spent a couple of hours with the djinn bride and human groom to explain to them some basic and essential rituals to be performed. It was made clear to the couple that there would be no elaborate rituals to adjust djinn and human time as the master intended and was fully confident that the ceremony would take less than five human hours. During the conversation, I tried, twice, to pay a compliment to the wisdom of that old djinn master but he ignored me. The meeting ended and all three of us, Ajee Shah, Tarru, and I, were content and had no burning questions left.

But something unexpected happened soon after the formal meeting ended. The old djinn master asked Tarru to leave and Ajee Shah to stay. Tarru left without any hesitation as she must have assumed that the master wanted to give some special instruction to Ajee Shah in private. Then the djinn master smiled mysteriously and asked Ajee Shah, 'Do you know who I am?' Ajee Shah, carrying out a search of his memory, answered, 'No sir, not at all. I only met you here for the first time, and, of course, I know that you are leading our wedding rituals.'

'No, we met before, at least a couple of times, if not more. Try to remember. You might recognise me,' he said. Ajee Shah was not much interested in that sort riddling conversation; it had always irritated him. But perhaps out of traditional respect for the elderly, he pretended for a while to stare at the face of the master and think hard about whether he recognised him. 'No, I have no idea when and where we met. I lose.' Ajee Shah declared his defeat so casually, clearly showing that it was not his game that he had lost. The old djinn master went silent for few moments and then said, 'I am the same python who used to appear sometimes in the back room of your house in your native village and your family called me Babaji.'

'Unbelievable! Unbelievable!' Ajee Shah spontaneously repeated the word many times. 'And I am also the one you encountered in the wilderness when you visited your agricultural land. I have been here on this earth for many hundreds of years but now my job is done. Or going to be done. My last assignment is to bond a human groom and a djinn bride who will generate a new phase in the relationship between the two races. The time has come when they must interact with each other with an open heart and cooperate in a manner not known to them before, so that their generations of the present and future will benefit in the new approaching age.' Ajee Shah and I, Kabuko the djinn, both were stunned.

But Ajee being Ajee could not bear his speechlessness and asked a very logical question that could only come into a human brain during that sort of situation. 'But both djinn and humans have engaged in wedded relationships in history. What is new in our marriage that you say it will be a landmark case?' The old djinn laughed and replied, 'Before these relationships were simply mating but this will be the first time that a human male and a djinn female are going to marry in a proper and legally-approved manner with the blessing of their respective ancestors in the other world.' After a pause that was not very comfortable for Ajee Shah, the djinn master continued, 'You are lucky, and Tarru is lucky too, but I am the luckiest one who has been entrusted to lead the ceremony. After this I will leave the surface and enter deep into the Earth where the kingdom of snakes is eagerly waiting for me as predicted by their holy ones for centuries.' Ajee Shah wanted to ask many questions, but before he could open his mouth again, the old djinn master said, 'I can't tell you more. Perhaps I have already told you a little more than I should have.' And he disappeared without saying goodbye. Ajee Shah was not in a mental state to even think about his rude gesture. He was lost in far-fetched thoughts.

The next morning I watched Ajee Shah carefully, and to my surprise, he was completely calm and there were no residues in his mind about the djinn master's mind-blowing revelation. There were no traces of any anxiety regarding the upcoming wedding or about losing the djinn princess of his heart forever after the birth of his first son. He was so calm and serene, as if he were a monk who had years of meditative energy inside him.

As the nearest, if not the dearest, person to him, I could not understand the reason for his composure. I asked and enquired from every source available to me but to no avail. I had come to this human body to get pure human experiences and wisdom but sometimes I wondered how it was that, instead of that, most of the time I seemed to be involved with my own kind. 'Kabuko, that is what they call life,' I consoled myself.

27

Marriage on a Mountaintop

The marriage ceremony started on time and all the guests reached the spot before midnight. They were not many but about a hundred of them, and I, Kabuko the djinn, was apparently the only non-human in the ceremony. All the guests were in their best possible human shape, and most of them, especially the females, were wearing designer clothes that were currently in fashion. I am sure that many boutiques in the country must have lost one or two of their most costly suits and the poor workers must have been blamed for that. Though some guests had arranged their human costumes through more dignified means as they were respectable and a few of them were even the heads of their clans. I guess that all the djinn attending in human shape and clothes was a precondition imposed by the ceremony master for Ajee Shah not to feel alone or alienated. It was a novelty that everyone was enjoying and they freely commented on the design and colours of their stolen and non-stolen dresses. One girl was cheekily telling the other girls that she visited many closed shops during the night time and took human shape and then tried many dresses to select the one that perfectly fit her human body.

On the other hand, Ajee Shah, though he looked dashing in a fitted three-piece suit without a tie, it was not a new one. His father had bought three such suits about a year ago from the market where they sold second-hand western clothes. A crafty and experienced local tailor had altered those suits to the sizes of the father, Ajee and, his older brother. All three suits were fully dry-cleaned before wearing to get rid of any germs from the original foreign owners. I did wonder what Ajee Shah's father would have thought about the suit being worn for his son's wedding to a djinn—but the laws of secrecy amoung her clan meant that Ajee Shah would never be able to tell his family the truth.

As soon as Ajee Shah entered the big marquee, which had especially been brought and put up there for the wedding, many of Tarru's girlfriends encircled him. They started freely touching and hugging the groom, checking the strength of his body, and smelling his human aura with such forwardness that Ajee Shah blushed. I became apprehensive when even the mature male guests looked inquisitively at Ajee Shah and indulged in scanning his thoughts to explore traces of his old memories. That could be dangerous as that sort of memory search sometimes leads to very personal information being divulged. Since I was the only one from the groom's side, it was my moral responsibility to deal with the situation. I scanned the thoughts of Ajee Shah and he was fully and wholly present in the ceremony with no trace of past memories or future projections. That made me comfortable and I started joking with my sweetheart Nirva who was pretending as if we had met for the first time.

The ceremony master was, of course, in human shape, but

either his aged costume or his responsible and tedious role made him look much older if not wiser than he had looked before. I had no idea what his actual age was, but my impression was in comparison to what he looked like at our last meeting. He started the ceremony with a speech that was more like a sermon and talked enigmatically about the beginning of a new era in the relationship between djinn and mankind. The wedding started. The groom and bride both faced north, and with sounds not decipherable to make any sense of and body movements not similar to any known human or djinn dancing gestures, the master started encircling the couple. Nothing was gradual. He began the ritual with full speed and maintained this in a way that only a being blessed with a constant flow of mysterious energy could afford. After every few unexplainable movements the master with his hands slightly pushed Ajee Shah and Tarru the djinn princess to come closer and change the direction they were facing. It did not take long and before the watching guests could get bored with the monotony of the ritual, the wedding couple were facing each other.

Ajee Shah was facing east and Tarru was facing west. At one point their bodies were so close to each other that the heartlessly cold Himalayan breeze could not penetrate in between them. The old master stopped suddenly. He instructed all present, including his two serious-faced assistants, to start taking any intoxication, whether permitted or not. He laughingly said that tonight you were free to forget yourselves and be whatever you wanted to be. 'And hurry up and don't waste any time as you have only hours,' he said joyously.

Everyone, without wasting a moment, started taking the intoxications that they had brought with them. I, Kabuko the djinn, had nothing with me as I was representing a human at the wedding and was not participating as a djinn. Nirva must have been observing me as she quickly, with the speed of a dove escaping a bullet, approached me and gave me three long, djinn-shaped roots to chew. I knew these roots and had had them twice before. Believe me human intoxications, spiritual or otherwise including hemp, cannabis, peyote, ayauasca, *datura*, or snake poison, have no match with djinn intoxications and especially the "stone roots" from the fire in the depths of volcanoes.

Except for the wedding couple, everyone was intoxicated in a short span of time. The two assistants of the master were as high as anyone else but still they performed their duties with all the required care to minute detail. They brought an old crystal goblet, holding it in their hands, and presented it with some style. The master took the goblet and with his own hands put it to the lips of Ajee Shah and Tarru to drink from the same, and when one was finished, the assistants poured more liquid into it and the master handled it the same way. After drinking twice from the goblet full of the finest intoxication, Ajee Shah and Tarru entered into a state that could be called, in human terms, a state of pure excitement. I, Kabuko the djinn, was amazed at how that traditional djinn intoxicating potion had the same effects on a human being. Either it was the power of the moment, filled with love, or the master had magically amended the ingredients and recipe to make it consumable for both.

The couple was enjoying their state, which was obvious from their body language. The master also took his time to imbibe some special substance that he himself had made for the event. Then without disturbing the guests, he took off Tarru's shirt and Ajee Shah's shirt, and with his sun finger rubbed a fragrant liniment in and around their belly buttons and stuck them together. After that, he started from their feet and bound them together with a special kind of silk thread organically and naturally produced and never touched by any djinn or man apart from the ceremony master. With the unifying influence of each round of thread empowered with a different mantra recited by the master, it seemed the two were actually getting closer and closer and closer. After many thousands of rounds, the silk yarn was wrapped around the groom and the bride up to their belly buttons.

They were joined as two beings ready to enter into each other. Then the assistant brought a yellow sheet with lots of red strings attached to it and the master related the history of that piece of fabric. It had belonged to Tarru's royal family and every red string represented a wedding in her family. The master put the sheet on top of the joined couple and beneath it their two bodies and souls were already experiencing the love of a lifetime. He fanned the strings with fast movements of his head from right to left and on occasions up and down. The movements were so magically fast that even I could not look at the master's head for more than a few seconds. He then stopped abruptly, removed the sheet, and asked for guests' attention.

Tarru and Ajee Shah at one glance looked like a single entity and at the next a loving couple. There was clapping and all sorts of hoo-ha. The master or Babaji or whoever he was at that moment, took it as appreciation for his hard work at joining the two entirely different souls. I, Kabuko the djinn, was observing every move of the master and was impressed at how he gave a human touch to every djinn wedding ritual and made it possible and bearable for Ajee Shah, a man made out of clay and a drop of semen.

After a while the master unwound the couple by carefully uncoiling the silk thread down their waists and gave a chunk of thread to one of his assistants for safekeeping. He gave a special drink to the couple to hold in their hands together and enhance their love intoxication. He made a final sound, which was too loud to bear, and all the djinn guests and the only man present their closed their ears to escape the velocity of its echo. The sound was a combination of hissing, bird singing, human calling, and perhaps many other unknown species known only to the master or an old python who could change shape and destinies.

Ajee Shah and Tarru were lawfully declared husband and wife.

28

A Predicted Regret

Two years passed. Tarru, the djinn queen, had a very handsome son from a man of the highest Muslim caste.

This happened only a few weeks ago, and, against all odds, there was no problem for a first-time djinn mother to deliver a baby created by a djinn and human fusion. These sorts of births are not unique but are obviously rare and predictably entail difficulties. Humans are more vulnerable than djinn. Their females, when having a djinn's child, often suffer mysterious complications, and, I am not very sure, but perhaps, their social situation and psychological frame of mind is to be blamed. I know this from my only experience of when I once had casual sex with a newly-wedded village girl. It was not my fault as the girl's husband had left her only a week after their marriage. He was a soldier in the British Indian army, and his unit had been ordered to move to a new front in the middle of war. He had no choice but to leave his bride alone to deal with the most maddening sexual urge introduced by him in only three nights. The virgin girl, when married, had, initially, not enjoyed sex due to her husband's robust size. Though before marriage she had heard a lot of stories and had had many interesting and eye-opening lessons from friends and experienced female relatives, yet still on her first night she just could not believe that her virginal capacity could ever entertain such a male organ. But during the fourth night, after a lot of bloodshed and suffering untold pain, she was convinced that nature is cleverer than mankind. The last three nights were progressively more enjoyable as the pain became more and more sweet.

After the sudden departure of her husband, the young girl, newly introduced to sexual pleasures, tried many ways to satisfy her sexual urges but she failed to acquire any real remedy. She was in torment when I, Kabuko the djinn, saw her by chance in a sugar cane field, squatting on the ground with her baggy trousers down. I took a chance, as any seducer in the world never wants to miss an opportunity, and appeared before her as an ordinary villager using the same field for the same purpose of relieving one's body waste. She looked at me as if I were a God-sent angel who had been sent to this earth just to alleviate her trouble. She only asked me one question in a meek voice, 'Which village do you belong to?' I answered with full confidence that I was a traveller and belonged to a far-off district. Next, she only said, 'Then what you are waiting for? The pearl is on the ground and do not waste any time to have it.'

So I had great sex with her and enjoyed it a lot. The only disturbance was when her friends finished their business and started calling her to hurry up. As a good will gesture, I gave her a long kiss and she panicked. 'Who are you?' she asked. I repeated the same storyline that I was a villager from another district but she did not believe me. She said, 'No one kisses like that in the whole area. Our males are always more interested in fucking and they never make love to anyone, even their beloveds for whom sometimes they have to give their lives. If you are not from the djinn world you are very strange.' I was amazed at her rustic observation. I had a small black stone in my pocket. I put it in my mouth and chewed it for a while so that it would absorb "me" in its core. Then I gave it to her and said, 'Whenever you need me most, chew this stone and I will somehow know and come.' She was an impossible woman. She was not scared at all and took the stone without saying thanks. I disappeared into the other side of the sugarcane field and watched her from a vantage point. She was so happy that until now I have never seen a girl so blissful just after a sexual session with an unknown male.

It was exactly six months after that lovely encounter that she called me to the same field with no sugarcane plants but the mustard seed plants blowing their yellow colour with an exuberant smell. She was pregnant and that was visible by her tummy. She was convinced that she was carrying my baby and told me that she was in real trouble as her body was refusing to accept an alien off-shoot. She was in a lot of pain and with complaints not related to human pregnancy. I felt guilty and asked her to meet me at the same spot after three days. I had heard of a djinn woman who had once given birth to a human child in the past and faced many problems, but I did not know her personally. After a lot of effort I located her and plainly admitted my misdemeanour and asked for help. She sympathised with me and appreciated my concern and that I was taking responsibility for my act. Finally, she gave me a powder made of different herbs and minerals along with the simple instruction of it usage. But in return for those herb and mineral powder, she took one dose of my semen from me, without any physical contact. She explained, without my asking, that she would use it for the benefit of other people in dire need and I did not bother to enquire any further, as that was no concern of mine. The soldier's wife, after using that powder, became very comfortable. I knew that she had given birth to my baby but I have never seen my baby girl and the mother never called me again. Perhaps, she lost my black stone.

Tarru, the djinn queen, had had no such hang-ups. The child was born out of her womb just like a pure djinn child. Ajee Shah had already visited Tarru and his son twice and took his son in his lap for hours. The elders of Tarru's clan had not yet decided the exact date when the final and last meeting between the couple would take place; to seal the marriage agreement by fulfilling the most undesirable and perhaps unworthy condition of permanently separating a loving couple. I, Kabuko the djinn, had smelt that they were secretly doing preparations and could bet, just on the basis of simply being a djinn, that the last meeting ceremony would also be conducted by the same old djinn master, known to Ajee Shah as Babaji, the python snake who lived in the darkest room of his Badi Ma's village home.

After the marriage, the frequency of our love-making trips was more or less the same. We would always go during the dark of night and both Tarru and Nirva always came to collect us. This arrangement was initially made as Ajee Shah being a man could not fly and Tarru had to hug him and take him to a love spot of her own choice hundreds of miles away. After the marriage, I offered my services but she flatly refused as she did not want me to come near to their love making place. She was paranoid but knowing her family's sad history no one could blame her for that. But despite all her secrecy, I happened to know that after the marriage she always took Ajee Shah to her own home and entertained him in that special protected place we djinn make for newly-married couples. I could easily read the mind of Ajee Shah to have access to this sort of information, and Tarru knew it. But she did not mind me having that second-hand information. I believed that now after such a long time and going through such an exceptional relationship, Tarru had a lot of faith in me and I am sure that I deserved it as I had earned it.

I often thought with some concern that after the final breakup of Ajee Shah and Tarru what would happen to my love affair with Nirva, as I was so much involved that I could not think of myself without her. Women, whether belonging to djinn or mankind, have some very mysterious inclination to that pragmatism which the male easily ignores and then suffers from this ignorant lethargy. Whenever Nirva and I discussed the future of our relationship, she took it very easy. Our conversation on this subject always ended on her hopeful note, 'When the time will come we will see to it.' In one of our meetings, soon after the birth of Ajee Shah's son, I said to Nirva, 'Why don't we make our relationship permanent and official?' 'Are you proposing to me?' she laughingly asked. 'Yes of course,' I answered.

She became lost in her thoughts and I also shut my mouth. I did not want to disturb her as I could feel that she was seriously thinking about it. 'I will answer you when we meet again and, Kabuko, no more conversation on this subject now.' She ordered me like a dominating wife and that made my day. I was sure that she wanted to discuss it with her friend Tarru and that they would come to a positive, affirmative conclusion.

After only a week, for the very first time, she came alone in the middle of the night and called me out. Ajee Shah was in a deep sleep and I was drowsy too. 'Don't be surprised,' she said in a low voice, 'I intentionally came alone. This matter is between me and you and no one should interfere in that. We must decide our future and decide it in complete freedom.' Her tone and words made me fully awake and I was so mindful and attentive that she smiled and said, 'Kabuko, relax' and kissed me. Her kiss was pleasantly prolonged. Then she took a deep breath and said, 'I am ready to marry you but I have only one condition, only one. I do not ask any more than that.' 'Yes, I know, I have to conceal my age and pretend to be so much younger that I am only few years older than you. So that your friends won't tease you that you have married an old man,' I jokingly said. She became serious. 'Kabuko, please do not joke. You do not have to conceal your age. I have the courage to face and rebut that silly crowd. My condition is very simple and straightforward. You have to leave Ajee Shah forever and settle with me, either within my clan or we will go and make our place in your clan or anywhere that suits you. In any case I am fully ready to face our future world. The decision will be yours.'

I, Kabuko the djinn, had never thought in my dreams that Nirva would come with that condition. Though I could understand the rationale and the expectations behind this condition, I was just not ready to think about it. I devoted many precious years of my life, more or less impeccably, to have a human experience and now when I felt that mature experience was on its way, how could I leave Ajee Shah and abandon my mission? That was impossible. I expressed myself with all the honesty I could muster, and said, 'My very dear Nirva, you know that is not possible for me.' Tears came out of my eyes and I did not even try to conceal them. She was calm, as if she had been expecting this answer. She said that the old wizard of their family had told her that I would refuse but had also predicted that I would regret my decision for a long time to come.

'Yes, I know I will regret it,' I said to her, 'but that is beyond my control. This is my destiny.' She said, 'I do not want to dishearten you and sound selfish, but I must warn you that our wizard has seen a big turning point in your life and your destiny will throw you on a completely new path and take you in a direction that was never in your mind. Though I am not superstitious, I believe my clan's wizard as he has never said anything irresponsible or mumbo jumbo. He has always been up to the mark.' Then after a haunting silence Nirva said, 'Kabuko, let us enjoy whatever time we have left,' and hugged me with the full force of her djinn energy. Soon we left the mundane world of negotiations and conditions and entered into the world of love, free of all foreboding and all mental and physical boundaries.

These were not the only big events to happen in the lives of Ajee Shah and me, Kabuko the djinn. Tahir Zaman, the editor, publisher, and proprietor of the weekly newspaper, passed away after being ill for six months. In those six months he hardly visited his office and everything was done by Ajee Shah. Ajee Shah would work very hard all day and during the evening visit Tahir Zaman at his home to take day-to-day instructions.

Then one day Tahir Zaman declared that he was on his last legs and could be called at any day to the other world. He said that he had no regrets as he had already fulfilled all the responsibilities in his life but he was not happy that there was no one in his immediate family with any aptitude or capability to run his newspaper after him. He was very impressed with the performance and honesty of Ajee Shah and decided to transfer the ownership of his paper to him and the property of the newspaper, which was basically an office building in a good location, to his only son who ran a petrol pump on the main GT Road. He went in his fragile condition to many offices in the district court many times and used all his old contacts to fulfil all the tedious official requirements. Only three weeks before his death, the paper's print line was changed to Ajee Shah's name and the property to his son's name. He came to office with a box of local sweets and celebrated the occasion. After that he was virtually bed-ridden and then one morning passed away peacefully. His funeral was a big one and hundreds of people belonging to many different areas of life attended it. Now Ajee Shah had more responsibilities as a manager than as a journalist. But soon he hired a part-timer, who worked during the day in a local school as a clerk. Ajee Shah noticed with a smile that he could no longer smell the ink odour from freshly litho-printed newspaper. He realised how unknowingly one gets used to these smells.

Bao Lohar now came only after many weeks and months to his shop which was now wholly and efficiently run by his so-called nephew. He was always in his long red cloak but most surprisingly there were no signs of any old age on his face and feet, the only parts that were visible. Sometimes he even looked in much better shape and a little younger than his previous appearance. Now he even smiled more and that too without any apparent reason.

On every visit Ajee Shah and Bao Lohar spent a lot of time together. During one such meeting they went out to nearby fields and there they sat down under an old tree. Bao took out from his side pocket the two small balls and showed them to Ajee. They were the same balls that had originally belonged to Ajee Shah's brother Karam Shah but their colour had changed and they did not look at all silvery. They had turned into a metallic red or a brackish red. One was of the same round shape but the other was triangular with roundness on all the corners. Bao Lohar explained to Ajee Shah that these balls had almost turned perfect and with his years of hard work, one ball had taken its individual triangular shape and had gathered around itself the roundness of five layers of the relevant dimension conducive to the object. 'Now it is a matter of only a couple of weeks and then with the help of these two balls you can invoke your *hamzad* without any effort on your part,' said Bao, 'and thus I will fulfil my promise to you and to your late brother Karam Shah.' Ajee Shah asked why one of the balls had turned triangular. Bao tried to make him understand but he used a very different type of vocabulary and terminology.

What I, Kabuko the djinn, could extract from that conversation was that there are two basic shapes—round and triangular—that are relevant to the occult or mystical work to invoke the double. Although there are many other sub shapes, those two represent the whole energy melodrama going on in our immediate cosmos. Ajee Shah spontaneously asked how big our immediate cosmos is. And Bao Lohar smiled and stretched both his arms and said, 'This big.' Then he tried to be serious but the smile still did not leave his face. He told Ajee Shah that no ordinary human being or djinn could even grasp the vastness of the immediate cosmos. 'You can ask Kabuko whether he can imagine the vastness?' I was a little afraid of Bao Lohar and his mysterious powers, so I answered out of respect, 'No, sir, I have no idea whatsoever.' Bao laughed. 'See, even this fire being does not know.' And then Bao Lohar changed the subject for no justifiable reason. I was curious as to why he always abruptly, and tactlessly, left his discourse unfinished on these subjects. It sometimes made me nervous as I thought that perhaps it was because of my presence among the two humans.

One day, to my surprise, at one of these meetings, Bao Lohar elaborated further and, as far as I could judge, he conversed to the end. I remembered that Bao told Ajee that ordinary folk always confuse the *hamzad* double with a djinn. Obviously the djinn are a separate species and the human double is one's own being, belonging to a corresponding dimension with multiple powers and mysterious accesses. According to Bao Lohar, the confusion stemmed from the fact that the *hamzad* could also perform many wonders similar to the djinn. When people saw those spirit workers, who had invoked their double, and others, who had access to a djinn's services exhibiting the same sort of wonders, they confused the djinn with the *hamzad*. Bao, in his own weird way, convinced Ajee Shah that successfully invoking his own double would multiply his mundane and spiritual powers and his whole life would become much easier as many of his impossible jobs could be easily performed by his very own self, his *hamzad*.

At last, Ajee Shah was convinced and ready to receive his gift from Bao Lohar to invoke his double in return for his brother Karam Shah's two magical balls. The deal was agreed and sealed. The only witness was I, Kabuko the djinn, whom no court of law in the human domain would ever recognise as a witness as we the djinn do not exist.

29

The Realm of The Double

It was on a Thursday, in the late afternoon, that Bao Lohar, Ajee Shah, and I, Kabuko the djinn, reached the dwelling of Sain Sidho deep in the woods. The ritual of preparing the hemp drink was at its peak and everybody was quietly excited as they awaited the holy intoxication. Sain Sidho gave a big and somewhat intriguing smile at seeing us and jokingly said to Bao Lohar, 'At last you have caught the child in your net. You iron monger, you are as stubborn as iron. You have increased my responsibilities. I already have enough to take care of. However, now you have brought him here so I'll have to do something.'

The dervish's welcoming remarks clearly revealed that he had to play an essential part in invoking the double of Ajee Shah and that some sort of arrangement had already been settled between Bao Lohar and Sain Sidho. Bao Lohar knew the deeper meaning behind dervish's words and took it as if he were not complaining but expressing his gratitude for bringing Ajee Shah into his fold. Bao replied in the same way, 'Sain ji, then throw water on your fire. It is not me but the flames of your fire that attract these kinds of souls to you. Do not blame me. Blame your fire.' The dervish laughed loudly, and his laughter danced with the rhythmic jingling of the bells that were attached to the hemp-preparing wooden staff. It made the atmosphere somewhat festive. As the imbibing time was getting nearer and nearer, the circle of *bhang* drinkers around the dervish was getting larger and larger.

Ajee Shah took three full bowls of *bhang* that evening but was still on his feet. Then the dervish did something that no one was expecting. He asked one of his followers to bring a *lungoot*, a piece of cloth worn, usually, by wrestlers, between their legs to conceal their genitals. The man brought a black *lungoot* and the dervish gave it to Ajee Shah and ordered him to go to the nearby woods and change into this. Ajee Shah took the *lungoot*, and had no problem with wearing one but pointed out a practical problem. 'Sain ji, I do not know how to tie a *lungoot*. My father only taught me to knot ties.' The dervish instructed another of his aides to go with Ajee Shah and show him how to wear and knot the cloth. The man who was instructed to go with Ajee Shah was in his early fifties and was so intoxicated with the hemp drink that he took quite some time to stand up. When finally he did stand up and accompany Ajee Shah towards the woods, he did not walk normally but slithered like a snake. Ajee Shah had no problem with walking straight but he preferred to follow him in the same way and tried to copy his footsteps.

Only few yards away, with the dervish's circle still in sight and the sounds of the gathering still audible, the man stopped and announced, 'I can't go any further.' He then addressed Ajee Shah in a harsh tone, 'You are a male, aren't you? Then why are we are going into the woods in the middle of night? A male has no shame from other males. Take off your clothes and I will show you how to knot a *lungoot*.' If that had happened a few days back, Ajee Shah would definitely have headbutted the obnoxious man, if not on the face then definitely on his chest. But now the magic of Tarru had changed him. He silently, with some embarrassment, started taking off his clothes and became naked. Then the man knotted the lungoot around his groin. When they came back, the dervish looked at him, laughed, and said, 'You look marvellous in this uniform.' Ajee Shah blushed.

The dervish, with his own hands, cleared the ground in front of his fire and made sure that there was no stone, wood, or anything else that would even slightly hurt the naked body. He took more time and care than the man who had knotted the *lungoot*. Then Sain Sidho instructed Ajee Shah to lie down on the ground that he had prepared for him, directly in front of his fire. He called Bao Lohar to sit near Ajee. After that, he took a handful of ash from the edge of his fire and started rubbing the ash on Ajee Shah's feet, first right then left. Then in the same order he rubbed the ash on every part of the body, including his face and head, but left a thin line between the left and right side of the body that clearly divided the body into two. Then the dervish took a full bowl of the hemp drink and started reciting some mantras in a low voice. Ajee Shah could make out that the mantras were in an old Indian language, like Dakani, as some words were very familiar to him. After fifteen minutes or so the dervish gave a long sigh of relief and declared that his initial job was over. He took the right hand of Ajee Shah and handed him over to Bao Lohar, and said, 'Now take him along and show him his *hamzad* and see what he says. Although he is now fully protected, you should still be very vigilant and careful. You know these outer things that belong to other dimensions Bao, don't you? They are really unpredictable. Do not panic in any situation as I am here watching all the time.' Now Ajee Shah, in spite of his new composure, became a little mystified but he was not fearful at all.

Bao Lohar held Ajee Shah's right hand and his tight grip showed his anxiety, as if he was not sure of himself. Ajee Shah stood up and they both walked towards dense woods; with each step forward Bao Lohar's grip loosened and, after a few yards, Bao Lohar was just loosely holding Ajee Shah's hand. They walked in the darkness for half an hour or so and then reached a clearing in the middle of woods. Bao Lohar stopped and let go of Ajee Shah's hand. He picked up a dried branch and with it drew a big circle on the ground and placed Ajee Shah in the middle of it. He instructed Ajee Shah to sit down on the ground and to keep his eyes open. Then, to my utter surprise, Bao Lohar ordered me directly, 'O Kabuko, the son of fire, come out of Ajee Shah and do not leave any of your residues in him.' I obeyed his order and gathered myself together as much as I could and came out. 'Okay now, sit on the left of Ajee Shah in the same way as he is sitting.' I sat down and made myself comfortable, although Ajee Shah and I were not used to sitting on the ground. Then Bao Lohar, with his hands, scanned Ajee Shah's whole body to make sure that there were no djinn parts left within him. 'Well done, Kabuko,' he said, 'you are now fully out.' Then, without wasting any time, Bao sat down on the right side of Ajee Shah and took out the two silvery balls from his side pocket. He handed over those small balls to Ajee Shah. This time the balls were very warm. Then Bao Lohar explained to Ajee Shah, 'Now these balls are fully active. I, with the help and blessing of the dervish, have done much work on these balls and completed the task that your brother, God bless his soul, could not finish in his life. These balls will bring to you your *hamzad* but you have to negotiate with your double by yourself. Do not agree to any of his conditions and always insist on invoking him unconditionally.' Then Bao Lohar took the balls from Ajee Shah and gave him back the first ball to hold in his left hand and the second in his right one. He explained that although the balls looked alike, they were very different from each other and represented the two opposite dimensions of the cosmos. 'Now be ready to experience magic that neither of you will ever have dreamt of.'

The last sentence of Bao Lohar said caused a cold wave to go down Ajee Shah's spinal cord but then he smiled and thought, 'Bao Lohar has no idea what my djinn wife Tarru had already shown me'. Suddenly Ajee Shah and I were both plunged into a silence that didn't even have the "sound of silence". We felt as if the whole universe was still and utterly quiet. Ajee Shah had experienced silence before but that had been different as it had a constant low vibrating sound as if of many grasshoppers singing together. He concluded in awe, that this silence was falling on him from another world—alien, mute, and impersonal. Ajee Shah became so apprehensive that he moved a little bit towards Bao in the circle, the boundary of which he could not witness but only roughly imagine. Ajee Shah's slight movement panicked Bao Lohar and he, for the first time ever, addressed Ajee Shah in a very strict tone, 'Don't you dare move! Your slightest movement could ruin everything.' Ajee Shah was not offended by the tone but became a little scared of the unforeseen. He didn't know what to expect in that haunting silence. Then Bao Lohar, with the same dried branch, made some doodles on the ground between them two while reciting something in a strange language that Ajee Shah had never heard before.

Bao Lohar was trying very hard to create some melody or at least some rhythm in his recitation but was failing miserably as three empty tooth spaces in his mouth were playing havoc with him. But until the end, he did try his best, ignoring his handicap. When the recitation ended, he took a deep breath and asked Ajee Shah to throw both balls at once with full force towards the sky. Ajee Shah did it, and Bao Lohar shouted out, addressing the magical balls, 'Now you are on your own. Do what you are supposed to do.' For quite some time nothing happened apart from the silence deepening. Then Ajee Shah realised that the balls that had been thrown up hadn't returned to the ground. That realisation inflicted an uncomfortable sensation in his body. He became serious. Serious and still like a dead person, who was still very much alive on a mysterious periphery. He waited in that state. I, Kabuko the djinn, was too excited and was looking forward to experiencing some unseen wonders, but I knew for sure that whatever happened would have nothing intended for me. I was a third party in the whole scenario, just taking a free ride. But still I was hoping for something more spectacular than our Tarru's magic.

Some time later the balls still hadn't come back but a shining red light started coming from everywhere. It was focused exactly in the circle. It eventually surrounded the whole circle and Ajee Shah, Bao Lohar, me, the ground under us, and the space over us, all became red. Now the red light made the circle clearly visible and showed up the spot's defined boundaries. Then the light increased and a time came when Ajee Shah and Bao Lohar both, exactly at the same moment, closed their eyes as they could no longer bear the scorching shine of the red light. From that point whatever they saw was through their closed eyes and in the background of utter silence. But I, Kabuko the djinn, never closed my eyes as the bright light was posing no problem from my vantage point—the left side of Ajee Shah. After a while, I noticed that the light was penetrating the body of Ajee Shah and the animal and other tiny spirits started moving around to escape the light. Then a sad thing happened and all the spirits inside Ajee's body, including the very small ones, fainted one by one. I, Kabuko the djinn, became upset. Although I was not in the body, and therefore was out of danger, I feared that the magical red light would eventually kill all my former dwelling companions. But then, to my pleasant surprise, the inner scene changed in a spilt second and now all the spirits were happy and enjoying the red atmosphere inside. They were behaving as if they were taking a bath in the light and making themselves clean to participate in a holy ceremony. All that happened only for a few minutes but half my life force was consumed by my fright of the unexpected. Then a very big parrot-like bird came from the sky and landed in front of Ajee Shah. Its feathers were red and green, but because of the shining red light the green colour was not dominant. It was overshadowed by the red. The parrot's beak was jet black and so smooth and shiny that it was as if it had been made for sliding. It rubbed its beak on Ajee Shah's forehead. Then it nodded its head many times. It didn't open its mouth but asked in the shrill voice of talking parrots, 'Are you ready to go?' Bao Lohar immediately put his index finger on his mouth which Ajee Shah saw in the brightness of the light, even with his eyes closed, and understood his instruction to say nothing. If Bao had not instructed him, even then Ajee Shah had no intention of answering the parrot as he had left everything to Bao Lohar. The big parrot repeated his question three times and then nodded so vigorously that his beak touched the lowest part of its chest. Then he moved his head around to look at the surroundings and nodded once again in agreement. The parrot closed his eyes as if in contemplation and then asked, 'So it means you are ready?' Bao Lohar nodded in reply. 'Sit on my back.' This time the parrot sounded like he was giving an order. Ajee Shah and Bao Lohar and I stood up slowly and over the tail of that parrot, or whatever he was, we climbed onto the back and lay down on our stomachs. The parrot left the earth towards the sky in a manner unlike any flying bird as he did not run along the ground to take off and nor did he spread his wings. He was flying towards North and going speedily towards sky but without moving his wings or apparently using any force of his body. I, Kabuko the djinn, was never afraid of falling and had no idea of what that human fear felt like but I noticed with surprise that Ajee Shah also had no fear of falling down even though he and Bao Lohar were not holding anything to ensure themselves of their safety.

After a time, that I could not even roughly guess, I suddenly realised that it was as if the parrot had crossed some unseen barrier and time had instantly changed. I knew that Ajee Shah also perceived the change but did not care about it as he was deeply enjoying his flight. This time change happened at least five times and every time it was different. At times it felt as if time was speeding up to become unbelievably fast and after another barrier it became so slow that I imagined that it would take a million years to travel a mile. Another more alarming phenomenon was that I, Kabuko the djinn, was slipping deep into my own being. A shocking thought passed through my mind that as the parrot, along with Ajee Shah and Bao Lohar, was going up and up, I was going deeper and deeper. After the third barrier crossing, it became clear to me that I had slipped into depths of my being of which I had been completely unaware.

Before I could make some sense of this new deep atmosphere, I noticed that I had company. She was a spirit, born naturally with me, and had always had a ready smile on her face. She was smiling now and came very close to me. She said in a polite voice, 'Kabuko, do not wonder. Believe me these depths were never there. These have been freshly created by this mysterious journey upwards somewhere.'

I asked her, 'Are you sure?' and she just smiled in the way one does at a child asking a silly question. The parrot stopped and I heard Bao Lohar asking Ajee Shah in a very low voice to open his eyes. He took his time to open them. Then the parrot very slowly stood up on his two feet and all three of us slipped down to the ground. We were sitting in the same circle and in the same order. Then I realised that it was not the same circle and even the ground was made of some other material. All around us was a shimmering fog. Suddenly I heard Bao Lohar giving instruction to Ajee Shah to cup his hands as the balls would be coming back at any moment. He immediately cupped his hands and the balls landed within them. Bao gave another instruction, 'Now hold these balls tightly in both your hands and wait for your *hamzad* to appear in front of you. And remember not to agree to any of its conditions. Insist on invoking it unconditionally.'

For a long time nothing happened but we were in a state as if we were not waiting for anything. Then in the dense fog-like atmosphere, a shadowy body appeared in front of Ajee Shah and became denser and denser and made itself quite visible. To me it seemed somewhat familiar but then I shunned this thought and reminded myself that we are in a magical world where anything is possible. Suddenly Bao Lohar, in a very concerned tone, asked the entity, 'Who are you?' He kept hysterically repeating his question until a telepathically delivered answer struck us. 'I am Kabuko. I belong to this world.' Bao Lohar then asked, in a clear and confident voice, 'But why, the double of Kabuko, have you appeared before us? We didn't call you. We didn't ask for you. Our waiting is not for a djinn double but the human double belonging to Ajee Shah. What brought you here?' The entity became so visible now that the features of its body and face were quite recognisable. I, Kabuko the djinn, could see some similarities with me but at the same it could have been an illusion. I was not sure of anything at that moment. I felt as though I were under some magical spell. The entity again telepathically answered, 'You are in a parallel world to your own but not in the human part of this world. This is the djinn sphere and the human realm is much above and beyond. Djinn never invoke their doubles, only humans are involved in this business. As my earthly double Kabuko was a part of Ajee Shah, this mishap has happened but now you have to accept this as at it is. You have invoked me and now I will become an integral part of Ajee Shah until his last breath on the earthly plane.' Ajee Shah looked calm but Bao Lohar was visibly disturbed by the answer. Then Bao Lohar nervously asked. 'What if we do not accept you?' This time the answer came verbally and all three of us could clearly see the movements of its lips as now it had fully materialised itself. It was me. Definitely me. My own double, without any doubt. 'You are now under the domain of the parallel world and here only its rules apply. Here the parallel world by itself decides everything and no outside will is allowed to interfere in all matters belonging to its domain. Once invoked, now I can not go back even if I wish to. This is now my destiny.'

Bao Lohar in his confusion called the parrot, but there was no sign of it, and my double was adamantly standing in front of Ajee Shah. Then we heard a voice that was loud but mixed with many types of weird sounds. It was Sain Sidho's voice. 'Let him come. Now we can't do anything about it. Let him come. Let him come.' Bao Lohar heaved a sigh and bowed his head and so did Ajee Shah. And I, Kabuko the djinn, followed them without thinking whether I was supposed to do that or not. My double instantly dematerialised itself and turned into a fog like substance with a silver lining that separated it from the foggy atmosphere. Then it entered the body of Ajee Shah through his belly button and merged with him. Ajee Shah shrugged for a moment but then remained stable. Bao Lohar watched Ajee Shah with full concentration, and I, too, looked at him with interest.

Ajee Shah suddenly stood up and so did Bao Lohar and myself, as if we knew that now he had to lead us. While standing, he raised both of his hands still holding those two magical balls and like a king making a proclamation announced;

> '*I, Ejaz Shah, son of Adam, have now become a djinn,*
> *a son of fire.*
> *I am a human djinn and I will remain so as long as*
> *I am on the earth plane.*'

Then he opened his hands and, dropping the magical balls, ordered, 'Go back to where you originally belong!' I saw the balls drop down and disappear into an abyss. Then Ajee Shah put his arm around my waist and the other around Bao Lohar and embraced us with an enthusiasm that lifted us up into the air with such ease as though we were weightless and hollow. He asked us to close our eyes and declared that we were going back to where we all presently belong.

Ajee Shah started flying and soon we crossed the same plane where I again felt the same changes of time and atmosphere as I had noticed on our journey on the back of the parrot. At last we landed at the same spot in the woods and exactly in the same circle that was made by Bao Lohar with the stick. We opened our eyes along with Ajee Shah. I sensed that it was the same time at which we had started our journey. Ajee Shah read my thought and I heard him say, 'Kabuko, it is the same time but it is not the same night. Seven days have passed.'

I, Kabuko the djinn, could now believe anything! Anything at all! Our world is very mysterious and we should believe in our world.

30

The Djinn's Eviction

Although our journey to the parallel world had not accomplished the precise objective of invoking Ajee Shah's double, I, Kabuko the djinn, was mystified and very much intrigued to know that I also had a double and that now we both were on this earthly plane. While travelling down to earth, many thoughts came to my mind about my future relationship with that alien entity supposedly belonging to me but then I comprehended that it was too early to make any assumptions. I had not yet been introduced to my double nor had I even spoken a word to him. Believing entails side effects; even if one believes in oneself.

After we landed, the moment I accepted the notion that I had spent a whole week outside my world without eating or drinking, I became devoid of energy, perhaps spiritually still exalted but physically exhausted. We were walking in the woods and Bao Lohar was leading, I could see he was a sad man. We were making our way to Sain Sidho's dwelling. I felt so tired that I thought it would be a good idea to enter into the body of Ajee Shah and have some rest to get rid of my fatigue. I tried to enter his body but to my shock, every possible entry point to the body was blocked. It had never happened before and I had no idea why it was happening now. After trying many times, I again started following Ajee Shah on foot and comforted myself that this must be the residual effects of the parallel world and that soon Ajee Shah would come out of the spell and everything would be normal again. But my heart was not ready to accept this simple explanation and was still filled with many doubts and much fear.

When we reached the dwelling, everyone except Sain Sidho was sleeping. Sain was waiting for us and was sitting at his usual place on the ground near to his fire place. He only answered our customary greetings and with a gesture of his hand asked us to sit near the fire facing him. We sat down silently. Sain ji, at intervals, keenly observed Ajee Shah and did not once look at Bao Lohar or me. Then he called one of his favourite disciples, who was sleeping nearby, and asked him to bring the clothes of Ajee Shah. The man went in the mud hut and brought out the clothes. Sain ji, while holding the clothes, asked Ajee Shah to take off the *lungoot* in front of him. Ajee Shah without any hesitation or shame took off the *lungoot* and gave it to him, who then threw it into the fire. The cloth instantly started burning just like dried wood and made such a fire-light that Ajee Shah's whole naked body was illuminated. Its burning created a strong unknown smell that put all the thoughts present in my mind to anarchic flight. I was unable to concentrate because of this havoc and believed that the same was happening to the others. After some time the intensity of the smell lessened and so did the chaos it had created. I noticed that Ajee Shah's glowing aura was so spread out that it enveloped not only me and Bao Lohar but Sain Sidho sitting on the other side of fire as well. The dervish looked at Ajee Shah and asked him to turn around and scanned his back with his eyes. He particularly looked at his groin area from the front and the back. He became relaxed and gave Ajee Shah his clothes to wear there and then. Sain ji asked the same man to bring a special drink that he had made with some herbs and minerals and give one bowl to each of us. That herbal drink made me suddenly so energetic that all my tiredness disappeared. It also changed the mood of Bao Lohar and now he returned to his normal self. Ajee Shah was calm and content with a sense of attainment. After a while, Sain Sidho suggested that we all take rest, not under the open sky but in his mud hut, and told his disciple to give us thin blankets to cover ourselves with. He instructed us to sleep with our bodies covered from head to toe. Though I, Kabuko the djinn, was in human form, Sain Sidho's disciple somehow knew that I was a djinn and was wary of me. He tried to make special and more comfortable sleeping arrangements for me.

We slept and slept and slept. We woke up together with only a difference of two to three minutes. We slept more than thirty hours as it was the next early morning and people at the dwelling were cleaning their teeth with small sticks of the Acacia tree called *muswak*. Under the strict instruction of Sain Sidho, the same disciple asked us to stay in the mud hut and not wash our mouths or faces. He immediately served us food that was not normally served for breakfast in that part of world. There were two dishes of red meat and warm bread freshly baked in a small clay oven built in the corner of Sain Sidho's dwelling. I was amazed to see the quantity of curry and bread. It was enough for a dozen people with healthy appetites. I asked myself what was happening here but no answer came from anywhere.

Ajee Shah ate thirty-two breads and his big bowl was filled at least nine times with the meat curry. I lived with the man and had never seen him eat more than two breads at a time. Bao Lohar consumed at least twenty breads with seven bowls full of curry. I, Kabuko the djinn, only ate three breads with one bowl of curry and my tummy was full. I could not believe my eyes and thought perhaps we were still in a magical world. But then the serving disciple announced that his guru was great and knew our hunger. That was why he had ordered a big fat goat to be slaughtered. The goat had been presented to him a couple of days ago by two strangers whose speaking style was so different, they must have come from some far away place. He told us that they just presented the goat to Sain Sidho and, without eating or drinking anything, went away. Strangely, Sain had not even asked them to stay or have something to eat or drink. When we finished our heaviest breakfast ever, the disciple conveyed the final massage of Sain Sidho in such an explicit way as if he was reading a court order. 'Do not wash your hands, mouth, or any part of your body for another two hours. Immediately leave the dwelling and never come back unless Sain Sidho calls you and invites you here by his own grace. I will accompany you to the end of the woods to where the river is, and if in our journey someone or something should call you, don't look back and ignore it completely.' Bao Lohar asked him to repeat all the instructions again so that everyone could remember it carefully. The man, without showing any annoyance, repeated the instructions. We stood up and started walking towards the river following the disciple. There were no unusual sounds in the woods and no one called us from behind. But, as we were approaching the river, I, Kabuko the djinn, heard a weird sound as if a bird was calling his mate and that sound filled my heart with sadness. I looked at Ajee Shah and Bao Lohar but both were just walking as if they had not heard anything. Reaching the river the man said goodbye and turned back and disappeared into the woods.

In the middle of the next night, when Ajee Shah was sleeping in his bedroom, I again tried to enter into his body. This time, a strange energy coming out of his body pushed me away with a force that even a djinn could not meet head-on. It was not only challenging but also intimidating. I did not give up and tried at least a dozen times more but every time the pushing power of that strange energy was more and more forceful. I said to myself, 'Kabuko, you are in real trouble'.

It was at that precise point when I remembered my darling Nirva's words when she had told me the predication of her clan's wizard about my changing destiny and that made me more uncomfortable. I sat down in a corner of Ajee Shah's bedroom in a confused state of mind. An idea came to me that I should read the thoughts of the sleeping Ajee Shah as that might give me some clue as to what was really happening inside him. For many years I had free and easy access to Ajee Shah's thoughts no matter whether I was inside or outside of him. I tried that but my access was completely blocked. That was the moment I realised the true horror of my situation. I had been virtually exiled by my own double! I had been made homeless and friendless with no idea as to what would happen next. I felt terribly lonely and alienated from my surroundings that only a few days back I had been so attached and familiar with. I was in dread and I cried.

The next morning, when Ajee Shah woke up, he seemed normal to me. He took a long shower and wore new clothes, even new shoes. Then he had his breakfast and did not eat any more than he usually did. He left the house with a big smile on his face and instead of going to his newspaper office, went to the nearby fields passing the well where he had first met the bathing djinn girl whom he had named *jal pari*.

In the middle of fields from where he could see nothing but greenery he sat down under an old tree, not at all caring for his new clothes. I was following him in my invisible mode and obviously took it for granted that he was unable to see me. I felt a severe urge to speak to Ajee Shah and was taking my human form when Ajee Shah removed the ground from beneath my feet and said, 'O Kabuko the stupid, you have no need to change your shape for me. I can very much see you and not only communicate with you but also wrestle with you if you want to test my muscles. Don't you remember that I have become a djinn now and perhaps stronger than many djinn clans? So stay as you are and tell me why you are so depressed and long-faced.' His frank tone encouraged me and I asked him, 'Why is a strange energy not permitting me to enter into your body? Why am I now being stopped from looking into your thoughts and feeling your emotions?' 'It is because of you. You are responsible for all of this,' Ajee Shah said and laughed. I did not like his answer as it confused and blamed me, and his laughter made me touchy as he clearly did not understand my terrible predicament. I became silent and serious and that was my protest. Ajee Shah broke the silence and delivered a long sermon, 'Look Kabuko, you lived in me, with me, and during some intervals, without me, for almost thirty years now. My grandfather granted you permission to stay where you stayed for all those years. I never asked you for any favours though I knew that djinn have the power to do many wonderful things that are miracles for humans. I never asked for anything in return. You came to me with your own free will and with your own set goal. You have learned many things from me and other humans around me. Now it is your destiny that wants to take you somewhere else. You will continue to live with me though not through your first part but through your second part that is called your double. Your second part has now fully merged into me and no one has any power to separate it from me until my physical death. I have no idea what will happen to me and your double after my death. We both only know stories of the other side, perhaps true, perhaps half-true or maybe totally false and fictitious. Now there is no way that you can enter into my body or read my thoughts, feelings, or emotions. You can take whatever shape you want and I will still see you because a djinn can't conceal its identity from another djinn. I did not call your double to come to me but I am inclined to think that perhaps he wanted to return the favour that my mystic grandfather gave you. So instead of my human double your djinn double appeared before us and he insisted on merging with me. You know very well that Bao Lohar resented your double's intrusion so do not make your situation worse by imagining yourself as a victim of these supernatural circumstances and try to understand this natural phenomenon. Karma has numerous ways to manifest itself and perhaps it was your karma that interfered to teach you something more precious than to waste your time with an ordinary human being.'

I didn't want to react as I did but I yelled, 'Bullshit, sheer bullshit!' I became hysterical and started flying over the tree under which Ajee Shah was sitting. I have no idea if it was defiance on my part or just a manifestation of my boundless frustration. I flew in every possible style a djinn could fly and made all those summersaults and trapeze-like flying movements I had learned in my early childhood but had never practised in my adulthood yet still remembered perfectly. I started laughing at myself. A flock of doves were heading towards the river where the woods concealed that dwelling of the mysterious mystic Sain Sidho and watched with interest my weird flight. One of the doves, the last but one in the flock, commented, 'Look at how that crazy djinn is flying'. I looked down at the dove and shouted, 'You are going to be killed. On both river banks human hunters are waiting for you. This evening your flesh and bones will be in a man's mouth.' She made a long call I suppose not to rebut me but to dispel my curse.

Many hours passed and I was still flying up that tree and expressing my frustration in my own way. Then I realised that if you express any emotion, good or bad or, in my case worst ever, you automatically release that emotion. Then I heard the voice of Ajee Shah. He was calling me down. I came down and, confronting him face to face, asked, 'Now what?' Ajee Shah did not take any offence and said in a calm and quiet tone, 'Kabuko, do not make a fool of yourself. I can match all your levitation and your clumsy summersaults but I do not want to. You are my friend, not a foe. Behave yourself and face your fresh reality with some grace.'

I believed that Ajee Shah could fly better than me as he had both djinn and human energies at his disposal. Believing seemed a curse to me now and I suddenly regretted cursing that little beautiful bird. Ajee Shah read my thoughts and said to me, 'Do not curse yourself Kabuko, my friend; you were right. That bird was heading not towards the river but towards its death. It was her destiny and no one can ever escape his or her destiny. You have no power to curse her but you were only foretelling her last departure from this world. So don't feel guilty.' I, Kabuko the djinn, did not know how to respond to that person who claimed to be a human and djinn at the same time.

Then Ajee Shah stood up but he did not brush his bottom to remove the dust. He said to me, while directly looking into my eyes, 'Kabuko, you are not a bad person. You are just like me. Half sane, half crazy and you have no power whatsoever, just like me, depending on which half of you is active and which inoperative at any given moment. So do not fight with yourself. No one on this earthly plane has ever succeeded in a battle with oneself. They always lose. If you are a warrior or wish to become one, this is the first and the last lesson you must remember. Never fight with yourself. You are your born ally and warriors do not fight with their own allies.'

I smiled and my smile was very much genuine as I knew that now Ajee Shah was speaking from his heart. He was in a saner mode. Real sanity always comes from the heart and is not a product of the mind. As such I was quite relaxed when Ajee Shah broke my heart. 'You can hang around me for as long as you want. But never try to interfere in any of my affairs. You can watch whatever you wish but with all the neutrality you can afford and, when you are tired of just watching and not interfering, then my friendly advice to you is to go back to where you originated from.'

Ajee Shah was not a friend as friends do not leave you like this. I had no friends and I had lost everything, my path, my fellow travellers, and even my own double. I was double-less now and my benefactor Kiya was not around. I was utterly alone. I gave a deep sigh, imitating humans, and flew over the head of Ajee Shah without saying goodbye to him.

Perhaps I was still not convinced that I had lost my last battle.

EPILOGUE

So, that's my story. For thirty years I underwent
myriad human emotions within Ajee Shah: living his
experiences, witnessing his friendships and enmities,
sharing his loves and hates, and in the end . . . I lost
out to myself.

Poetic justice, you say? Maybe. I'd have even
laughed at this ironic nature of my defeat had I not
been feeling such nostalgia and despair. For the first
time in my life I understood why humans and djinn
sometimes commit suicide. I always used to think of
those unfortunate beings as a spineless breed that
could not face up to their situations. But now I very
much know how desperation really works. Where
could I turn now?

I went to visit Nirva, in the hope that in her
soft arms I would find solace. She kissed me many
times, and I did not see any change in her feelings
towards me, but when I jokingly asked her, 'Are
you still ready to marry me?' she laughed it away by
saying, 'O my dearest Kabuko, it is too late now.' I
was a little surprised by her answer, and, keeping my

voice light and playful, asked, 'What has happened during these few days that has made me so late? Have you been engaged to someone or have you given your heart to a younger man? Tell me the name of my rival and I will fix him up.' She became serious and said that she knew the story of what had happened in the parallel world.

'I have lost you, my Kabuko,' she said. I really did not understand what she meant, so I asked her, 'What do you mean that you have lost me? I am very much alive and sitting in front of you. If you permit me, I will propose to you right here and now.' She said, 'Kabuko, you don't understand. Now you no longer fully belong to yourself. Ajee Shah, with your double, is also Kabuko now. I know this because I have met him twice, once with Tarru and once alone, to sort out this very strange and mysterious happening. Ajee Shah is already married to Tarru and they have a son. If I marry you then it means Tarru and I would be sharing the same husband, though in two separate bodies, and it will not only complicate our relationship, but may also hurt one or all of us. You know that I love Tarru and I don't want to hurt her at any cost. So marrying you is out of the question. Let us remain friends, but no more love-making. If you need me for anything else, at any time, you will find me by your side.'

To force myself to accept her excruciating rejection, I asked in jest, 'Which side will I find you on, right or left?' She laughed loudly, but a single tear slipped from her eye, and said, 'Of course on your left side. Now forget the right side.' During our whole relationship, whenever we made love, Nirva always insisted on lying down at my right side, as this was her habit. Our meeting ended on this bittersweet note. We kissed and I said goodbye to her with tears in my eyes. So even the path of love was blocked to me. I felt even more alone and desolate.

I flew over the city, feeling sorry for myself and bemoaning my fate. Eventually, I landed on a tree at a shrine on the outskirts of town. Having no idea why, I started imitating the calls of various birds when they cry in sorrow. I was so involved in that futile activity that I imitated almost all those birds whose sorrowful cries I could remember. Then I suddenly noticed that a few birds had come near me and were moving from one branch to another in frenzy. Either they had been disturbed by my imitating cries or they wanted to help me. I stopped and became still and silent, pretending that I had died and that those cries had been due to my last pangs. That worked well and after only a few minutes, the birds retreated to their places—perhaps with newly sorrow-filled hearts. Yet again I was alone, but this time I was relieved too, because I had realised I was unable to put up with any company, no matter how sympathetic it was.

I woke up the next morning with the call from the mosque for morning prayers and found I was sweating terribly. This state was because of a weird dream that I had experienced just before waking up. I remembered it clearly. In my dream a dervish had appeared in front of me. He gave me a clay bowl full of milk and told me to drink all it all in three gulps. I could not refuse and drank it just as I had been told. I gave the empty bowl back and he broke it into pieces by throwing it on the ground with full force. Then he said in a polite voice, 'Kabuko, do not do this to yourself. You came to get human experience and you have had your fair share. You are not a failure but now your destiny has changed your path. You are now equipped with a very precious thing, the pain of separation, and that was the most important experience you have ever had. Accept this with grace and believe me, there are many more exciting times waiting for you. You have drunk all the milk from the bowl and you do not

285

need that bowl any more so I have broken it.' Then with a big smile on his face, the dervish disappeared and I woke up.

The dervish's words gave me some strength and I decided, at last, to visit Ajee Shah. Ajee Shah was sitting on his bed and his eyes were open. He welcomed me and said, 'Kabuko, I waited for your return.' Then, he stood up and hugged me with full force as he used to hug his school friends when he was a child. He reminded me of the late Hafiz Sahib from whom we used to take Koran lessons in his childhood. 'Kabuko, you remember Hafiz Sahib was scared of me and always openly admitted that small Shah was a djinn and he could not stand my staring? Perhaps he knew that one day I would become a real djinn. Thanks to you, Kabuko, it is all because of you.' And he hugged me again, but this time a little gently. He brought his breakfast in and we ate together.

Two weeks had passed and I was still hanging around Ajee Shah. I had now accepted my situation but was yet undecided about my future course of action. I thought hard but had no answer to my predicament. Whenever I went too near Ajee Shah that force, which had now settled in his aura, pushed me away. This "pushing away" happened so many times in those two weeks, as I always forgot to keep my distance from him, that it hurt me a lot. Not physically but emotionally. Gradually I learned to keep a reasonable distance from Ajee Shah and my subconscious eventually learned to respect the newly-laid boundaries.

Occasionally Nirva, Tarru, and Ajee Shah's boy would visit us. The child had Ajee's good looks and made me feel quite emotionally vulnerable with the memories he stirred in me. He was not given over to crying and screaming like other babies; in fact, he seemed quite relaxed and almost wise. The nearest I had come to this sort of energy was the human spirit, but I knew it was not that within him which I sensed because he was also a djinn. It was easy to love this child and I did worry about how Ajee Shah would cope when the elders of Tarru's clan would insist on the last meeting between them, after which he would have to leave his wife and child forever. It made my heart ache every time I thought about it. Now that I knew what separation felt like, I did not wish it on my worst enemy, much less my beloved soul twin . . .

One late afternoon, when I was practising being apart from Ajee Shah by exploring a copse of trees by a local stream, he came to find me. He was not in his human form but came as a fully developed djinn. He invited me to come with him, and we both flew along the stream towards the river. He flew perfectly, just as a djinn would, but was as fast in flying as he had been in walking and running in his human life. We sat on a secluded part of the bank where we could see the young boys swimming, splashing, and making noise on the other side of the river. Ajee Shah was silent for a while and then said, 'The date has been announced for the meeting, and Kabuko you have to accompany me as your attendance is vital.' 'What meeting?' I pretended. 'You know very well. Do not try to fool me. I can read your mind as you have been reading mine for the last three decades.' I nodded.

We sat there, remembering many forgotten events. Both making sure that our last one-on-one meeting was so enriched that we would remember it with joy for the rest of our lives.

It was the night between Saturday and Sunday. When the middle part of it had passed, we entered the ceremony site for the meeting with the elders of Tarru's clan. First went Tarru, by virtue of being queen; then her son, the future head of the clan, whom Nirva was holding in her arms; after that Ajee Shah; and lastly I, Kabuko the djinn. The old ceremony master was the same shapeshifter who had conducted the marriage ceremony. All the elders of the clan were gathered around the main dais.

When the five of us were in front of the ceremony master, he watched Ajee Shah with interest, smiling with his eyes, and then proceeded with his address. When he finished speaking, Ajee Shah, without wasting a moment, raised his left hand to indicate that he had something to say. The master smiled again but this time everyone present could see him smiling. He allowed Ajee Shah to speak. Ajee Shah, speaking confidently, said, 'I married your Princess Tarru as a human and you were all kind enough to give us permission for that. Of course, you have your old customs and at the time of the marriage you had a lot of reservations. To make our marriage happen I, with full sincerity, agreed to your strictest condition that I would not see my wife after the birth of our first child, but that condition applied to a human only. I now declare that agreement null and void on the basis that I, while remaining human, am now a djinn too. So I claim my wife and my son not as a human but as a djinn. I have every right to be with them and to live with them freely, without any restrictions.'

The audience was stunned and in front of all the elders Ajee Shah changed his shape and became a djinn! Then he addressed the master and said, 'You can make sure by all means that what I have said is the truth.' There was a long, tense silence that was broken by the master and he just said, 'Yes, we can see it.' Elders are elders and even when faced by the most unexpected of events, they have to stay calm. They shared some signals among themselves and after that the chief elder bowed his head to the master.

The old master again smiled and declared that from now on Ajee Shah, the djinn, had no need to follow the separation clause of the agreement. He kissed Tarru, Ajee Shah, and their son one by one and congratulated them.

Then he called me, embraced me, and said 'O Kabuko, the son of our bird clan, I bless you that all your pains turn into pleasures and your pleasures into your happiness and your happiness into your bliss.' Closing the ceremony, he climbed down from the platform and promptly disappeared. Soon the women-folk of Tarru's clan started singing and dancing. I did not stay for the celebration. I did not say goodbye to anyone but I caught Nirva's eye and she looked at me in a way that I promised never to allow myself to turn into a hazy memory.

I began my flight back home very slowly. With the first ray of the Sun, I will reach my destination—or should I say "destiny". I can already hear the voices of my clansmen saying, 'Look, our Kabuko has come back!'

ACKNOWLEDGEMENTS

I would like to thank Shikha, Pooja, Monica, Sankalp, and everyone else at Fingerprint! Publishing for their patience, talent, and hard work as publishers of this book.

I'd also like to thank my family for copious amounts of love, tea, and support:
Paro for everything, always;
Tania, Pawan, and Munazza for giving and receiving advice, almost always graciously;
my grandchildren, Sara and Hassan, for often yelling to each other "Don't disturb Nana, he is writing!"
and Noreen, Shuja, Tariq, Anita, and Amir for having faith in me.

Of course, another family member who must be thanked is Bunty the rabbit, for kindly not eating the manuscript.

Thanks are also due to my friends Amin Mughal, Nuzhat, Abbas, Amarjit, Kaiser, Roma, Sahar, and Andrew for their encouragement and kind words.

My gratitude goes out to authors Adele Nozedar, Ross Heaven, Poorna Bell, and Shihab Salim for reading the book and providing testimonials.

I would also like to thank Isabel Atherton, Tridivesh Singh, and Tahir Malik for their persistent belief in my work and helpful suggestions.

Hamraz Ahsan is a seasoned journalist and syndicated columnist with over 30 years' experience in Urdu print media. He has researched and written on various social and anthropological subjects, including work on the remote tribes of Punjab. He is a published poet and is author of *Tibbiaan Uttey Chhaavaan* (Shades on Dunes), a collection of Punjabi poems; *Muqeem Bi Masafar* (The Settler is also a Nomad), a collection of Urdu poems; and *Par Samundraan Walley* (Trapped on the Other Side of the Ocean), Punjabi short poems about the immigrant experience in Britain. He is also the author of *Harf-e-saadaa* (A Simple Word), a collection of his Urdu newspaper columns. His most recent poetry book is a book of Punjabi Sufi-inspired quatrains.

He currently lives in London and writes for newspapers around the world.